ALSO BY FRANCIS DUNCAN

In the Mordecai Tremaine Series

Murder for Christmas

So Pretty a Problem

Behold a Fair Woman

In at the Death

MURDER Has a MOTIVE

FRANCIS DUNCAN

sourcebooks
landmark

Published by Sourcebooks Landmark, an imprint of Sourcebooks, Inc.
P.O. Box 4410, Naperville, Illinois 60567-4410
(630) 961-3900
Fax: (630) 961-2168
sourcebooks.com

Originally published in 1947 in the United Kingdom by John Long. This edition
issued based on the paperback edition published in 2016 in the United Kingdom by
Vintage Books, an imprint of Penguin Random House UK.

Library of Congress Cataloging-in-Publication Data

Names: Duncan, Francis, author.
Title: Murder has a motive / Francis Duncan.
Description: Naperville, Illinois : Sourcebooks Landmark, 2018. | "Originally
    published in 1947 in the United Kingdom by John Long. This edition issued
    based on the paperback edition published in 2016 in the United Kingdom by
    Vintage Books, an imprint of Penguin Random House UK" -- Verso title page.
Identifiers: LCCN 2017023611 | (pbk. : alk. paper)
Subjects: LCSH: Actors and actresses--Fiction. | Serial murder
    investigation--Fiction. | GSAFD: Mystery fiction.
Classification: LCC PR6007.U527 M89 2018 | DDC 823/.914--dc23 LC record
available at https://lccn.loc.gov/2017023611

Printed and bound in the United States of America.
VP 10 9 8 7 6 5 4 3 2 1

1

Lydia Dare was dining with a murderer.

If she was afraid, there was no trace of her fear in the hazel eyes that were regarding her companion across the snowy table with its scintillating burden of silver and glassware, polished and displayed, as she knew, in her honor; nor was there any tremor of the surface of the liquid to betray a nervous unsteadiness of the slender fingers in which she held the glass she was raising to her lips.

She sipped appreciatively and turned the glass against the light so that golden pinpoints of reflection danced in her eyes.

"There are people who say that champagne doesn't deserve its reputation," she observed, "but this would make them all converts, Martin. It makes you feel light and gay as though you were walking on air. How on earth did you manage to find it?"

That the man facing her was delighted with her praise was evident, but he strove to conceal his pleasure with an exaggeratedly deprecating shrug.

"I moved mountains," he returned lightly. "After all, champagne is for special occasions, and for very special occasions there should be a very special champagne."

"I can't think, my dear," he added quietly, "of any occasion more special than this—to be here alone with you, even if for all too short a time."

Lydia's eyes softened. Impulsively her hand reached out to his.

"Sometimes, Martin," she said, "I think you're the nicest murderer I know."

Martin Vaughan smiled.

"It's been fun, Lydia. I didn't think I could have enjoyed anything so much."

He did not have the appearance of a murderer now. Or rather, since murderers are found among all sorts and conditions of men and are not as a rule marked out from their fellows by any definite peculiarities of form or features, he had the appearance of a very boyish and yet distinguished-looking one.

Boyish on account of the air of enthusiasm that he had momentarily acquired and that had smoothed the years from his brow and distinguished on account of the wide proportions of that same brow and of the slightly graying although still thick and crisply curling hair that was brushed back from it.

Martin Vaughan was proud of the fact that his age was not visible in his face—unless one took account of the tiny wrinkles around the blue-gray eyes that had looked out upon forty-five years of existence—and that his thick-set frame and heavy shoulders had not degenerated into the fleshy obesity of that dangerous combination of middle age and success.

Rigorous exercise and the near tropics had preserved his waistline. Archaeology and the study of ancient civilizations were his hobbies, and he had made a number of extensive tours of Mesopotamia and the Eastern Mediterranean. Several works he had published on the difficult and skilled task of locating and excavating age-old cities and burial grounds, and of extracting their story from the mists of unrecorded history, had become recognized as standard treatises and had gained for him the reputation of being an authority in such matters.

He had been able to indulge in his hobby because success had come to him early. Gold, South Africa, and a forceful, adventurer's personality had been the rungs by which he had climbed. Not a great deal of gold as vast fortunes are reckoned, but he had sold out his holdings at a figure that had enabled him to choose his own way of life.

Something of his past was still evident in him despite the conventional evening clothes and the subdued but undoubtedly expensive comfort of his surroundings. The adventurer was lurking yet in the depths of the blue-gray eyes that seemed to hold a hint of storm-lashed seas; in the powerful lines of a jaw that appeared to be thrusting itself forward a little more pugnaciously than was really necessary; and in the thick, confident fingers of his powerful hands.

Studying him, Lydia was lost for a brief space of time in a panorama of boom towns and lusty, crowded, tempestuous days in which a man's fists had to act as his claims to life and in which humanity was a raw thing pulsating near the surface of existence. She found herself thinking, as though she had not really known him before this moment of instinctive comprehension, that Martin Vaughan could be ruthless, that what he wanted he would take, and that his revenge could be a dreadful thing. Ten years in the peaceful beauty that was the south country village of Dalmering had given him background but had merely overlain, without removing, his primitive beginnings.

Her eyes must have betrayed her thoughts. Her companion's somewhat wry chuckle broke in upon her involuntary musings.

"So you think I *am* capable of murder, my dear?"

"Of course not," she said hastily, but with the very spontaneity of her answer and the quick flush of color giving her the lie. "I was just—just thinking how exciting your life must have been before—before—"

She broke off uncertainly, but he was aware of her discomfort and went to her aid.

"Before I turned myself from a rough diamond into a gentleman of leisure?" he said, amused. "You blush charmingly, my dear, but you don't lie very well. As a matter of fact, you're quite right. I've been in unpleasant places where I've had to be a little—unpleasant—myself. At least, if I wanted to go on living—as I usually did. Perhaps," he added slyly, "that's why I make such a good murderer!"

"Now you're developing the immodest ego of the successful actor," she returned accusingly, but her attack left him unshaken.

"I believe I am," he told her. "And speaking of murder, I've an idea that Pauline Conroy was near it at yesterday's rehearsal."

"She thinks you're deliberately trying to act her off the stage and steal her thunder."

"Poor Pauline! As the only professional of us all she takes herself very seriously! She certainly seems to have her mind set on making a success of the play. She'll probably have half the critics in London down for the opening night. Maybe she imagines she'll be able to persuade them to believe that they've found a Sarah Bernhardt in a village hall!"

Lydia smiled.

"When you say the 'opening night' I take it you mean the *only* night! Seriously, though, Martin, acting in a murder play can't really be much of a consolation for you. Don't you get bored with living here? Don't you find it horribly dull?"

"Why should I?" he countered. "I lead a very comfortable existence. I've all I want—books, music, my research. And an occasional trip abroad when I feel in need of a change."

"A trip for what? To dig up moldy old bones in a desert?"

Vaughan leaned back in his chair, and his deep voice was vibrant with genuine enjoyment.

"I believe you're trying to prize the oyster out of his shell. I *like* digging up moldy old bones in a desert. It's my idea of enjoyment. Anyway, bones are interesting things. They can tell fascinating stories. They can tell of what the poet called 'old, unhappy, far-off things, and battles long ago.' They can tell of thieves in the night, willing to risk desecrating a tomb in order to make themselves rich, and of great kings, buried with their courts around them and all the things they might need in the afterlife placed ready to their hands. But don't think, my dear, that I'm just an old fossil too, only interested in the dust and ashes of a few thousand years ago."

He rose to his feet, and, crossing to the window, drew back the heavy velvet curtains. Through the darkness, as though they were bright stars sprinkled down out of the skies at random, they could see the lights of the little group of period houses that had been scattered—for profit, but by a builder with at least a lingering respect for the decencies—among the beauty of Dalmering.

"No one could be dull—or even a fossil—with so much

to see and hear and study. Look—behind all those lighted windows there are living people. There's Pauline Conroy's window, for instance—since we were speaking of her just now. I wonder what she's doing at this moment? Perhaps she's rehearsing her lines in front of her mirror. And there's a light in the house to the left where Karen Hammond lives all the week—and where Philip Hammond lives at the weekend when he can get away from business. What is *she* doing now? Is she trying on the new hat her husband bought her in town this morning?

"How do any of us know what strange creatures our neighbors become when they go into their houses and shut their doors upon the world? How do we know what people are thinking and saying behind all those innocent-looking facades? There's the very stuff of drama lying all about us—a score of human beings, all loving, and hating, and laughing, and crying, just as those other humans who once animated those moldy old bones you were decrying did in their lifetimes ages of time ago."

Lydia was looking at him wonderingly, her lips slightly parted, held by his air of elation, deliberately half-suppressed though she could tell it to be. She had never seen him in quite such a mood before.

"The oyster didn't need much prizing, Martin. You're almost lyrical."

"It was my speech for the defense," he said, drawing the curtains again and turning to her. "The bones are only part of the story. Remember Pope—'The proper study of mankind is man.'"

"'The glory, jest, and riddle of the world,'" she added.

"Not really much of a riddle, my dear," he said, and now his voice held a serious note that had not been evident before.

"The same old emotions are still running around loose. You asked me if I found it dull here in Dalmering. It hasn't been dull here for one moment. Of all the places I've ever known, Dalmering is the loveliest. You know why, Lydia. *You've* been here. You know—you know that I'm in love with you?"

"Yes," she said quietly. "I know. I'm sorry, Martin—"

There was a look of contrition on his face at that.

"I don't want you to be, Lydia. I didn't intend to be the skeleton at the feast. It was just that—just that I couldn't help myself. I didn't really intend to say anything—except that I think Farrant is a lucky man and that I hope you'll be very happy."

"You're very generous, Martin."

Vaughan made a visible effort to make his voice sound normal.

"Nonsense, my dear. It isn't really surprising that you preferred not to spend the rest of your life tied to an old roughneck like me. I've been smoothed out a little, but I'm still liable to revert to type at awkward moments! And I appreciate your coming here tonight—especially as you knew all about my hopeless passion."

"It was the reason I came," she said, admiring his attempt to speak lightly, and with a little ache at her heart because of the misery in his eyes that he could not conceal.

"I hope Farrant won't mind your being here."

"Of course he won't. Gerald knows we're old friends. Besides, I'm thirty-five. I'm an old woman, not an inexperienced young girl whose honor is in peril!"

The big man took her right hand in his own powerful one and, stooping, kissed her fingertips with a gallant little gesture that seemed oddly out of keeping with his heavy frame.

"As long as you look as beautiful and charming as you're looking now," he said, "you'll never be an old woman, Lydia."

He added, after a pause, "It's the conventional thing to say on these occasions, but you know that I'm in earnest. If ever you need me, if ever there is anything I can do, you have only to ask and I'll be there."

It was clear that Lydia was conscious of the strained situation between them. Conscious of it and of the dangers it possessed and anxious to bring it under control before it proved to be beyond her power.

"I won't hold you to it," she said jestingly. "I don't want to embarrass you when you meet the only girl in the world."

"I've already met her," he responded quickly, and then, as if he, too, realized the strength of the emotions that were beginning to ride perilously near the surface, he went on, "I suppose it means that you'll be leaving Dalmering?"

She nodded.

"Yes. Gerald has to live in Edinburgh."

"I was afraid of it," he said, with mock resignation. "It means I'll have to go searching for some more old bones. Lions in Africa for some, deep-sea fishing off Florida for others, and bones in the desert for me!"

But it seemed that his efforts were wasted and that Lydia was not listening to him. A queer, puzzled frown had come into her face.

"I used to think that I would hate having to leave Dalmering," she said slowly. "But now I'm glad I'm going. Martin, have you noticed anything about this place lately? Has it seemed—different?"

Vaughan's attention was caught by the oddly urgent note in her voice. He looked at her curiously.

"Different?"

"I can't explain it," she said helplessly. "It's just that there's a strange feeling in the air—a horrible sort of feeling, as though everybody is frightened of everybody else, and people are watching each other, waiting for some dreadful thing to happen."

"Nerves," he told her. "You've been overdoing things—worrying about details and letting all the excitement get you down."

But the idea had gained too firm a root in her mind for her to be so easily comforted.

"No, it isn't nerves. There's something wrong. Things aren't normal anymore."

"You aren't going to tell me that there's something rotten in the state of Dalmering!"

A little to his dismay she took him literally.

"There is, Martin! Something—something rotten. Something ugly and horrible and obscene. And I'm afraid. I know it sounds stupid and hysterically feminine of me, but sometimes I wake up at night panting and terrified, feeling that there's some awful black power brooding over us all, just waiting for an opportunity to strike."

A ragged note of fear had crept into her voice, and Vaughan's big hands went out protectively to her shoulders.

"Steady, my dear—we can't have you going to pieces like this! You'll have me beginning to blame my champagne!"

He refilled her glass, and she took it from him with a half-ashamed little smile that was the product of a determined effort at self-control.

"Sorry, Martin. *I'm* the skeleton at the feast now. Perhaps it *is* the excitement. I'll be giving way to schoolgirl giggles next."

The glass was partway to her lips when she shivered involuntarily.

"Cold?" he said quickly. "I'll switch the fire on for a few moments."

"No, I'm not cold," she told him. "Just frightened."

It was the truth she was speaking, for there was momentarily a look of sheer panic frozen in her eyes. She emptied her glass mechanically, as though she was not tasting the sparkling liquid.

"There were icy fingers on my spine," she said, with an attempt to regain her composure. "I'd like another, please, Martin."

"Of course, my dear."

There was a watchful, somehow guarded look upon the big man's face as he took the glass and refilled it. He had seen that fleeting betrayal of her inward terror, and it had left him disturbed and uncertain.

But despite its apparent intensity, her emotion seemed to have been a transient one for it did not recur. The pallor left her cheeks. She became the gay, charming companion he had always known.

They had many things to discuss, and time became of no importance—until Lydia looked down at the tiny gold watch gleaming against the white of her slender wrist and gave an exclamation of dismay.

"A quarter to eleven. I'll have to fly, Martin."

"Does Cinderella have to be back so early?"

"I promised Sandy I'd be in by eleven. She'll be waiting up for me."

"Patient Sandra! She's going to miss you, Lydia."

"Not so much as I'm going to miss her," returned Lydia. "She's been my fairy godmother and guardian angel combined."

Vaughan fetched the short evening cloak she had brought and placed it about her shoulders with just a touch of possessiveness.

"I'll see you back to the house."

"No, Martin," she said quickly. "I'd rather you didn't. After all, there *are* the proprieties to think about—even in Dalmering. People will probably talk enough as it is about my coming here alone. Besides, it's only a few minutes' walk; it isn't worth dragging you out for such a short distance."

She saw that he was going to raise objections, and her voice became coaxing.

"Please, Martin. Just this last service—to round off a perfect evening."

He was unwilling to acknowledge defeat, but defeat it was. He shrugged his shoulders in helpless acceptance of it.

"When you attack me like that you leave me no defense."

"Thank you, Martin," she said softly. "For tonight—and everything."

For several reasons Lydia Dare was glad that she was alone on the short walk back to the attractive half-timbered cottage she shared with Sandra Borne. Her mind was a confused tangle of impressions that she wished to sort out and label before their chaos overwhelmed her.

It was not that she had any doubts as to the wisdom of her marrying Gerald Farrant in preference to Martin Vaughan. She had known that Vaughan was in love with her before she had accepted his invitation to dine with him. As she had told him, it had been one of the reasons why she had gone.

But now she was not quite certain whether her action, which had sprung from a vague desire to make things easier for him—some kind of repressed maternal instinct she told herself wryly—had been a wise one. She had underrated the situation. She had imagined it to be perfectly simple and easy to handle, and instead it had proved to be bristling with psychology.

Martin Vaughan was not a stranger. She had known him for so long that she could anticipate his ideas and his moods and the way in which he would react. At least, so she had believed. Now she was not sure.

She had become aware that his was a powerful personality; that although his strength might be latent, concealed beneath the veneer of a placid existence in a small country community, he could be masterful and dominant—all those things, in fact, that women are reputed to desire in men.

She was conscious of a disturbed, unsettled feeling, a

sensation of disaster in the air. She hesitated and looked about her, as if to gain comfort from her surroundings.

It was a quietly peaceful early summer night. There were still odd lights dotted here and there to reveal that Dalmering was not yet wholly abed, but most of them marked the homes of the colony.

Dalmering consisted of the old village, with its tiny cluster of houses and its handful of miniature shops, lying along the main road; and a much more recent outcrop of larger houses that were the homes of its temporary residents, the weekenders and the city businessites who had discovered its unspoiled beauty. It was in these latter that the lights were to be observed. The older Dalmering, the true Dalmering, which had endured through the centuries with an impassive tranquility, facing birth and death and the catastrophes of war and nature with equal undismay, was already enveloped in darkness and sleep.

Even the moon seemed to be aware of the division. Motionless banks of cloud hung in the sky, obscuring its rays from certain angles, so that while the newer houses were clearly outlined, as though to indicate that their inhabitants were in no hurry to retire, the old village was an undisturbed pool of ink in the midst of the radiance.

The sighing rustle of the waves on the shingle came plainly to her ears. The sea was no more than a mile away, and although the air was almost still, the salty tang and feel of the water was all about her.

Beauty was about her, too. Dalmering typified the real loveliness, the unbearable heartrending beauty of England—a beauty of flared sunsets and silver sea; of lonely moors and winding, dusty roads; of shady lanes, straggly roofs, and scented hedgerows—a beauty that she could feel and that rose in her throat like a sweet agony and yet for which she was without words.

To reach her destination she had first to cross the open ground rather like an extended, haphazardly shaped, and uneven version of the ancient village common, around which Martin Vaughan's and the other houses were placed, and then walk along the narrow but well-worn pathway that traversed a small copse about twenty or thirty yards in depth before it made contact with the roadway leading to the old village— and, incidentally, her cottage.

She made her way at a quicker pace down the slope leading to the wooden bridge over the stream that zigzagged an apparently aimless way across the common and in a few moments had reached the copse.

As she entered it the moonlight ceased and the shadows rushed upon her. The first few steps she took were blind and hesitant. Although she had trodden the path countless times before, it was as though she had walked into an unknown world of darkness in which she was lost and alone.

Something rustled close at hand. So close that it startled her and she stopped abruptly, her heart thudding.

Her first reasoned thought was that Vaughan had followed her, after all. She knew that he had not been behind her as she had crossed the common, but although he would have had a greater distance to cover, it would have been easily possible for him to have gone around by the roadway and reached the copse before her.

"Is that you, Martin? You shouldn't have bothered."

She tried to speak casually, but her voice was unreal and a little desperate. It surprised her with its shrill uncertainty.

There was no sound in reply. All around her it was still and somehow dreadfully silent.

And now there was fear at her side. The darkness was becoming less intense, but the shadows that were detaching themselves from the deeper blackness were grotesque and ugly and menacing. They were no longer the shadows of friendly things but were alien and distorted, reaching up to her, stretching out greedy fingers to drag her down.

She knew that it was a lie born of an imagination no longer under her control, but momentarily she was incapable of restoring her conscious reason. She gave a stifled sob and began to run.

It might have been the signal for all the power of the evil she had been secretly fearing for so long to rise up against her. For suddenly she was no longer alone on the path.

She turned against her will to see that horror was there. A twisted, devilish horror with insatiate eyes in the impossible mask of a fiend. An incredible horror which paralyzed her body and which her mind refused to believe.

And as she stared, incapable of movement, it resolved itself into a searing, sharp-edged pain—a pain that both pierced her through and enveloped her in its intensity. It screamed through her nerves to a fierce and terrible climax, and then there was no feeling anymore—no pain, no fear, only a great, embracing silence, in the soft arms of which she lay utterly still.

2

Even in his early sixties Mordecai Euripides Tremaine still preserved many of his boyish enthusiasms. One of them was a delight in all kinds of travel, even when the countryside through which he was passing held no undiscovered treasures for him.

It was a source of secret amusement to the other occupants of the compartment in the electric train that was carrying him swiftly southward from Victoria to observe the eagerness with which he surveyed the rapidly changing landscape. Villages, farmhouses, green countryside—all appeared to have the same fascination for him as for a child seeing all these wonders for the first time.

His fellow travelers so far forgot the conventional reserve of the English using a public conveyance as to express their surprise at his obvious animation by exchanging glances among themselves. They would have had more surprise to express had they realized that they, too, came within the scope of his intense interest. Mordecai Tremaine had developed the

valuable asset of being able to take comprehensive and sometimes devastating stock of his neighbors without giving them
the least suspicion that he was at all interested in them.

It was not a gift that had descended upon him unawares
but was the result of a deliberate and often painstaking policy, sustained over a long period. To observe without being
observed, and to observe accurately, had been the goal toward
which he had striven with a persistence and faithfulness of
purpose any potential martyr might have envied.

There was, of course, a reason for this somewhat unorthodox ambition. Within the shell of a slightly built, harmless-
looking citizen with graying hair, pince-nez, and a regrettable
but pronounced tendency to become garrulous, there dwelt a
personality with attributes that were in violent contrast to the
carpet slipper body that was displayed to the world. During
the years when he had stood behind the counter of his tobacconist's shop, dispensing packets of twenty, pipe cleaners,
and the brands of tobacco most favored by his customers,
Mordecai Tremaine's mind had not been on those mundane
means to a moderate livelihood. Instead, his thoughts had
been traveling a darker, more savage, and yet infinitely more
exciting road.

Murder and Mordecai Tremaine had the sound of strange
bedfellows, but nevertheless murder was his hobby. Many a
night after the last customer had been satisfied was spent in

the cozy room over the shop, discussing the latest crime to horrify a public that openly decried but secretly welcomed blood with the breakfast newspaper. That his discussions had been with an acquaintance whose position as a police surgeon brought him into intimate contact with the details of such crimes had put an edge to his enjoyment and had lent point to the rows of books on criminology that filled his bookshelves.

The days of the tobacconist's shop were over now. When he had judged that his profits would provide enough for his moderate needs, Mordecai Tremaine had wisely retired. He had invested his capital with a careful eye to the maximum of return for the minimum of worry over the fickle variations of share prices and had settled down to his hobby in earnest.

It was not so much the retired businessman who looked out upon the world from behind the old-fashioned pince-nez that seemed to be always on the point of slipping to disaster as the keen criminologist and eager student of human nature. His relaxation was sought now not in the closely printed pages of his books after working hours but in the study of his fellow men and the complex and fascinating emotions and passions by which they were swayed. The fact that the gods of chance had seen fit to involve him in two real-life murder cases since his retirement and that he now numbered among his friends two inspectors of police, including one from Scotland Yard itself, had served to enslave him more.

He glanced around the compartment at his companions, thereby compelling them to make self-conscious efforts to appear as though they had not been furtively eyeing him. There seemed to be nothing of particular significance in his manner, but when he turned back toward the window his preoccupation was not with the landscape but with the mental exercise of placing the four people whom his brief examination had covered.

Three were men and one a woman. This last was middle-aged, cheerful-looking, and, judging from the filled shopping basket, returning from an expedition to the market town two stations up the line where she had joined the train. The mother of a family of healthy young animals, he decided—probably the wife of one of the local farmers, out with the object of supplementing her home-baked farmhouse fare.

Of the men, two responded equally easily to analysis. One was a parson—too easy that, he decided; the collar left no opportunity for theorizing. The second, from his neat, pinstriped suit, a little shiny at the elbows, and the leather briefcase in various papers taken from which he had been engrossed, was almost equally obviously a city businessman paying an out-of-town call.

The third man presented more of a problem. Tremaine

had been trying to affix a label to him for some while, for he had already been in the compartment at Victoria when he himself had entered.

He was a middle-aged man, whose round, bespectacled face and plump figure—enclosed in a well-cut if somewhat creased blue suit—should have suggested good-humored prosperity and yet somehow failed to do so. The cheeks that should have been smoothly aglow with well-being had a faint trace of flabbiness, and there were little lines of strain etched into their folds. The eyes behind the spectacles had a darting, worried quality, as though some urgent problem was pressing upon their owner and he was searching frantically not so much to solve as to evade it.

Mordecai Euripides Tremaine (his name was a legacy from parents in whose minds had dwelt a hazy but fervent appreciation of the Arthurian legends and the Greek classics) gave him a great deal of thought but without the satisfaction of the said thought crystallizing into a sound theory. He had not, he told himself regretfully, achieved the skill of a Sherlock Holmes, whose agile brain and sharp eyes would have required no more than a few moments in which to give the stranger—to use a phrase from Shakespeare—both a local habitation and a name.

The next station was that at which he was to alight. As he stepped down to the platform, he squared his shoulders and breathed deeply and deliberately. He fancied already that he could smell the sea—he had made up his mind that he would do so before he had left the compartment—and although he had never sailed the ocean in anything more substantial than his imagination, a hint of salt in the air was always enough to set his blood racing.

He recognized the much-traveled little saloon car standing in the station courtyard in the same instant that he himself was recognized. He waved a greeting to the middle-aged couple, evidently husband and wife, who had been awaiting him, and Paul Russell came toward him and reached for his hand.

"Glad to see you, old man," he said warmly.

Tremaine returned the grip, smiling into the kindly eyes in his friend's weather-beaten face.

"You're looking well, Paul," he told him. "How is everything? Are all the Dalmering babies being born at a respectable hour now instead of dragging the unlucky doctor out of his bed in the middle of the night and robbing him of his beauty sleep?"

Jean Russell came through the car to join her husband.

"Talking about babies in a public place is no fit way for a bachelor to behave," she said, with mock severity. "I can see you're still a problem child, Mordecai, despite your gray hair!"

A busy country practice and a great deal of voluntary social work left neither Paul Russell nor his wife a great deal of time for relaxation, but Mordecai Tremaine had made their acquaintance on one of their rare holidays, and he had enjoyed their friendship ever since. Tolerant and easygoing and yet with the ability to work desperately hard, very much alive to social evils and doing what they could to combat them and yet possessed of a cheerful good humor, the Russells had made an appeal to him that he had found irresistible. Although it was several years since he had been able to spend any length of time with them, they had corresponded regularly.

As he was climbing into the saloon, Tremaine saw Russell nod a greeting to someone who was just passing the car, and he saw the passerby raise his hat to the doctor's wife. It was the plump man in the blue suit who had puzzled him in the train.

"One of the locals?" he asked curiously.

"Yes and no," returned Russell. "His name's Shannon. He lives about half a mile up the road from our place. Why? Do you know him?"

There seemed to be just a trace of a sharper note of inquiry in the doctor's voice than the original question had appeared to warrant, but it was so faint that Tremaine was uncertain whether it possessed any significance or not.

"We were in the same compartment coming down from Victoria. I was amusing myself trying to guess what he was and where he was going."

"Did you discover the answers?" asked Jean. "If you did

you'll be able to give *us* some information. Howard Shannon's one of our mystery men."

Tremaine gave her a quizzical look.

"You sound as though he's one of several."

"So he is," she told him. "Dalmering's population is like Gaul in being divided, only it's divided into two parts and not three. There's what you might call the indigenous population—the people whose ancestors lived here—and the visiting population, the people who come down periodically, for weekends and so on. They arrive one day and go back the next, and although we're used to seeing them about, we don't really know them—not in the sense that we know who their families are and what they do for a living. Shannon comes down at all sorts of irregular intervals. He's not a stranger, and yet where he goes when he leaves the village and what he does when he gets there we haven't the faintest idea."

"You're making Dalmering sound an interesting place," said Tremaine.

"Perhaps it is," said Russell, and once again there seemed to be an odd note in his voice.

They drove out of the station yard and down the sun-lit road leading to the village. It was early summer, and the countryside—beautiful at all times in this quiet corner of Sussex—was almost poignantly lovely. Green fields with a fragrance upon them; tree-shaded roads with a copse appearing here and there to prevent any jarring suggestion of pattern or regimentation; ancient cottages intermingled with variedly modern houses, designed to blend into their surroundings as if nature had set them there and not the normally heavy hand of man, and each with its riotous blaze of color where lupins, delphiniums, and peonies bloomed—it was an enchanted land lying between the silver border of the sea and the smooth shoulder of the Downs, which rose up behind it to merge into the blue of a sky hazy with warmth and pregnant with suggestion of droning insects and long, still summer hours.

Mordecai Tremaine sat silently enthralled in the back of the saloon, avidly drinking in the scene as though he was fearful of missing some portion of its loveliness if he moved or spoke, his sentimental, romantic soul reaching toward an understanding of how it was that poets and artists throughout the centuries had been constrained to express such magic in words or in color so that something of it should always remain.

Bordering the road on the left he saw a long, redbrick building with a low, thatched roof. There was a noticeboard outside it, and Tremaine caught a glimpse of a printed poster as they passed. It was enough, brief though it was, for him to read the bolder lettering.

MURDER Has a MOTIVE

A Play in Three Acts
By Alexis Kent

"I see you go in for drama in Dalmering," he remarked with a smile.

"Yes," returned Russell, "we do."

Once again that odd note seemed to be in his voice, but he did not offer to elaborate upon what he had said.

They turned a corner in that moment and came within sight of the village itself. It lay in a hollow a little below them, and in the brief instant in which the car was on the crest of the road before beginning the gentle run down, Tremaine thought that he had never looked upon a view so lovely.

The light summer haze gave an unreal appearance to the land. The contrasting greens of grass and trees, the pleasantly uneven common land with its winding stream and rustic bridge and with half-hidden cottages and houses spaced around it, all seemed to merge into a picture possessed of an enchantingly insubstantial air. Tremaine felt momentarily like a man who gazes into an image framed in the depths of a pool that is still and yet not quite still and who is afraid even to breathe lest he should disturb the surface of the water and destroy the vision.

The car coasted down the slope and reached the level road again. They ran through the deserted "square" that was the local shopping center and in a moment or two were passing a copse lining the roadway that temporarily hid the common from view.

Tremaine drew a deep, sighing breath, as though reassured that now he could do so without disturbing the peace and tranquility that lay almost tangibly about him.

"It's a beautiful spot," he said, his heart in his voice.

The doctor spoke over his shoulder, without taking his attention from the wheel.

"It's where they found the body," he remarked quietly.

So quietly that Mordecai Tremaine was not at first certain that he had heard him correctly.

"The body?" he echoed, a little stupidly.

"The body," repeated Russell. "The body of Lydia Dare. She was found stabbed to death in the early hours of this morning on the path through the copse we've just passed."

Tremaine looked blankly from one to the other of his friends.

"Not—murder?"

"Murder," said Jean Russell, and the hardness in her voice gave the word a flat, ominous sound that seemed to shatter the illusion of tranquility like a steel hammer disintegrating a flawless sheet of glass into splintered fragments.

She turned in her seat so that now she was facing him from the front of the little car.

"Lydia was a friend of ours—a dear friend. That's why we want to do something—why we feel, Paul and I, that we *must* do something. That's why we didn't wire you not to come today although we knew that it wasn't likely to be a holiday for you since it's obvious that Dalmering will be full of police and newspaper reporters."

Mordecai Tremaine tried to imagine dark, brutal murder, with all its inevitable camp followers of endless publicity and inquiries, of screaming newspaper headlines and remorseless police investigations, of relentless, sometimes sordid, searches for news and clues, and found that his mind refused to measure up to the task of connecting those things with Dalmering. They seemed so utterly opposed, so completely incompatible.

But it was quite clear that Jean and Paul Russell were grimly serious. He knew them too well to have any doubts as to their sincerity.

And he thought he knew, also, what had been in Jean Russell's mind when she had told him that she had deliberately refrained from advising him not to pay his projected visit to Dalmering in view of what had happened.

He waited, not quite certain whether or not to assume his conjecture to be the right one, and the problem was solved for him.

"You know what we're trying to suggest, don't you, Mordecai?" said Jean, her eyes searching his face.

"I'm not sure," he said, deliberately dull.

"We want you to find the murderer," she told him bluntly.

He still fenced, although it was the reply he had expected.

"But surely it's a matter for the police? They don't like amateurs getting themselves involved in these things."

"You're not an amateur now," she persisted. "You can't offer that excuse—not after all the nice things your friend Inspector Boyce said about you after the Queen's Newbridge murder."

Mordecai Tremaine tried to overcome the feeling of complacency that was struggling to creep over him and endeavored to look unimpressed.

Inspector Boyce (of Scotland Yard) had had no direct connection with the murder that had thrust the little west country village of Queen's Newbridge into the limelight of publicity. Officially the crime had been solved by Inspector Rich of the Westport and District Constabulary. But Rich, being an honest man and knowing that Mordecai Euripides Tremaine was acquainted with Boyce, had written privately to his colleague at the Yard and had given him a full account of the part Tremaine had played in the solution of the mystery.

"Suppose you tell me all about it when we reach the house," he temporized. "It's a complete surprise to me. The murder must have been reported too late to be in the newspapers. I didn't read anything about it in the *Gazette*."

They had almost reached their destination by now—it was one of the smaller of the modern houses, although set, like its neighbors, in its own well-tended garden—and the doctor slowed down in order to swing over the road and drive through the gateway into the brick-built garage that was just beyond the house itself and pleasantly concealed by a rustic archway in which the roses were just beginning to appear. As he cleared the gate, with an expert certainty born of much practice, he nodded in recognition to a woman who had halted to allow him to pass.

Tremaine did not see her features clearly, for she was wearing sunglasses, which created a partial effect of disguise, but she carried herself gracefully, and her superb figure was emphasized by the lines—plain but not forbiddingly severe—of the white summer frock she wore. Her hair, shoulder length, was silkily blond to a degree that caught the attention, framing as it did a clear-featured face that was healthily suntanned. Her eyes, Mordecai Tremaine told himself, his sentimental soul in full command, would almost certainly be blue.

He realized a little guiltily that he had been openly staring and that Jean Russell's eyes were upon him with a quizzical air.

"Karen Hammond," she told him, anticipating his question, and added, wickedly, "I'm afraid she's married."

They had come to a halt outside the garage, and Tremaine made use of the few moments it took him to climb from the car to recover his self-possession.

"Is she one of the regulars or one of the weekenders?" he asked, with a carelessness as assumed as he could make it.

"Both," returned Jean. "She's here quite a lot, but her husband is more of a bird of passage. His work appears to keep him busy in town. Sometimes we see him down here at weekends and sometimes he seems to manage to get down during the week, but he's very erratic. You never quite know whether he's here or not."

"What does he do?" asked Tremaine, and Jean Russell smiled.

"*You're* the detective," she told him. "All that we know is that he's something in the city—which isn't very helpful."

Tremaine was in the act of framing another question when they heard a step on the gravel path and a figure came from the direction of the garden at the rear of the house.

"Hullo, Paul," said a new voice. "I just looked in to ask Jean if she—" The voice broke off as its owner became aware of the presence of a stranger. "I'm sorry. I didn't realize you had visitors."

"That's all right, Sandy," said Russell's cheerful tones.

"Come along and be introduced. We want Mordecai here to get to know Dalmering, and of all the people in the neighborhood you're one of the first we'd like him to meet. After all, you're something of an institution!"

He ushered his visitor forward so that Tremaine and the new arrival were face-to-face.

"Mordecai, this is Sandra Borne, one of our near neighbors. Most of us call her Sandy—she prefers it. Sandy—meet Mordecai Tremaine, an old friend of ours."

Tremaine found himself shaking hands with a bright-eyed little woman over whom he appeared to tower although his own height was no more than average. He estimated Sandra Borne's age as something near forty, but he was aware that when it came to guessing how old any woman was, he was on dangerous ground, and he refrained from setting his mind upon any definite figure.

She was not by any means good-looking, but there was a certain attractive vitality about her. She had the air of a capable, intensely "busy" person, the kind of hardworking enthusiast who is responsible for organizing fêtes and pageants and all the numerous social activities of village life.

Her forehead was wide, and its breadth was further accentuated by the piled-up dark hair, streaked with gray, that surmounted it, so that her head seemed a little too large for her short body. A small, straight nose with flared nostrils, a wide, mobile mouth, a rounded but firm-looking chin, and brown eyes that appeared to possess just the faintest suggestion of green but that he could not assess definitely because of the horn-rimmed spectacles she wore completed the overall impression Tremaine received in the first moments of greeting.

When the introductions had been made he had an opportunity of studying her more closely, and he saw then that her appearance of vitality was an artificial one; she was struggling to maintain it, as though she felt it to be expected of her, but it required a constant effort to keep up the pose.

Her eyes were not as bright as he had at first imagined them to be; there was in their depths a mixture of strain, anxiety, and other emotions he could not read, and they were faintly ringed with shadows. When she was off her guard her smile took on a fixed, mechanical quality, and underneath it the lines of distress were visible.

The reason was soon made clear to him.

"Sandy and Lydia Dare shared a cottage," said Paul Russell.

He gave the information almost casually—with what was, Tremaine realized a little belatedly, a deliberately assumed air of unconcern. Sandra Borne's reaction was much swifter than his own. She glanced quickly at the mild-looking man with the old-fashioned pince-nez to whom she had just been introduced and then back to the doctor.

"He knows—about Lydia?"

"Yes, he knows," agreed Paul Russell.

"They've just told me," interjected Tremaine, finding his voice at last. "I only arrived from London a few minutes ago. There was nothing in the newspapers before I left. I take it that Miss Dare—it was Miss?" he added, turning to Russell. The other nodded and he went on, "I take it that Miss Dare and yourself were very close friends? It must have been a great shock for you."

"It was," said Sandra Borne in a low voice.

It was clear from her face that discussion was painful to her and that it was taxing her self-control to endeavor to remain unmoved. She turned to the other woman as if feeling the need for support from her own sex.

"I'm afraid I'll have to fly, Jean. There's a—there's a lot to be done."

"We understand," said Jean Russell quietly. "If there's anything we can do to help you mustn't be afraid to let us know."

"That's an order, Sandy," said her husband.

Sandra Borne's eyes were a little misty.

"You're both awfully good," she said.

Her voice trembled dangerously. Abruptly she turned and went down the path as though she dared not linger in case her emotion betrayed her. They watched her slight figure as she instinctively straightened as she reached the gate, determined to show a brave face to the world.

"I think," said Mordecai Tremaine thoughtfully, "I'd like to know the whole story."

Jean Russell glanced significantly at her husband.

"While I'm getting a cup of tea ready," she observed, "you two men can talk."

The doctor led the way into the cool drawing room, its half-drawn blinds toning down the heat of the sun and transforming its glare into a soothing twilight, and settled his guest into a comfortable lounge chair.

"I'll do my best to be as dispassionate as possible," he said, seating himself opposite Tremaine, "but as I told you, I knew Lydia—and I was called in when they found her this morning. So you'll have to make allowances if I seem to be showing too much heat."

"Let yourself go, Paul," observed Tremaine, "and don't be afraid of saying what you feel as well as what you know."

The other nodded, but he did not begin his story immediately. A hesitant look had come into his face now.

"Knowing that you were coming down," he said haltingly, "Jean and I have been wanting to talk to you about it all day. And now that you're here I don't know where to begin."

"Try the beginning," said his friend. "Murder begins a lot

further back than the actual crime—at least, it does in most cases. How long had Lydia Dare lived in Dalmering?"

"About eight or nine years. I believe her people live in Yorkshire—she used to go up to visit them several times a year."

"So that she was quite an old inhabitant? Most of the houses nearby seem to have been built fairly recently."

"Yes, I suppose she'd be what you might call one of the oldest of the new crowd. Her cottage—hers and Sandy's—was put up before the main estate was developed. Most of the houses were built about six years ago—it was a commercial scheme run by a private company."

Having found a point at which to embark upon his narrative, the doctor soon began to develop his theme, and Mordecai Tremaine—interjecting an occasional question—listened intently while Paul Russell told him what he knew of Lydia Dare and her way of life and of her last hours upon earth. And as he listened, he knew with a growing certainty that somehow, with the police or in spite of them, he would have to do what he could to find the assassin whose vicious hand and twisted mind had been responsible for the horror that had overtaken Lydia Dare in the darkness of that lonely path. For the murder seemed so utterly without reason, so utterly a deed of foul, useless, and bloody villainy.

Possibly he did not fully realize it even himself, but it was the fact that she had been engaged to be married and that her death had been encompassed almost upon the eve of what was to have been her wedding that weighed with him most. It was that which revolted and horrified his sentimental soul.

A bachelor himself, Mordecai Tremaine's sympathies were yet on the side of romance. He was the sworn friend of lovers. One of his chief delights was the reading of the admittedly highly colored but at least refreshingly idealistic fiction offered by *Romantic Stories*. It was a trait that had more than once rendered him an object of suspicion to cynical chambermaids who had discovered copies of that magazine in his room, but he was a romanticist unashamed.

To strike at the happiness of those who were patently in love was to arouse him to wrath. It awoke all the smoldering, deep-seated chivalry of the Galahad who dwelt within him. And hearing now of the pitiless, swift destruction of all the hopes that must have flamed so brightly in the hearts of Lydia Dare and the man she was to have married and of how the chill darkness of a shroud had so ruthlessly replaced the clinging warmth of a bridal gown, he was conscious of a deep and terrible anger.

He hardly knew that he was drinking the tea that Jean had brought in to them. He replaced the cup mechanically on the tray on the trolley at his side and looked across at his hostess who had joined her husband and himself.

"Do you mind if I slip out for half an hour or so, Jean?" he asked diffidently. "I'd like to have a look around."

"Of course not," she told him. "Would you like Paul to go with you?"

"No, don't bother, Paul," he said, turning to the doctor. "You'll probably have to attend to your surgery very shortly anyway, and I'd prefer to wander along on my own for a little while. I'd like to straighten things out in my mind."

There was no hesitation in his manner as he turned out of the gateway and walked down the roadway in the direction of the village and the copse in which Lydia Dare's murdered body had been found. He walked like a man whose mind was unclouded by doubts, but it would have surprised—and possibly dismayed—his friends to realize that he had in fact no clear plan of action. There was only a somewhat nebulous idea within him that he must see the place where the murder had been committed as his first step.

He had walked about two hundred yards when a dismaying thought came thrusting an imperative way into his mind with the same chill effect as an immersion in cold water.

He halted involuntarily. Murder had been done. He was on his way to examine the scene of the crime. The police, of course, would have no comment to make. They would calmly allow a stranger to the village, a stray visitor with no official status, to wander at will about the spot marked X without uttering a word of protest.

Or would they?

Mordecai Tremaine shook his head reprovingly and sorrowfully, one half of himself a source of pitying regret to the other. Despite all he should have known, despite all that his previous experience should have told him, he had been behaving like an uninformed amateur, meandering thoughtlessly toward disaster.

There was less spring in his step as he continued on his way. A cold doubt had begun to paralyze his mind. It was true that he had played a part in the solution of two murder mysteries. It was true that in doing so he had won (so he had reason to believe) the esteem both of Inspector Rich of the Westport and District Constabulary and of Inspector Boyce of Scotland Yard.

It was true that his friendship with the Scotland Yard man had been continued, both by correspondence and by an occasional meeting, ever since the conclusion of the first case in which he had been involved and in the course of which he had encountered Boyce. It was true that Inspector Rich for his part had thought so highly of him that he had taken the trouble to write to Boyce singing his praises, therefore increasing that gentleman's already high regard for him.

But these things did not make him *persona grata* with

every police force in Britain. They did not open all official doors to him. They did not mean that he could assume himself to be possessed of the powers to carry out investigations where he chose.

Besides, even if he could rely upon Inspector Boyce to back him in his actions, it would be of no avail here. Scotland Yard's writ did not run in Dalmering—or would not run until the local police had called in the Yard's assistance.

The copse lay between the house the Russells occupied and the village, and in a very few more moments he had drawn level with it. A little wooden gateway gave on to the road, and there was a path beyond it, leading through the trees.

There was no other human being in sight. He had seen no one during the short time it had taken him to walk down from the house. The village appeared to be deserted. He was aware of a feeling of surprise, and he realized subconsciously that he had been expecting to find the neighborhood of the crime barricaded off and guarded by burly and uncompromising policemen.

He peered over the gate. The path ran between ash, elm, and hazel for perhaps five or six yards and then took a sharp turn to the right so that its course was not visible from the road.

Its very emptiness was inviting. Mordecai Tremaine was

conscious of a wild desire to go through the gateway and see whence the path led. Swayed by some new, exciting emotion, he felt his indecision drop from him. His hand went out to the wooden latch.

And then he heard a cough—a warning, official cough, which was deliberately produced and not the involuntary result of any medical condition. His eyes became aware of the presence among the trees and bracken of a pair of boots that seemed to be planted into the ground with an authoritative solidity. From the boots, his startled glance traveled toward a pair of gray serge trousers and from the trousers to the face of their owner.

There it remained fixed. Recognition opened his mouth incredulously. Standing regarding him, as though his thoughts of a few moments previously had conjured him out of space and time, was the stocky, bullet-headed figure of Inspector Boyce of Scotland Yard!

3

Boyce stood without moving for an instant or two longer, the shrewd eyes in his expressionless official face devoid of any readable emotion.

And then: "Are you man or ghoul?" he asked.

And when Mordecai Tremaine still gaped at him, unable yet to divine whether he was dealing with friend or foe, he added: "They should call you the murder magnet." His voice seemed to hold a sorrowful regret. "You appear to attract crime. Whenever anyone gets killed you either find the body or else you're somewhere near at hand. How do you manage it? I've been a policeman for twenty years, and in all that time I've never been the first person to find a body nor even lived in the same place as a murderer."

Mordecai Tremaine made a strenuous mental effort and compelled his mind to belabor his vocal chords into activity.

"I've only just come here," he said defensively. "I was in London when it happened. The murder was all over before I arrived."

Boyce smiled disbelievingly and infuriatingly.

"I suppose you had a telepathic message that there'd been a murder here and came straight down like a homing pigeon?"

But by now Tremaine had recovered from his surprise and he went over to the offensive.

"What are *you* doing here, anyway?" he asked. "I thought Scotland Yard didn't handle these cases unless it was called in officially."

"It *has* been called in," said Boyce gently.

A great load lifted itself from Mordecai Tremaine's soul and went careering away into the abyss of troubles past.

"You mean," he said, "that *you're* in charge?"

The exultation in his tone brought a wary look into the Yard man's face.

"Suppose I am," he said suspiciously. "Where does that take us?"

"You mean where does it take *me*?" said Mordecai Tremaine. "I want to help you find the person who killed Lydia Dare."

"What," said Boyce quietly, "do you know about Lydia Dare?"

"I know that she was killed within a few feet of where we're standing, that the murderer used a sharp-bladed weapon— probably about nine or ten inches long—which hasn't so far been found, that death must have been instantaneous, and that it occurred before midnight last night. I know that the last person to see her alive was Martin Vaughan, who lives in a house about ten minutes' walk away. I know that she had no obvious enemies and that the police seem to have a difficult job on their hands."

A frown appeared between the Yard man's eyes.

"Where did you learn all this?" he demanded.

"From the doctor who was called in to examine the body," returned Tremaine, dropping his bombshell with a nice accuracy upon the center of the Yard man's official armor.

"The devil you did!" Boyce took a quick, angry step forward, so that now he was facing the older man across the wooden gate. "I'll see that that talkative numbskull gets his knuckles rapped! Has he been opening his stupid mouth all over the village?"

"I don't think so," said Tremaine mildly. "Nor," he went on, "do I think you will find it necessary to rap his knuckles when I explain why he told me. Dr. Russell is a friend of mine. I'm staying with him. He told me what he knows because he's aware of my—interest—in these things."

"It's irregular," grumbled Boyce, but it was clear now that he was mollified.

Had Mordecai Tremaine been any ordinary visitor to Dalmering his wrath would have remained unassuaged. But he knew that he could never remain out of temper for long with the retired tobacconist who looked so inoffensive and yet who could reveal the tenacity of the tougher breed of bulldog. Besides, Tremaine wasn't simply a vulgarly, morbid snooper of the type who made a nuisance of himself by perpetually getting in the way; he had a genuinely professional interest in crime. And in addition, Boyce told himself a little wryly, he had a habit of being infernally right when it came to arriving at the solution of murder mysteries.

By which it may be seen that, despite his somewhat frigid reception of him, Inspector Boyce had a warm corner in his heart for Mordecai Euripides Tremaine and no small appreciation of his capabilities.

"I suppose," he added sarcastically, "you imagine that now *I'm* going to tell you all *I* know?"

Deliberately blind to the sarcasm, Tremaine pretended to take him literally.

"After all," he responded mildly, "it will certainly make things so much easier if we're frank with each other. We both want to get at the truth—you because it's your job to do so and I because I want to help my friends. They were very fond of Lydia Dare, and this is a bad business. She was going to be married, you know."

Boyce was well aware of the incurably romantic streak in his friend's nature. He gave him a shrewd, understanding glance.

"So that's one of the things that have got your back up, is it?"

Mordecai Tremaine considered the position for a moment or two. He was, he thought, on safe ground now.

"I don't suppose you've had time to get down to any inquiries," he said reflectively. "I may be able to pass on some useful information to you. Paul Russell gave me a pretty comprehensive account of things in general. He's lived here for some years, and as the local doctor there isn't much he doesn't know about the neighborhood."

"You don't," said Boyce, "have to use so much camouflage. You know that although it's strictly against the regulations and that I'm a fool for doing it, I'm going to let you take a hand and look around if you want to. But for Heaven's sake be careful. Don't let any of the locals suspect that I'm aiding and abetting you or else you'll have the chief constable coming down on me, and letters written in vitriol will be going up to the Yard complaining that I'm allowing unauthorized persons to interfere in police matters."

"Thank you, Jonathan," said Tremaine, and the fact that he made use of the Christian name was significant in that it revealed that he considered now that all doubts had been cleared away. "You know you can rely on me to use discretion. I know your position is a difficult one."

Made bold by his new feeling of security, he ventured to ask a question that had been puzzling him.

"Just now you were accusing me of being a murder magnet,"

he said. "But how did *you* come to be here so quickly? I didn't think that the murder was discovered until this morning."

"It wasn't," returned Boyce. "But Major Rennolds, the local chief constable, is a man of good sense. He called in the Yard at once instead of waiting until the scent had grown cold and everything had been thoroughly messed up."

"You mean that it didn't take him long to come to the conclusion that his men were up against a problem they wouldn't be able to cope with?"

"Not exactly. This place, as you probably know since you've obviously been busy since you've been here," said the Yard man, unable to resist the dig, "has a semipermanent population, whose interests are in London and who spend a good deal of their time there. And since Lydia Dare's friends were largely drawn from the London 'colony' Major Rennolds decided that it was a crime for which he would probably need the Yard's assistance anyway. He called us in at once."

"A very wise step," said Tremaine approvingly. And added, after a pause, "Do you think I might take a walk along the path with you?"

"You don't lose any time, do you?" grumbled Boyce, but there was a twinkle in his eyes as he said it, and he opened the gate to allow his companion to go through.

The Yard man led the way along the narrow path until they came to a point about half a dozen yards beyond the right-angled turn. It was quiet and cool and so screened by trees that no exit from the copse was visible.

Tremaine looked inquiringly at his companion.

"Here?"

"Here," agreed Boyce. "To be precise—*here*."

He indicated a spot at the side of the path where the crushed bracken revealed that something had lain. Tremaine looked curiously about him.

"By now, of course, you'll have given the ground a good comb-over. Did you find anything?"

"Little enough," returned Boyce. "Whoever did it must have waited behind this bush until his victim came along." He gestured toward a clump of bramble bordering the path. "There was a cigarette butt lying there—or, rather, half a cigarette. It had been pinched out, as though someone had stopped smoking it in a hurry before they'd had time to finish it. It wasn't squashed flat or stubbed out against the ground."

"Any footprints?"

"You can see for yourself that the ground's too hard to give much away. But we did find a couple of prints." The Yard man drew aside a straggling length of bramble and pointed. "There's a patch of softer ground—must hold the water longer. You can see two heel marks. It's not much, but at least it's something."

Tremaine bent to examine the indentations that were just visible in the earth. There seemed to be a limited patch of ground with a swampy tendency a foot or so beyond the bush, and it was possible to make out the imprints of a pair of heels. They were much deeper at the back than at the front, and the soles had left no impression at all.

"Looks as though they were made by a man," he observed, straightening. He waved a hand to take in the immediate surroundings. "Judging by the signs, it must have been over very quickly. There doesn't seem to have been much of a struggle."

"She couldn't have had a chance to offer any resistance," said Boyce. "Whoever did it must have taken her completely by surprise and struck before she knew what was happening."

Tremaine glanced about him, peering among the trees and up and down the path.

"I expected to find policemen everywhere. Hasn't the path been closed to the public?"

"Temporarily—yes," nodded Boyce. "Although we've got what we want in the way of photographs and measurements. I've a man watching the point where it joins the common. I've sent the man I had posted at the roadway end off to get his tea. As a matter of fact I've taken over from him."

"Oh." Tremaine regarded his friend searchingly. "So that's why you were standing there when I came along. You were on the watch for anyone trying to use the path—but without allowing them to see you until they'd made their intention obvious."

"That," agreed Boyce, "was the idea. The news is all over the village now, of course, and it's common knowledge that we're here, but there's always the hope of picking up something. Lucky for you I happened to be there," he added. "Otherwise you'd have been facing a cross-examination from Newland—he's the chap who's been on the watch there— and he'd have sent you away with a flea in your ear."

"I was born," said Mordecai Tremaine complacently, "under a lucky star."

He prized an old-fashioned pocket watch, not without difficulty, out of the depths of his waistcoat and opened the case.

"I'll have to be getting back to the house. I said I wouldn't be much more than half an hour." He replaced the watch and glanced inquiringly at his companion. "Are you staying in the village, Jonathan?"

"Yes. I've a room at the Admiral. Pub down the road. But don't come asking for me there," added the Yard man warningly. "Partly because it won't do for us to be seen together in case the locals kick up a fuss, and partly because if you're not suspected of being a friend of mine you'll stand a better chance of getting to learn things. People are likely to tell you all sorts of village gossip that they wouldn't think of passing on to me."

"So I'm to be your sounding board," said Tremaine. "All right, Barkis is willin'. I'll keep my ears open. But there's a price, of course."

"Don't worry," said Boyce. "You'll be told if there are any developments. We'll need a meeting place, though. Any suggestions?"

Tremaine considered for a moment, and he recalled the low, redbrick building just beyond the village, outside which he had seen the advertisement for a play. He described the place and Boyce nodded.

"I know it—the village hall. I'll see you there at eleven. We'll compare notes. Now I'd better see if the coast is clear."

He led the way back down the pathway in the direction of the road. Tremaine kept well in the rear, and it was as well that he did so, for he was able to slip out of sight among the trees at his companion's hasty signal and Boyce's deliberately noisy progress served to cover the slight sound he made.

The reason for going to ground became obvious a moment later. Tremaine heard a new voice. A somewhat imperious voice with an underlying note of harshness.

"You the fellow from Scotland Yard?"

"I *am* from Scotland Yard," agreed Boyce quietly.

"Good. Heard you were here. My name's Vaughan."

The voice stopped—expectantly, as though the speaker was waiting for some reaction. If he was, he was disappointed. Boyce remained silent, obviously leaving it to him to do the talking.

Cautiously, Tremaine peered out from the shelter of the

trees and undergrowth. Boyce was standing by the gate now, facing the man who had addressed him.

Fortunately the newcomer's entire attention was focused upon the detective, and he did not give a glance in Tremaine's direction, which afforded that gentleman an opportunity of studying him in comparative safety.

As the last person to see Lydia Dare alive, Martin Vaughan was evidently destined to play an important part in the case. He would, therefore, well repay close observation.

Paul Russell's description of a powerfully built man of middle age, above the average height and looking as though he could still, if he chose, be physically a tough customer, was accurate enough. To that somewhat vague outline Tremaine added a pugnacious jaw that spoke of a forceful, determined character, a straight nose with just a hint of undue breadth about the nostrils, which gave his whole face a slightly ruthless appearance, and eyes that, beneath bushy eyebrows already inclining to gray, were regarding Jonathan Boyce with a challenging stare.

"I'm Vaughan," the big man repeated, as though he believed that since the inspector had made no response to his first statement he could not have heard it. "I was the last person to see Miss Dare alive."

"So I understand," said Boyce quietly.

"Well?" The word was sharp. "Don't you want to ask me any questions?"

Boyce stirred at that. His voice took on a deprecating quality.

"All in good time, Mr. Vaughan," he returned. "We like to take these things in order."

"I would have thought," said the other, and it seemed that he was keeping his tone level only with an effort, "that in that case one of your first actions would have been to question me in an attempt to narrow down the circumstances surrounding the crime."

"We haven't overlooked that," said Boyce. "We appreciate that your evidence may be important, and there are a number of questions we would like to ask you—later."

Martin Vaughan's great bulk surged up to the wooden gate, eliminating the space between them in one flood tide of movement.

"By thunder, man! Don't you know a woman's been killed? Somewhere her murderer's walking around as free as you or I, hugging his devil's secret and laughing at all of us, and you're standing there as if time wasn't important, doing damn all about it!"

And then the storm slowly subsided. They saw him fight to bring his passions under control, his thick fingers clamping down on the woodwork of the gate. He looked at Boyce.

"Sorry, Inspector. It is Inspector, isn't it? I'm afraid I'm a bit under the weather. The shock—after dining with her only last night—" He drew a deep breath, as though to steady himself. "Have you—have you discovered anything?"

"It's my job," said Boyce, "to discover things."

Vaughan's glance flickered past him, rested momentarily on the path through the copse, came back—guardedly it seemed—to the Yard man's face.

"When you want me," he said, "I suppose you'll know where to find me. I live at 'Home Lodge'—just across the common."

"Yes," said Boyce, "I know."

For a little space of time longer Vaughan stood looking at him, as though uncertain whether he should say what was in his mind. And then: "There's something evil in this place," he said, intensity clipping his words so that his voice seemed to vibrate with hardly controlled power. "It's peaceful and lovely and normal to look at, but underneath it's rotten—rotten and festering and corrupt. All the reeking powers of darkness and evil are hidden in it. She knew it. She tried to tell me of it, but I wouldn't listen. God, if only I'd believed her! If only I'd insisted on going back with her when she told me she preferred to go alone!"

He leaned forward. His voice was level enough, but his eyes had a wildness in them.

"It's too late for that now, Inspector. We can't put back the clock and live yesterday again. But we *can* find out who killed her. We can find him and feel his throat in our hands"—the thick fingers had begun to work—"and hear him try to squeal for mercy and see his obscene murderer's eyes blaze with terror and come bulging out of their sockets as he knows the life is being choked out of him!"

Boyce made no movement. His features remained expressionless. But: "I must point out, Mr. Vaughan," he said quietly, "that the law has its own machinery for dealing with these matters."

Martin Vaughan drew back. He laughed. It was a strange, faintly mocking sound that came from deep inside him.

"Of course," he said. "Of course. What I was trying to say, Inspector, was that you can rely upon me to give you all the assistance I can. I shall welcome any opportunity to help you. But no doubt you're busy, and I'm taking up your time. My apologies for the outburst just now."

"No apologies are needed," said Boyce. "I understand how you feel."

"Do you?"

The words were quiet. Vaughan gave him a queer sideways glance and then nodded and turned away.

Boyce stood watching him until he judged that the big man was out of earshot, then he looked around for Mordecai Tremaine.

"What," he said, "do you think of our Mr. Vaughan?"

"I'm not sure," said Tremaine reflectively. "Is he mad—or clever?"

"Don't," said Boyce patiently, "try to be the mysterious and great detective. Just say what you mean."

Mordecai Tremaine looked guilty.

"What I mean," he said, "is that you seem to be receiving a surprising number of offers to help. First of all from me, and now from Martin Vaughan. *I'm* easy enough to explain," he added modestly. "But why Vaughan?"

"*You're* the brilliant, unorthodox investigator," said Boyce maliciously. "All right—why?"

"It might be," said Tremaine, "because he's mad. Because his mind is obsessed with the one idea that he must find Lydia Dare's murderer and take his revenge for her death. Because he thinks that by offering to help you he will be able to share any information you may obtain and achieve his purpose more quickly. Or it might be because he's clever. Because he killed Lydia Dare himself. Because he wants to keep level with your investigations in order to safeguard himself."

"In other words you're suggesting that he was deliberately putting on an act just now?" Boyce shook his head. "You're a long way ahead of me, Mordecai. I'm just a policeman. I have to stick to facts. I can't afford to start romancing."

He added, after a pause: "All the same, there may be something in that suggestion of yours that he's mad. He's an archaeologist—done a lot of excavating and written books about what things were like thousands of years ago. A fellow like that, buried in the past, might get hold of some queer and bloodthirsty ideas—about revenge and human sacrifice and so on. All that stuff about the powers of darkness, for instance, didn't sound like the talk of a mentally healthy man."

"Precisely," agreed Mordecai Tremaine, in a manner, however, that allowed the word to mean anything.

Boyce was frowning, his toe prodding in a dissatisfied fashion among the bracken.

"But where's the motive?" he asked. "What reason would Vaughan have, either for killing Lydia Dare or for wanting to revenge her murder so badly? Do you know, Mordecai," he went on, in a sudden burst of frankness, "what I've always been most afraid of? Ever since I can remember, I've been scared that one day I might meet a motiveless crime, that I might be called upon to solve something with no reason behind it, something just plain senseless, something that would beat me just because there wasn't a mind or a motive I could track down. And I've a feeling that this," he finished grimly, "is going to be it."

Mordecai Tremaine looked carefully up and down the road. It was quite clear. He opened the gate and passed through.

"You're getting morbid, Jonathan. It's because the case has

only just begun and you've not found anything yet to get your teeth into. This is murder. And murder," he added sententiously, "always has a motive."

4

Efficiently Mordecai Tremaine had effaced himself. Once the inevitable introductions had been made he had gradually withdrawn from the conversation, and his own action and the fact that one subject was occupying the minds of his companions to the exclusion of all others had combined to give him the position he desired of the unnoticed spectator.

The scene was the drawing room at "Roseland," which was the attractive name the Russells had given to their equally attractive and invitingly cozily furnished house. Eight people were seated around the room, perched on the arms of chairs where it was not possible to adopt a more orthodox position, making themselves comfortable in the easy, informal manner of those who are on terms of familiarity with each other. It was evident that Jean and Paul Russell had been in the habit of keeping open house and that Roseland was an unofficial center of Dalmering's social life.

Outwardly it was a friendly little gathering. But it had not taken Mordecai Tremaine long to sense that under the apparent calm, the atmosphere was dangerously electric. The surface of the relationship between the men and women talking so casually was perilously brittle; occasionally it would break for an instant and reveal the ugly storm of fear and mistrust that was sultrily brewing beneath it.

The reason lay in one menacing word. Murder. All these people had known Lydia Dare. To a greater or less degree all their lives had been bound up with hers. And now that she was dead and her murderer was walking abroad undetected and probably in their midst, suspicion had become the dominating factor in their contacts with their neighbors. Guilty or innocent, consciously or subconsciously, they were on guard against each other, on the alert for a chance word that might possess a grim significance, quick to read some damaging meaning into what would otherwise have been an ordinary phrase.

Women, Mordecai Tremaine noted, were in the majority. In addition to himself and Paul Russell there was only one other male member of the party. Russell had introduced him as Geoffrey Manning. Tremaine judged him to be in the middle twenties—a quietly spoken young fellow whose rugged features and big-boned frame effectively prevented him from laying any claim to being handsome but who was possessed of a quick smile that gave him a frank and likeable air.

It was true that he was obviously suffering from the same sense of strain that obsessed the other members of the group, but even so there were occasions when his engaging grin relieved the underlying tension, and momentarily the conversation would become free and unrestrained. Inclining, as always, to the side of youth, Mordecai Tremaine found himself liking Manning on sight. He had to remind himself that it would be unwise for an investigator engaged upon what must necessarily be a grim search after truth to allow his judgment to be swayed by first impressions and personal prejudices.

The same self-discipline was necessary in respect of the girl on the arm of whose chair Manning was seated. Phyllis Galway was a highly attractive brunette, and her appeal was of the type—usually somewhat inadequately described as fresh and unspoiled—to which Mordecai Tremaine was especially prone to fall a victim. She approximated so closely to the charming image he carried in his heart of the daughter he would have liked to have.

The girl was frowning now, but it was a thoughtful, puzzled little frown that increased rather than detracted from her youthful good looks. She was, thought Mordecai Tremaine, wondering to himself what was wrong with Geoffrey Manning that he showed no sign of being aware of it, wholly adorable.

"It's very difficult," she said doubtfully, "to know what to do for the best. What do *you* think, Pauline?"

The question was addressed to a woman who was seated

opposite her. Tremaine had found his eyes straying very frequently toward Pauline Conroy. If Phyllis Galway's beauty was typical of the eager, fragrant appeal of youth, Pauline Conroy's was of the variety best described by the hackneyed word *striking*.

There was, Mordecai Tremaine decided, something about her that was slightly larger than life. Undeniably she was a beautiful woman, but her beauty had an air of being just a little more obvious than was consistent with good taste.

Her dark hair, curled at the ends and just sweeping her graceful shoulders so that each studied movement of her head revealed the slim column of her neck, was of a blackness that was boldly Spanish in its intensity. Her flawless skin; the vivid dark eyes, shaded by their long lashes, which could obviously flutter with the maximum of effect; the full red lips, parting when she smiled to display almost too even white teeth, reminded Mordecai Tremaine of a glossy photograph in a film magazine.

Photogenic. The word projected itself on to his mind as though a camera shutter had clicked. She was Hollywood with trimmings. She was languorous grace upon a background of velvet luxury.

It was not, of course, surprising that she should create such an impression. Pauline Conroy was an actress. Not, as yet, a star. Not, as yet, one of the dazzling lights of the firmament whose radiance could attract adoring crowds to the box offices. But possessed of ambition, consumed by the desire to climb the difficult slopes toward the angels.

Which meant that she was consistently playing to an audience—consistently, in fact, overplaying in order to draw attention upon herself. Her talents as yet unrecognized, she was compelled to display them lavishly. Not yet could she afford to hide modestly behind the dark glasses and the assumed name of a million-dollar success.

She did not make any immediate reply to Phyllis Galway's question. Tremaine was not sure whether her hesitation was part of her pose or whether it was due to the fact that she found it genuinely difficult to frame an answer.

"I think we should go on with the play," she said slowly. "After all, we owe it to the public. And I think it's what Lydia would have wished us to do."

She stopped. She looked around her. Her air was a little guilty, as though she herself felt that she had been a trifle too stereotyped, as though she had adhered too closely to the lines written in her part by convention.

Mordecai Tremaine had heard enough of the conversation that had been taking place to be fully aware of the situation that was under discussion. His mind had been presented with the memory of the noticeboard he had seen outside the building Jonathan Boyce had described as the village hall.

Murder Has a Motive, the play that had been advertised, was being produced by the residents of Dalmering's "colony" for the benefit of a local charity—an orphanage situated on the outskirts of Kingshampton, the seaside resort some five miles away. The production had been extensively advertised in the district, and the play was due to be performed in a fortnight's time. The question at issue was should it be postponed—or even canceled—in view of the murder that had shaken the village?

Lydia Dare had not been playing any actual part, but she had been acting as stage manager and had done a great deal of the inevitable behind-the-scenes organizing. Her death in any circumstances must naturally have cast a gloom over the remainder of the company, and coming in the stark and ugly manner in which it had, its effect had been doubly felt.

There was a brief silence after Pauline Conroy had delivered her judgment. And then: "I think," said another voice, hesitantly, "I think it would be better to drop the whole thing."

It was Karen Hammond who had spoken. She was not wearing the dark spectacles now, and Mordecai Tremaine had been able to confirm the truth of his assumption that her eyes were blue. He had confirmed, too, his first estimate of her beauty—Dalmering appeared to be singularly fortunate as far as the good looks of its womenfolk were concerned—and he had made in addition the discovery that she was in a bad state of nerves.

Occasionally he would observe a twitching at the side of her mouth, a restless movement of her hands. She herself was clearly unconscious of those things—or, if she was aware of them, they had become so much a part of her that she took them for granted. The glimpse of her that he had obtained from the car as they had reached the house that afternoon had been too brief for him to do more than assimilate the obvious—which meant her looks, dress, and graceful bearing—but now he was certain that if ever a woman was a prey to a continuous, nagging anxiety, it was Karen Hammond.

There was sudden antagonism in the glance that Pauline Conroy bestowed upon the woman whose blond loveliness was in such striking contrast to her own flamboyantly dark beauty.

"Why?" she asked sharply.

The slender fingers of Karen Hammond's right hand nervously twisted the artistically chased circle of gold on the wedding finger of her left. The words came from her reluctantly.

"It's all—all so horrible. Everything's so different now that Lydia's been—now that she's dead. It's become sordid—and—and beastly. There'll be inquiries—publicity. We'll have

newspaper reporters asking questions—prying into everything we say or do. Don't you see"—there was a breathless,
appealing note in her voice—"if we go on with the play the
newspapers are sure to write about it. They'll think it's good
copy—they'll want to know what she was going to do and
who's taking her place and every little detail there is. It will
make it all so—so tainted."

"I don't," said Pauline Conroy coldly, "see why it should.
Suppose the newspapers do get hold of the play and make news
out of it? Publicity is what we need. We want the play to be a
success, don't we? We all know that it was what Lydia wanted.
And as for the reporters asking all sorts of questions"—there
was an edge of malice in her tone—"there's no need for us to be
afraid of that. We none of us have anything to hide, have we?"

The final question was a barely concealed challenge. The
foil was all but off the rapier. Karen Hammond stiffened.
Again there came that momentary twitching born of agitation, and beneath her suntan, her face had whitened.

"Of course not. That wasn't what I meant. It was just that
I wanted to save any more trouble than we shall have to face
in any case. I thought it would save pain for everyone—for
all of us here, for Mr. Vaughan and Mr. Shannon—and for
Mr. Galeski."

It was clear from her attitude—expectant and defensive—
that she knew that the last name would produce a reaction.

She was right. Fire blazed viciously from Pauline Conroy's eyes before she could control herself and the long lashes had swept concealingly down.

"I don't think," she said, through lips that had temporarily lost their soft allure and become a thin, harsh line, "that Mr. Galeski will object to answering any questions—from anyone."

From the way in which she accented the last word, it was evident that it was "Scotland Yard" she meant to convey. Hostility crackled dangerously between the two women.

Paul Russell leaned forward, metaphorically gloved hands holding the naked wires tactfully apart.

"Of course he won't," he observed. "Serge is as ready as any of us to do what he can to help."

A faint, warning bell was echoing distantly in Mordecai Tremaine's brain. But before he could grasp the meaning of what was happening, before he could pin it firmly to the wall of his mind, it was happening no longer. Russell had brought back normality into the room. He had turned toward Sandra Borne.

"The best thing we can do, Sandy, is to leave this to you. You were closer to Lydia than any of us. You should be the one to decide."

Sandra Borne had been taking little part in the conversation. Tremaine had been watching her as she had sat, sad-faced, in one corner of the room. Her eyes had traveled restlessly from one to the other of the faces of her companions, but she had made no effort to express any opinion. She had a listless air, as though the vitality had been drained out of her by some emotional turmoil that had left her exhausted.

Sympathy for her had flooded Mordecai Tremaine's soul. Sandra Borne and Lydia Dare had been more than friends; they had shared not only the same house but the same tastes and interests—almost the same thoughts. There was about her the look of one who had been crushed beneath a fate in which she had trusted unquestioningly and that had suddenly overwhelmed her for a reason she did not comprehend.

Russell's remark, addressed directly to her, brought her around to face him. The doctor's friendly, weather-beaten countenance seemed to give her courage, and Tremaine was conscious of the illusion that he could see the life slowly flowing back into her dispirited body.

"We ought to carry on," she said firmly. "We've worked so hard and achieved so much that it would be a pity to stop now. Lydia"—the hesitation over the name was only brief—"Lydia wanted the play to be a success."

"That's settled then, Sandy," said Russell. He looked around at the others. "Are you all agreed?"

There was a murmur of assent. Even Karen Hammond, apparently prepared to yield to the fact that she had been overruled, gave a nod of acceptance.

Pauline Conroy flashed her a triumphant glance.

"Sandy's right, of course," she said. "We owe it to Lydia's memory to go on and do our best."

"Does that mean rehearsal tomorrow as usual?" Phyllis Galway asked. "We'll have to let Mr. Vaughan and Mr. Shannon know."

A look of concern came into Sandra Borne's face at that.

"I'm afraid I'd overlooked Martin and Mr. Shannon," she said apologetically. "We ought to consult them first."

"I'm sure they'll be willing to fall in with the rest of us," said Russell confidently.

"Shannon probably will," interjected Geoffrey Manning impulsively. "He's usually ready enough to accept any suggestions. It might be a bit difficult for Vaughan, though. After all, he was in—"

He broke off abruptly, as if he had realized that he had been on the point of saying something that would have precipitated a crisis. He reddened, made a clumsy attempt to retrieve the situation.

"He was in a bad state of nerves when I saw him this evening," he finished hurriedly. "Seemed to be taking it to heart."

There was a silence as he broke off. An uncomfortable silence, which gradually became more uncomfortable and more oppressive. And then several people began speaking at once.

Paul Russell signaled desperately to his wife. She rose.

"It's time for a cup of coffee," she observed, and Karen Hammond snatched at the straw.

"I'll come and help you, Jean."

The few moments of bustle and moving of chairs that were occasioned by their exit served to turn what had evidently been a dangerous corner. Tremaine glanced unobtrusively about him and saw the relief coming into faces that had been revealing traces of strain.

He knew now that Lydia Dare's death had not been as a stone thrown wantonly into what had been a placid millpond of village life. It had stirred into movement the dark and secret things that had been already in being beneath the calm of the surface. It had not brought evil into existence; it had revealed its presence.

There was only one person in the room who appeared to be unaffected by the general atmosphere of strain. Tremaine had observed that not only did Edith Lorrington appear to be unaffected by it, but she even appeared to be blissfully unaware of it.

She was an elderly spinster. Her thin gray hair, tied in an old-fashioned bun, and her blouse, fastened high around her neck and held by a large and ornate brooch, emphasized her prim plainness. She was faded Victorianism dwelling diffidently among colorful modernity.

She was not, however, of the vinegary spinsterhood that, robbed of fruition, turns its claws upon its more fortunate sisters. Here, indeed, was the mask of tragedy, not of envy disguising itself as righteous indignation. The man who would have been her husband had died of malaria in West Africa while she had been preparing her trousseau, and opportunity had not passed her way a second time.

After the cable that had meant the end of her dreams had reached her, she had never known youth again. The years had watched her become more dowdy, plainer in looks and dress, until now she was a harmless, ineffectual shadow, taken for granted in life and unlikely to be missed when she eventually faded unobtrusively into death.

Exactly what part Miss Lorrington was taking in the production of *Murder Has a Motive*, Mordecai Tremaine was not certain. She was the sort of person who inevitably moved vaguely in the background of such events without apparently serving any specific purpose.

Oddly enough it was she—seemingly tranquilly unaware of the forces she was helping to unleash—who threatened to recreate the taut, explosive conditions that had so narrowly been dispelled.

"We're all Lydia's friends here," she announced suddenly. "It's up to us to help the police."

She might have been opening their eyes to catastrophe. No one moved or spoke. Even Paul Russell seemed momentarily at a loss.

It was Sandra Borne who first found words.

"What do you mean, Edith?" she asked quietly.

"I mean that we should do all we can to find out who committed this horrible crime." Miss Lorrington was sitting very upright in her chair. Her hands were clasped in her lap, and on her face was the rapt, innocently engrossed expression of a child who sees things simply and very clearly. "Lydia was murdered. She was our friend. We can all help to avenge her."

"How?"

It was Pauline Conroy's voice—a little harsh, a little—fearful? Mordecai Tremaine was not sure. As yet he was still groping, still assimilating facts, still feeling his way in the morass of human emotions into which he had deliberately tried to sink himself.

Edith Lorrington turned to regard her questioner. Her eyes were shining. Deep inside her old instincts were stirring. The shadow was taking on substance.

And then, quite suddenly, the fire died down. The habit of self-effacement, engendered by the passage of more than forty years, overcame her brief resolve. She made an ineffectual gesture.

"I—I don't know," she said helplessly.

Over Pauline Conroy's dark head Paul Russell's eyes caught Mordecai Tremaine's. Their glances held—significantly.

"Perhaps," he said, "Edith's hit upon a sound idea. Perhaps we *can* help the police. We know Dalmering—we know the people who live here. It's by the putting together of all the simple things, all the apparently unimportant details, that the police solve crimes. It's like a jigsaw puzzle. One tiny piece can make the whole thing fit. If we pool our knowledge we may be able to uncover something that will give us a clue as to who killed Lydia."

"But who," said Sandra Borne, bewilderment struggling with horror in her voice, "who could have *wanted* to kill her? Lydia didn't have any enemies."

"You mean," said Russell quietly, "that she didn't have any enemies—*as far as we know*." He accentuated the last words, giving them a grim significance. "I'm afraid this is likely to be painful for you, Sandy," he went on, "but if we want to arrive at the truth it means that we've got to ask each other questions. At what time did Lydia leave the house last night?"

"The police," she said, "will ask questions. In fact, they've already started. So you don't have to worry about me, Paul. To answer questions among friends will be a help. A sort of dress rehearsal," she added wryly. "She left just before seven o'clock."

"You knew where she was going?"

"Of course. She was dining with Martin. It was still quite

light when she left. She must have been seen by someone on her way there."

"I saw her crossing the common," said Karen Hammond, who had made a brief reappearance. "From my bedroom." She shivered. "It—it was the last time I ever saw her."

Paul Russell gave her a curious glance as she went out again, and Mordecai Tremaine wondered just why she had made that last remark. It had had the ring of an alibi.

"Did Lydia say what time she was coming back?" asked the doctor.

There was just the faintest suggestion of hesitation in Sandra Borne's manner before she shook her head.

"No—she didn't say. I stayed indoors, knitting and listening to the wireless. I didn't notice how the time was passing. I felt myself getting sleepy so I went up to bed—it must have been after eleven. Lydia had her key, of course. It wasn't until this morning that they told me—that I heard what had happened. It was Briggan who came. He said that they'd—that they'd found Lydia…"

Briggan was the local constable who had been immediately roused by the farm laborer who had discovered the body in the early hours of the morning on his way to his work.

Russell nodded sympathetically.

"That seems clear enough, Sandy."

But to Mordecai Tremaine it didn't seem clear. Not at all

clear. There were two questions at least he would have asked of Sandra Borne.

He would have said, "*Was it usual for Lydia to stay out so late on her own?*"

And: "*Didn't you become alarmed when she didn't come back?*"

For it seemed to him that there was something missing in Sandra Borne's story. Was it likely that if her friendship with Lydia Dare had been so close, she would calmly have gone to bed without taking any steps to discover why she had not returned at a very late hour? After all, it was reasonable to assume that Lydia would at least have left a tentative time of her return with her companion. There was, he thought, room for elaboration of the story Sandra had told.

The reentry of Karen Hammond with a tray bearing a number of coffee cups that she proceeded to set out upon a small table served to terminate Russell's cross-examination. There was a brief silence while everyone watched the setting out of the china in the self-conscious manner of people who are searching for something in which they can pretend an interest in order to hide their unease.

"Was Philip here last night, Karen?"

There was a clatter. A cup rattled noisily against its saucer. Karen Hammond's hand was still shaking as she replaced it. It was a moment or two before she replied to Paul Russell's obviously casual question, and Tremaine saw that even then her nerves were not quite steady.

"Yes," she said breathlessly. "Yes, he was here. Why do you ask?"

"Just friendly curiosity," said Russell, with a smile. "After all, we're neighbors, you know. Has he been able to get down tonight?"

"He's at home now. He had to bring some work away with him from the office. That's why he didn't come along."

She gave the explanation hurriedly, as if she feared that it would be challenged. She had the same hunted expression she had worn during her brief duel with Pauline Conroy a few moments previously. Ostentatiously she busied herself with her task. Her fear was evident in the taut lines of her body.

Pauline Conroy was regarding her oddly. "I saw Philip's car come in this evening," she said. "He's been in town all day?"

Karen Hammond compelled herself to look around with an appearance of unconcern.

"Yes. As a matter-of-fact he's been very busy lately. He wasn't at all sure that he'd be able to run down here tonight."

"He must have left very early this morning. I usually hear his car going off."

Pauline Conroy's dark eyes had opened wide in an innocent, questioning stare. But it was, Mordecai Tremaine noted shrewdly, a little more innocent, a little more bewildered than the situation required. The alluring Pauline was overplaying again.

But by now Karen Hammond had succeeded in gaining a hold of herself. Blue eyes met dark without faltering.

"I don't suppose you did hear him go this morning," she said levelly. "He had to leave very much earlier than usual, and he did his best not to disturb anyone."

Instinctive suspicion replaced cultivated innocence in the dark eyes. But it was an obvious stalemate, and Pauline Conroy did not try to press the point.

In a few moments the coffee made its appearance, and while it was being handed around there was another opportunity of relieving the tension. But primitive emotions were too nakedly exposed for them to be covered up too easily or for long. Once again Mordecai Tremaine was conscious of the feeling that the shadow of evil lay heavily over the loveliness of Dalmering; that its beauty was threatened by black horror.

It surprised him to find the remembrance of Martin Vaughan vividly in his mind and the echo of the words he had used in his ears. He saw the big man as he had stood facing Jonathan Boyce, his powerful hands tightly clenched and that strange, half-wild look upon his face.

Sandra Borne was slowly stirring her coffee. She had lost

something of the birdlike appearance he had noticed at their first meeting. Her pale face was pinched and haunted.

"There was something worrying Lydia," she said. "There was something on her mind. She was glad that she was leaving Dalmering. She was afraid…" She looked up suddenly, and her voice sharpened, became possessed of a shrillness that verged on hysteria. "That was it. She was afraid! She knew that something was going to happen! She said—she said that underneath Dalmering was evil and rotten!"

Once again it was an echo of Martin Vaughan that Mordecai Tremaine heard. He would have liked to have asked the questions that were clamoring at the back of his mind. He would have liked to have known with more certainty what it was of which Lydia Dare had been afraid. But he feared that if he spoke it would inevitably draw attention to himself, and then the resulting remembrance that there was a stranger among them would effectively close the conversation between his companions. And if it closed—or, rather, became stilted and guarded—he would hear no more of interest.

Geoffrey Manning was leaning forward, a trace of excitement in his manner.

"When you say that Lydia was afraid, Sandy, do you mean that she was definitely afraid of *someone*?"

Sandra Borne shook her head.

"Not exactly that. She didn't speak of any particular person. It was just a vague sort of idea she seemed to have."

"What's in your mind, Geoffrey?" asked Paul Russell.

"Have any of you noticed a stranger about the neighborhood?" asked the other man. He glanced inquiringly around him. "A short, ferrety-looking fellow in a pair of gray flannels and a sports coat?"

"Don't think so," returned the doctor slowly. "At least, I don't remember seeing him. I've been too busy with my old patients to have the time to go around looking for likely new ones!" he added with a smile.

Sandra Borne gave a little cry.

"Yes—I remember him, Geoffrey! I saw him talking to Lydia. It was a few days ago. They were standing just outside the cottage."

"Did Lydia say anything to you about him?" asked Manning.

"No, she didn't. It was rather strange. It seemed as though she didn't want to talk about him. So, of course, I didn't ask any questions."

"I've seen him, too." It was Edith Lorrington who spoke, and her words shifted the center of interest toward her once again. "It was one day last week. He asked me where Mr. Hammond lived."

So engrossed were the others with what she was saying

that Mordecai Tremaine thought that he was the only person in the room who heard the faint, stifled gasp that came from very near at hand.

He gave a cautious glance sideways, taking care not to be observed. Karen Hammond was bending over the trolley. She was pretending to be busy with the empty cups and her blond hair had fallen forward so that her features were partially concealed.

But from where he sat Tremaine could see that beneath her suntan her face had become possessed of a taut, deathly paleness and that the blue eyes held the pleading terror of a creature who could see the remorseless closing of a trap.

5

There was still enough light to make walking easy, so that there was no question of stumbling blindly into ditches and hedgerows, and yet it was dark enough to encourage thought. Or so Mordecai Tremaine considered as he strolled pensively in the direction of the village hall and his rendezvous with Inspector Boyce of Scotland Yard.

He eyed the twinkling pattern of the stars reflectively. His first evening in Dalmering had undoubtedly been a full and intriguing one. And not the least of its incidents had been the arrival at "Roseland" of Martin Vaughan and Howard Shannon.

The two men had arrived just in time to save Karen Hammond from embarrassment—from what might, indeed, have proved more than mere embarrassment. Edith Lorrington's statement that the stranger in the gray flannels had asked for Philip Hammond had brought the limelight of curiosity full upon his wife.

Critical eyes had searched her face. Tremaine

acknowledged admiringly that, despite the agonized, hunted look he had surprised, she had faced the situation with courage.

"That's odd," she had said. "He hasn't called at the house. Are you sure he asked for Philip?"

Nevertheless, it had been a desperate moment for her. There might have been other questions. Pauline Conroy, for instance, might have fastened upon it, and her overpitched but compelling tones would have played viciously and cunningly upon tight strong nerves, extracting the last grain of drama, searching for a weakness in the defenses through which the flood of her malice could pour.

The sudden, shrill sound of the doorbell must have echoed through Karen Hammond's mind with the raw clamor of an unexpected reprieve. It had halted the questions for a few painful seconds, and then it had been too late for questions because Martin Vaughan had arrived.

The big man's entry into the drawing room had been something in the nature of a challenge. He had stopped on the threshold and surveyed the gathering as though he was facing potential enemies whom he had determined to intimidate by taking the offensive from the start. And then he had smiled and had introduced himself easily, with no suggestion of antagonism.

"Hullo, everybody. Sorry I couldn't get along before. I've

been entertaining Scotland Yard. I bumped into Shannon along the road, and we finished the journey together."

Paul Russell had looked at him inquiringly.

"Entertaining Scotland Yard, Martin?" he had asked, and Vaughan had waved a big hand carelessly.

"I've had a visit from the Yard detective who's in charge of the case. Routine, I suppose."

And then he had looked around, and there had been an odd note in his voice as he had added, "His name's Boyce—Inspector Boyce. For when *your* turns come along."

He had not waited to observe the effect of his words, but his big frame had loomed its way across the room through a suddenly awkward silence.

As though there had been nothing of significance in his tone, he had found himself a seat on a small folding stool that had been tactfully ignored by the others as offering too cramped a resting place. It had disappeared incongruously beneath his bulk so that he had appeared to be sitting on air.

Sandra Borne had been his neighbor. As he had greeted her his massive hands had temporarily engulfed her tiny ones in an enveloping but sympathetic grasp, and Tremaine fancied that the hardness in the big man's gray eyes had softened.

"How are you, Sandy?"

Sandra Borne had smiled and used Vaughan's Christian name in her reply. But somehow there had been a hint of insincerity in her voice. It was almost, Tremaine had thought, as though there had been a trace of repugnance in her attitude.

And yet, Paul Russell had told him, Martin Vaughan and Sandra Borne were good friends. Had he been mistaken in thinking that he had sensed hostility on the part of the eager little woman who had been Lydia Dare's closest companion? Had he misinterpreted something much simpler and more easily explained? Or had he indeed been presented with a brief clue to yet another of the secret feuds that lay beneath the falsely peaceful surface of the village community?

Mordecai Tremaine listened subconsciously to the quietly echoing sound of his own footfalls as he crossed the open space in the center of the old Dalmering, passed the dark and shuttered Admiral, and went on up the road toward his rendezvous. It was like listening to the measured pad of insistent facts across his mind—facts that marched in a steady circle, so that although they lured him to follow them, they led him nowhere.

Howard Shannon had joined Karen Hammond among the people who had left him facing a question mark. The plump-faced man in the crumpled blue suit whom he had seen in the train had been a negative quantity at the side of Vaughan's aggressiveness. He had not attempted to thrust himself into the limelight as Vaughan had tended to do. As Geoffrey Manning had forecast that he would, he had agreed without argument to the decision to continue with the production of the play. He had seemed anxious not to become involved too deeply in the conversation lest he should be called upon to answer questions.

Or was that conclusion fair? Tremaine considered the matter as dispassionately as he was able. Yes, Shannon had displayed a certain nervousness; he had shown a certain inclination to withdraw into his shell of silence when questions had been in the air.

On the other hand he had seemed overeager to explain that he had not been in Dalmering at the time when Lydia Dare must have been killed.

"I had to go to town yesterday," he had said. "On business. As a matter of fact, I wasn't keen, but it was a chance I couldn't miss. Fellow I've been trying to get in touch with for weeks happened to be in London with an hour or two to spare. I stayed overnight—didn't get back until this afternoon."

"There was a pretty bad storm last evening so I'm told," Vaughan had put in casually. "I was talking to a friend of mine in Kingshampton who happened to be in town and was caught in it. He told me he was soaked in a few minutes—he hadn't expected it, didn't have his raincoat or an umbrella with him. That's the worst of these unexpected English summers of ours. You never know what's likely to happen for five minutes at a time. I hope you weren't one of the unlucky ones, Shannon?"

"No," the plump man had replied, hesitantly. "No, I—I took a taxi from the station and missed the worst of it."

And then his eyes had alighted upon Mordecai Tremaine. He had stared at him, obviously not quite certain, and then, when he had convinced himself that he had made no mistake, a smile had spread over his podgy features. It had been like the incredulous, unutterably relieved smile of a man who had been encompassed about with perils and who had suddenly been shown an avenue to safety.

"Why—didn't we share the same compartment coming down from Victoria today, Mr.—er—Mr. Tremaine?"

Paul Russell had introduced them when Shannon had entered the room, but the plump man had been so evidently preoccupied that he had given no sign of recognition. His words of greeting had been quite mechanical, and his mind had clearly been elsewhere.

"Quite right, Mr. Shannon," Tremaine had replied. "A pity neither of us knew the other's destination! When I saw you get out at Dalmering I asked Paul if you and he were neighbors."

The other had seemed taken aback at that. A plump hand had nervously and ineffectually made a pretense at smoothing the creases from his rumpled clothes.

"Oh—yes, yes, of course. Paul and I are quite old neighbors now."

That had been all. There had been nothing to startle,

nothing to afford sensation. And yet Tremaine had been aware of a feeling that there was something wrong.

It was odd that Shannon should have seemed so ill at ease, odd that he should have leaped so obviously at the opportunity of supporting his alibi with an independent witness.

If he had left Dalmering for London long before Lydia Dare had been killed and had not returned until the following afternoon, then obviously he had nothing to fear. *If* he had left…

Tremaine pulled his mental wanderings to a halt. This was undoubted romancing, the kind of idle weaving of baseless theories that would call down the wrath of Jonathan Boyce upon his head.

He quickened his pace determinedly, and, just ahead of him, in the deep shadow of the hedgerow opposite the village hall, he saw the red pinpoint of a cigar.

"Is that you, Jonathan?"

The pinpoint moved.

"It is," came the Yard man's voice in reply.

The end of Boyce's cigar glowed brightly as he took a step forward out of the darkness of the hedgerow, bringing with him a rich aroma of tobacco leaf.

"I'm a fool for being here," he said morosely. "I'm breaking all the rules and laying myself open to a dishonorable discharge. I'm throwing away the prospect of a perfectly good pension. What do you suppose the commissioner would say if he knew I was meeting you like this for the purpose of giving away official information?"

"I expect," said Mordecai Tremaine mildly, "that he would decide that you were showing outstanding initiative and would mark you down for the next superintendent's vacancy. You've been brooding again, Jonathan—upsetting your nerves. Don't forget you've already told the commissioner about me. In one of your letters you said that you'd had a chance to mention my name to him when he was in a good mood, and that provided I kept out of the way and didn't try to gain any publicity he didn't mind my having a look around with you sometimes—if *you* wanted it and on a purely unofficial basis. You said that he was enterprising and unorthodox and that he wasn't afraid to go outside the regulations if he considered it would be worthwhile."

"Did I say all that?" Boyce shook his head in mock dismay. "The trouble with you, Mordecai, is that you remember too much."

"Did Vaughan tell you anything?" asked Tremaine.

The detective's stocky figure stiffened warily.

"What makes you think I've seen him?"

"He's been along to the Russells' tonight," returned Tremaine. "He told us that you'd been to see him."

"I didn't get very far," said Boyce. "Lydia Dare arrived

somewhere between seven o'clock and half past—he wasn't sure of the exact time—and left about eleven. He wanted to accompany her back to her cottage, but she insisted on going alone. He said good night to her at the door of 'Home Lodge,' and that was the last he saw of her."

"Did Vaughan say whether she made any mention of what time she'd promised Sandra Borne she would be back?"

"Yes. According to his story she left in rather a hurry because she said that she'd promised Miss Borne that she'd be back by eleven."

"H'm."

It was an indeterminate grunting sound. It might have served to cloak something significant. The Yard man eyed his companion suspiciously.

"Anything special about that?" he demanded.

"I don't know," returned Tremaine.

Briefly he told Boyce of the suspicions that had come into his mind when Sandra Borne had told her story. The detective listened to him carefully. His eyes were thoughtful, and he made no attempt at interruption until the recital was finished.

"You seem to have had a pretty full evening," he observed. "I mean from the point of view of learning about the people who live around about here. Suppose you give me an account of what was said and who said it."

"I'll try," said Tremaine. "I'll give you the essence of it, anyway, although I can't swear to the exact words."

As well as he was able he gave the other a summary of the conversation that had taken place at "Roseland." He added his personal observations. He made a special point of describing with as much detail as he could remember the outwardly polite but secretly fiery exchanges between Karen Hammond and Pauline Conroy. He laid emphasis on Karen Hammond's undoubted state of nerves.

But despite his subtle underlining of the part the two women had played in the evening's minor drama, it was Martin Vaughan in whom Boyce seemed most interested.

"When Vaughan came into the room," he said, "what sort of mood was he in?"

"He seemed—aggressive. Almost as though he thought he was under suspicion and was trying to brazen his way out of it."

Boyce gave a little murmur of satisfaction.

"Like his attitude when we saw him down the road and when I called on him at his house this evening. He answered all the questions I put to him without making any fuss, but he gave me the impression that he was on his guard all the time and trying to hide it by taking the offensive."

"Did he offer any proof of his story?" asked Tremaine.

"Not directly. But he pointed out—as though he didn't

want me to overlook it—that he has a manservant living with him."

"Sounds like the buildup to an alibi," observed Tremaine, and Boyce nodded.

"That," he remarked, "is what *I* thought. I questioned Blenkinson—that's the fellow's name—and he said that he saw Miss Dare leave the house—alone."

"Definitely an alibi." Tremaine sniffed gently at his companion's cigar, as though he fancied that its fragrance could soothe his mental processes. "Did you ask Blenkinson whether his master went out at any time after Lydia Dare had left?"

"As far as he knows," said Boyce slowly, "Vaughan didn't leave the house."

"But," prompted Tremaine, "he can't swear to it because he didn't actually see him. Is that it?"

Boyce carefully removed an inch of ash from the end of his cigar. He eyed his companion thoughtfully.

"Blenkinson's story is that he remained downstairs—'tidying up,' as he expressed it. Vaughan went to his study, and Blenkinson didn't see him again until about half an hour later, when he came out, said good night, and went up to bed."

"Is the study on the ground floor?"

"Yes," said the Yard man, in the tone of one who knew what was coming.

"So that Vaughan could have left the room by the window, could have made his way to the copse—either by overtaking Lydia Dare along the path over the common or by doubling around by the roadway and reaching it ahead of her—could have killed her and been back in the house in well under half an hour—all without Blenkinson knowing anything about it and believing him, in fact, to be still in the study."

"Could be," said Boyce. And added, "But there's no proof."

"Yet," said Mordecai Tremaine.

He sensed that the other was on the point of putting a pertinent question and was only hesitating while he found the words in which to frame it. He went on hastily: "Any other alibis?"

"Two," said Boyce unwillingly. "Three if you count the Hammonds' alibi as two. I've not been able to consolidate the inquiries yet—this is just a sort of preliminary look around. Mr. and Mrs. Hammond didn't go out at all last night. Mrs. says that Mr. was tired—had been working hard at the office. They went to bed early because he had to leave first thing this morning."

"That was what she said in the house just now," observed Tremaine. "There seems to be that feud I mentioned going on under the surface between Karen Hammond and Pauline Conroy, and Pauline didn't look too convinced."

"She's my other alibi," remarked Boyce. "Newland checked

up on her. She stayed indoors, too. Must have been a sort of holiday at home here last night. Her maid corroborated her story. According to Newland—"

He broke off. He stared up and down the road in the darkness.

"Did you hear anything?" he asked.

"No." Tremaine shook his head. "I was concentrating on what you were saying. Why? What was it?"

Boyce stood in a listening attitude for a few moments longer. They heard the telephone wires humming softly above them. A long way off a car hooted once, twice. The faintest of breezes rustled the leaves in the hedgerows. The detective relaxed.

"Thought I heard someone moving about," he said. "Must have been mistaken. What was I talking about? Oh, yes—according to Newland this Miss Conroy is an overpowering young lady."

"She's an actress," said Mordecai Tremaine, as if that explained all.

"Talking about actresses," said Boyce, "maybe it's a good idea from our point of view that they've all decided to carry on with the play over there." He jerked an expressive thumb in the direction of the darkened village hall on the opposite side of the road. "Keeps everybody together. We'll know where to find them if we should want them in a hurry."

"There's something in what you say, Jonathan." Tremaine's voice was exasperatingly noncommittal. "By the way," he went on, as a scrap of the conversation to which he had listened at "Roseland" came back into his mind, "have you had any dealings with anyone called Galeski yet?"

"Galeski?" Boyce frowned. "Can't recall the name. It isn't one you'd be likely to forget if you'd heard it. Who is he?"

"I don't know," returned Tremaine cheerfully. "Beyond the fact that he has some connection with Pauline Conroy. I dare say we'll come across him sooner or later." He moved away from the shadow of the hedgerow into the roadway. "That seems to be about all we can cover tonight, Jonathan. I'm supposed to be taking a quiet stroll for a breath of fresh air before turning in. I'd better get back before Paul starts sending out a search party to make sure I've not become Dalmering's second victim!"

"The doctor and his wife don't know you've come out to have a talk with me?"

"No. They know that I write to you, and Vaughan mentioned your name tonight when he said that you'd been to question him. But they didn't make any comment, so they may not have noticed it."

"They will soon," said Boyce. "You'll have to give them the tip not to spread it around the village, otherwise all these new acquaintances of yours will be shutting up like clams."

"Don't worry about Jean and Paul. They're safe enough. Well, I'll be on my way, Jonathan."

They said good night, and Tremaine set off down the road, walking at a brisk pace. Although he had learned nothing new during his conversation with Jonathan Boyce, with the exception of what he had been told of Martin Vaughan's statements, he felt that he had cleared the air. He had been enabled to marshal what facts he had so far gleaned into some sort of sequence. He had been enabled to sort out and label his impressions of the people he had encountered. He felt that even if he had not succeeded in fitting the oddly shaped pieces of the puzzle into their correct places, he had at least prevented them from wandering haphazardly into the wrong ones. They had all been firmly pinned down where he could examine them at his leisure.

He had walked about a hundred yards, engrossed in his thoughts, when he became aware of a flurry of movement among the deep shadows bordering the road. A figure detached itself from the gloom. He heard the quick sound of footsteps.

"Mr. Tremaine!"

The voice, although edged with urgency, was a soft, huskily feminine one. Mordecai Tremaine felt his heart slide back into its normal position. He turned.

"Why—Mrs. Hammond!"

His tone revealed his surprise as he recognized her. She took a step toward him.

"I had to see you," she said, hurrying her words as though she feared he would not otherwise listen. "I've got to talk to you. I heard you tell Jean before everybody left that you were going for a stroll later on, and I waited outside the house until you came out and then followed you."

Tremaine peered at her, trying to read the expression on her face.

"But why didn't you speak to me when you saw me leave the house?"

Karen Hammond did not make a direct reply to the question.

"You're a friend of Inspector Boyce, aren't you?" she said quickly. "The detective from Scotland Yard. You've just been talking to him."

Mordecai Tremaine experienced a sudden cold dismay.

"What makes you think I know Inspector Boyce?" he asked.

"Jean used to talk about you. She said that you knew a Scotland Yard detective whose name was Boyce and that you had helped to solve several murders. And when you came today and then Martin said that a detective called Boyce had been to question him I knew that it must be the same man.

You were talking to him along the road just now. I—I wanted to see if you were going to meet him."

So Jonathan Boyce had not been mistaken when he had thought he had heard something. It had been the sound of Karen Hammond's approach that his keen ears had detected. She must have been near at hand, concealed in the darkness of the hedgerow, while he and Boyce had been talking. It was a disturbing thought. Tremaine wondered what Boyce would say when he knew. If Karen Hammond was aware of his interest in crime and of his acquaintance with the Yard man, how many others of the village's inhabitants also knew?

"Suppose," he said slowly, "I *have* been talking to Inspector Boyce. What then?"

"Have they—have they found out anything?" she asked him.

"Policemen," he returned reprovingly, "don't go around telling people things like that, you know."

She caught his arm impulsively.

"You've got to help—you've got to find out who killed Lydia."

"That's what the inspector has come here to do, Mrs. Hammond. And he *will* do it—no matter how long it takes."

"But you don't understand! It mustn't take a long time! It must be done quickly—quickly!"

She was standing quite close to him. He could feel her breath soft upon his cheek. Her agitation seemed to be enhancing her beauty in some strange way, making her elusively desirable. Oddly, Mordecai Tremaine the elderly bachelor knew a faint moment of jealousy toward the man on whose behalf this exciting creature was showing herself so disturbed.

Was it a man? That, of course, he did not know. His conjecture might be wildly astray.

"Why is it so important that the murderer should be found quickly?" he asked her quietly. "I mean important for *you*?"

"The longer it goes on the more inquiries there will be," she told him. "It will be questions—questions—all the time. Newspaper reporters will be here, photographers, searching and prying. Nothing will belong to us any more. We'll have no rights, no thoughts even. Everything will be dragged out and shown to the public, just to make a story. Nothing will be private. Nothing will be respected. Philip—"

She stopped. She bit the word off abruptly, vehemently, as though she had realized that in her headlong expression of her feelings she had been in danger of betraying herself.

"Yes?" prompted Tremaine, but she evaded him by replying with another question.

"You *will* help, won't you? It's terribly important."

"I'm sure that Inspector Boyce will do all he can," he replied. "That's his job—to find the murderer as quickly as possible."

Karen Hammond looked full into his face, and once again he was aware of the unsettling but pleasurable sensation that her beauty was swaying his reason.

"It's *you* I mean," she said. "*You* could find out who did it."

Before her urgent pleading Tremaine's sentimental soul wavered.

"I'll do anything I can to help, Mrs. Hammond," he told her. He felt her reach for his hand.

"Thank you," she said, a little catch in her voice. "I knew from what Jean said about you that you would help me. You don't know what it means—you don't know…"

He felt the soft, grateful pressure of her fingers on his, and then, quite suddenly, she was gone. Without another word she had turned and had almost fled from him. Back through the darkness that had enveloped her, the hurried patter of her shoes on the roadway came to tell him of her haste.

There was, obviously, no point in pursuing her. Karen Hammond had said all that she intended to say—for the time being at any rate.

Tremaine walked on slowly. Why had she followed him? She had told him nothing—nothing to justify her approaching him in the agitated manner in which she had done—and yet some urgent reason must have been driving her.

Philip—evidently she had meant her husband. What was

it she had almost said before prudence had overtaken her distress? What was there about Philip Hammond that his wife was so anxious that the mystery of Lydia Dare's death should be solved quickly—and not by the police?

On the surface, of course, it indicated that both Karen and Philip Hammond were innocent of any connection with the murder. But, on the other hand, it might merely be part of a subtle move to cover their guilt. Jonathan Boyce had said that their story was that they had spent the night of the crime at home together; the alibi of each supported the alibi of the other. Karen Hammond's action might have been intended to throw dust in the eyes of the law. After all, she had not approached Inspector Boyce, the professional. She had come to Mordecai Tremaine, the amateur.

Had she done so because she secretly believed that the amateur, his reason blinded by his friendship with *her* friends, would offer less danger than the dispassionate policeman who would ruthlessly tear her alibi to pieces if necessary?

It was not exactly a complimentary thought. Tremaine grimaced, as though he had taken a dose of a particularly unpleasant medicine. He hoped he didn't give the appearance of being quite such a fool. The advancing years had brought no diminution of his dislike of seeming ridiculous in the eyes of a beautiful woman.

He stopped suddenly. Startled, he drew back. Another

figure had loomed toward him out of the shadows at the side of the road.

Visions of a crumpled body being discovered in the early hours of the morning flashed across his mind. His heart thumping, he yet managed to clench his fists and summon up the resolve to sell his life dearly.

And then leaping fear was replaced by relief.

"Excuse me. Have you a light?"

It was a quiet, diffident voice. Its tone carried an apology.

"Yes—certainly," said Tremaine, hoping he did not sound as unnerved as he had momentarily felt.

He searched in his pockets for his matches and struck one a little fumblingly, cupping his hands to shield the flame.

The other leaned forward, his cigarette in his mouth. But his attention seemed to be only half upon the task of lighting it. Tremaine felt the man's eyes searching his face, peering at him across the flickering glow of the match, as if he was intent upon making sure that he would be able to recognize him again.

He stared back. He saw a pair of narrow, inquisitive eyes; a sharp, beaklike nose; a face in which the features were thin but prominent and possessing an air of wizened cunning. And their owner was wearing a sports jacket and gray flannels.

Mordecai Tremaine's mind went back to "Roseland."

Geoffrey Manning was speaking: "*A short, ferrety-looking fellow in gray flannels and a sports coat…*"

"Thanks."

The cigarette was drawing now. The ferrety one seemed to have finished his scrutiny. He turned back toward the hedgerow. Tremaine saw that he had evidently been leaning against a small stile like the entrance to a footpath across the fields, for it was to this spot that the other returned.

He stood irresolutely. This, beyond doubt, was the stranger to whom reference had been made. The stranger who had asked for Philip Hammond and at the mention of whom Karen Hammond had betrayed such fear—or, at the least, such agitation. And it was evident that he had been following her and that his sole purpose in asking for a light had been in order to obtain a good look at the man to whom she had been speaking.

Tremaine stared toward the shadowy figure by the stile.

"It's a beautiful night."

"Yes. Thanks for the light."

The ferrety one made it ostentatiously obvious that he intended it to be his last effort at conversation. Since to persevere would merely serve to arouse suspicion in the man's mind without accomplishing anything constructive, Tremaine gave a rueful shrug and walked on.

Despite the intriguing nature of his dual encounters, it was not the thought of the man he had just left or even of Karen Hammond that occupied his mind. He had not, indeed, taken many steps before both of them had been temporarily forgotten.

Something had been lodged at the back of his brain. Something that had been disturbing him, worrying him ever since he had left "Roseland." He had not spoken of it to Boyce because he had not been able to give it a name.

But now he knew what it was. Unbidden, since he was no longer fretting after it, the revelation had come to him.

He could hear Martin Vaughan and Howard Shannon. He could hear the big man speaking of the storm that had broken over London; could hear him speaking humorously of the vagaries of the English summer that brought rain clouds without warning; could hear him asking: "*I hope you weren't one of the unlucky ones, Shannon?*"

And he could hear Shannon's reply. Could hear him saying that he had missed the worst of it because he had taken a taxi from the station.

That was what was wrong! There was the jarring note!

For Mordecai Tremaine himself had been in London then. *And he knew that over the whole city not one drop of rain had fallen.*

6

Dalmering was in the public eye. From the front pages of the daily newspapers, the story of the murder of Lydia Dare beckoned to a world of hurrying human midgets with the tidings that one of their number had been lifted out of anonymity by the violence of her passing.

The crime had coincided with a temporary lull in the storms of home and foreign politics, and the morning newspapers had featured it prominently. It did not occupy the main headlines, but such details as were known had been made the basis for a long account in each case.

After breakfast on the morning after his arrival at "Roseland" Mordecai Tremaine retired to the garden with half a dozen of the leading London journals. Jean Russell had told him that anticipating his desire to read as many as possible of the opinions that would certainly be expressed upon the murder, she had requested the local newsagent (who was also the grocer and the chemist; specialization had not so far penetrated to the Dalmering backwater) to provide all the additional newspapers he could. Despite what must have been a greatly increased demand he had responded gratifyingly.

It was a beautiful morning—in the best sense of that hackneyed phrase. The sun had risen untroubled in a clear blue sky, and although there was a faint suggestion of overbrilliance that gave a forewarning of uncomfortable heat later in the day, at the moment the village lay smilingly in a caressing warmth.

Paul Russell, with an apology that he had to leave his guest to his own devices, had disappeared into his surgery to face the day's round of wheezing chests, muscular rheumatism, and the countless, but routine, minor ailments of a G.P.'s existence. Tremaine could sympathize with his friend. Paul, he knew, would have preferred the life of research, the exciting pursuit with the microscope in a laboratory, the thrill of accomplishment in pitting his skill against the minute organisms that threaten the continuance of the human miracle of nerve, bone, and muscle and in gaining the victory over yet another obscure aspect of disease. But finance and the responsibilities of marriage had forced the replacement of the microscope by the stethoscope, had compelled the abandonment of the uncertain glory of medical research for the steady if uninspired income of the G.P.

Tremaine settled himself in a deck chair and began to read. As he had expected, he learned nothing new. The newspaper reporters were aware of no facts he himself did not know; he was certain, on the contrary, that he knew considerably more than they. But it molded his deliberately pliant mind into the desired pattern; made it easier for him to reflect in the manner in which he required to do so.

He took out his pipe. A little self-consciously he lit it. As usual it cost him three matches and a burnt finger.

He smoked a pipe on principle. For a long while his smoking had been limited to the ritual of three cigarettes a day, after meals. He had been unable to settle down to a pipe; at each experiment his stomach had rebelled bitterly.

Nevertheless, he had persevered. A pipe was essential. It was, he felt, the kind of thing a detective was expected to do. Eventually he had conquered nature to the extent of being able to hold his own, but still he lacked real professional enjoyment, and it was a source of trivial annoyance with him that he always had the air of an amateur, that his attempts at packing and lighting the tobacco were invariably clumsy. Sometimes, indeed, the smoke penetrated his throat in a stinging wave and caused him to cough.

He coughed now. And looked up to see Jean's eyes upon him, a twinkle of amusement dancing in them.

"Rotten tobacco," he explained carefully. "I haven't been able to get my usual brand."

Her amusement widened into a smile.

"Don't mind me, Mordecai," she said, in the tolerant voice

of a woman who knew what eternal little boys the most adult of men were in their hearts. "I'm used to watching Paul. He likes to smoke a pipe whenever the vicar calls to talk over the affairs of the parish. He says it lends him dignity."

Mordecai Tremaine looked down at the tumbled walls of his defenses. Then he saw the humor of it and smiled back.

"Don't give me away, Jean. I'm playing the great detective."

He puffed conscientiously at his pipe, allowing his thoughts to drift, passing in slow review the various actors in the drama. Karen Hammond, Howard Shannon— Martin Vaughan.

Vaughan. The memory of the big man rose before him— dominant, somehow ruthless. He saw the thick fingers clamping down upon the gate at the entrance to the path where Lydia Dare had died. Vaughan had the appearance of a man whose passions might break the bonds of his self-control and drive him to excesses, of a man who had lived hard and who might react in violent ways to any emotional strain.

But why should he have wanted to kill Lydia Dare? Tremaine puffed out a smoke cloud and admitted that he did not know.

He spent a pleasant if hardly profitable couple of hours smoking, reading, and thinking. He had reached the point where he knew that he could not allow his limited knowledge to form the basis of any more theories lest they should lead him into the dangerous realms of pure invention, when he saw Paul approaching him.

"Hullo, Paul. All the cures completed?"

"Well, I've prescribed all the pills and iron tonics," returned the doctor, with a smile. "I usually spend a few moments pottering around the garden just about now. Helps to keep down my waistline and saves me from ordering any digestive tablets for myself."

At the end of the garden was a little potting shed and toolshed. Russell pushed open the door.

"I think I'll arm myself with a trowel," he observed. "A little bending wouldn't do me any harm."

He disappeared inside the shed. Tremaine heard him give a sudden exclamation.

"What's the trouble?" he asked.

"I'll swear I'm cursed with a poltergeist," said the doctor, reappearing. "Look there!"

Tremaine lifted himself from his deck chair and peered into the interior of the shed.

"What's the poltergeist been doing?"

"Those boots." Russell pointed. "Two days ago I hunted high and low for them, and there wasn't a trace of them anywhere. Now here they are, under my nose—grinning at me."

"You probably looked at them without seeing them. You know how easy it is to do that sort of thing."

"No—I'm certain they weren't there the last time I looked."

Tremaine glanced down at the articles in question, lying untidily where they had evidently been carelessly thrown in the middle of the wooden floor. They were roomy, wooden-soled Somerset clogs that fastened with a strap. He bent to examine them.

"They're ideal for the spring and autumn digging seasons," he remarked.

He smiled to himself as his eyes roamed casually around the shed. It was to be hoped that Paul was not so careless of his surgical instruments when he was called upon—as he sometimes was—to perform a minor operation at the Cottage Hospital just outside Kingshampton as he appeared to be of his gardening implements.

Rakes, forks, spades, and various-sized trowels were in an entangled heap in one corner; in another a tumbled pile of flowerpots and watering cans were gathering dirt and cobwebs. Wooden trays that had been used for seed were lying everywhere.

Through the half-open window he saw Jean come out of the house, a bag on her arm, and walk toward the gate, evidently about to make a shopping expedition to the village.

"There's your poltergeist, Paul," he told his companion. "Jean's probably been tidying up after you."

"Maybe," returned Russell cheerfully. "I'd like to think

it really was a poltergeist though. What an alibi! It would help to explain why I'm always upsetting things and leaving things about!"

He began to busy himself with a nearby flowerbed, loosening the soil and weeding with a surgeon's quick precision among the banked lupins and antirrhinums.

"Any theories yet?" he asked, over his shoulder.

"Dozens," returned Tremaine. "All useless. I've been thinking," he added, "about Vaughan."

"Vaughan?" Russell looked up. "In what way?"

"Oh, no particular way—just generally. He and Lydia Dare seem to have been pretty good friends."

"I suppose you might say that of most of us. We've been a happy little crowd down here."

Was there a note of insincerity in Russell's voice, something that did not ring quite true? Tremaine thought of the surging emotions of which he had caught a brief glimpse on the previous evening and was not quite sure. Loyalty and an unwillingness to admit that the Garden of Eden possessed its serpents could be keeping a guard over his friend's words.

"I suppose so," he said noncommittally. "Do you think he was at all—well, what you might call disturbed over Lydia's engagement?"

"Good lord, no. He was delighted—as we all were."

"Her fiancé—Gerald Farrant—has he met Vaughan?"

"Yes. Several times. Why?" Russell had straightened from his weeding operations and was looking at him with a doubtful, puzzled expression. "You don't mean to tell me that you suspect—*Vaughan*?"

He brought the word out with an air of unbelief—as though the thought was too incredible to harbor.

"I didn't say I suspected anybody," returned Tremaine quickly. "I'm just asking a lot of questions in case some of the answers turn out to be useful." He changed the subject quickly without allowing the other to pose any further queries. "I'd like to meet Philip Hammond some time, Paul. When would be the best opportunity?"

"That's easily arranged," said Russell. "There's a rehearsal tonight. Why don't you come along? You'll meet everybody there—including Philip. At least, you will if he's down here. He isn't always at rehearsals. It's awkward sometimes when he can't turn up, but his business keeps him in London quite a lot. He usually rings Karen up in the afternoon when he can't get away."

They had begun to pace together along the garden path as they talked. The doctor seemed to have forgotten his intention of persevering with the weeding of the flowerbeds.

"How's the play going?" asked Tremaine. "Are you satisfied with results so far? *Murder Has a Motive*—I don't recollect the title. It hasn't been put on in the West End, has it?"

"To be perfectly honest I'm not certain," confessed Russell. "Vaughan could probably tell you more about it."

"Vaughan? He's playing a part in it, is he?"

"Yes. Playing it well, too. It was his suggestion that we should tackle the production. He thought it would be a good idea to do something in that line to benefit the orphanage, and we all agreed. He produced the play from somewhere. We formed a committee, allocated the various parts—and that was that."

They had reached the end of the path now and were within a few yards of the roadway. They were about to retrace their steps when a voice called to them.

"Good morning, Paul."

The doctor looked up.

"Oh, hullo, Edith. Good morning."

Edith Lorrington gave a smile and a friendly nod in Mordecai Tremaine's direction, and that gentleman smiled back.

"Good morning, Miss Lorrington. I see you're out enjoying the sunshine."

"Yes, it is beautiful, isn't it? I'm just going along to see if I can catch Sandra. I've just finished a novel I feel sure she'd like to read. I get them from friends of mine in Kingshampton, you know. They keep a bookshop, and they always let me know when anything really special comes in."

Mordecai Tremaine wondered just what Edith Lorrington meant by the phrase "really special." She gave him the impression that her reading choice would be a very narrow one.

"How did you sleep last night?" put in Russell.

"Much better," she told him. "That medicine you gave me yesterday was splendid—not like the tablets I had before. They never seemed to do me much good. I slept for seven hours right off, and yet the night before I had to get up and go out for a walk before I could get off to sleep. It was nearly twelve o'clock before I went indoors."

"You'll have to take care, Edith," said the doctor seriously. "I don't think it will be wise to go wandering around on your own so late at night in the future."

"Who would want to molest an old woman like me?" she said lightly. "Anyway, it isn't so lonely. People don't go to bed as early as you think. Mr. Galeski was still up. So was Mrs. Hammond. And so was Sandra, of course. She was waiting for Lydia and listening to the wireless—they were playing swing music. It always seems to me to be so late for that sort of thing."

Quite suddenly Mordecai Tremaine became aware what it was she was saying. Edith Lorrington had been walking calmly about the neighborhood at the very time when Lydia Dare had been murdered!

"Did you see anyone while you were out, Miss Lorrington?" he asked.

"Oh no," she said simply. "It was very quiet—like it always is, you know." She looked brightly from Tremaine back to Russell. "Now I really must be getting along. I missed Sandra the last time I called, and then all this terrible affair over poor Lydia drove it out of my mind."

She nodded and smiled again. They watched her walk down the road, primly correct.

"What," said Mordecai Tremaine, "do you know about that?"

Paul Russell shrugged.

"Edith suffers from insomnia. It's quite usual for her to go out for a walk at night when she can't sleep. She's a strange mixture," he went on ruminatively. "Sometimes she seems as trusting and as innocent as a child, and then she'll come out with some shrewd observation that makes you wonder just what is going on inside her mind. This business of walking around the neighborhood late at night, for instance. Most women would be as nervous as kittens alone on these dark roads, but it doesn't seem to trouble her for a moment. I met her once when I was coming back from a late call—that's how I got to know of her habit of going out—and she was as unconcerned as if she was taking a stroll in broad daylight down the main street of Kingshampton."

Tremaine gazed thoughtfully after the slight, old-fashioned figure that was now nearly out of sight.

"Have you been treating her for insomnia for long?"

"Off and on for months," said Russell casually. "There isn't really a great deal one can do with these cases."

"Do you think," said his companion carefully, "she really did sleep a good deal better last night? I know a doctor isn't supposed to discuss his patients," he added hastily. "I don't want to put you in a false position."

"Under the circumstances I don't think it could be called an indiscretion," returned Russell, smilingly. "It's very probable that she did sleep well. Until yesterday I'd been giving her barbitone tablets, and the trouble with barbiturates is that they're habit-forming and that people get used to them."

"So yesterday you tried something different?"

"Yes. I gave her chloral hydrate. It has a very unpleasant taste."

"And it's a common belief that the more horrible medicine tastes the more good it's likely to do." There was a twinkle in Mordecai Tremaine's eyes. "You think that psychology sent her to sleep?"

"Well, it has happened," said Russell diplomatically.

They strolled back through the garden, and when they reached the flowerbed where he had left his trowel, the doctor stooped to retrieve it and replaced it in the toolshed.

"I'm afraid that's the end of my exercise for this morning, Mordecai. I've several calls to make before lunch."

Tremaine nodded understandingly.

"There was a time when *I* had to work for a living," he observed.

He spent the rest of the morning undisturbed in the garden, but he went in to lunch with a vague feeling of dissatisfaction with himself. He felt that he had accomplished nothing; that valuable hours had slipped irritatingly through his fingers.

But that was only the conscious side of his mind. Deep inside him he knew that the morning had not really been scattered unproductively. Although he had achieved no definite result, the fact that his mind had been actively working upon the problems set by the death of Lydia Dare would sooner or later prove of value. Sooner or later—in all probability when he was thinking of something entirely different—the fruits of his labors would be delivered.

Over lunch Jean had an item of information to pass on.

"Gerald Farrant's here," she announced.

Tremaine looked up quickly from his salad.

"The fiancé?"

"The fiancé," she agreed. "He's staying at the Admiral. He came down today."

"I take it," said her husband, reaching for the salad dressing, "that this tidbit of gossip is the result of your visit to the village this morning?"

"It is," she told him and added shamelessly, "To pick up any gossip I could was the reason why I went out."

"I've been wondering about Farrant," said Tremaine. "I was thinking this morning that it was odd he hadn't shown up. After all, the wedding was to have been quite soon, wasn't it?"

"There's a simple explanation," she told him. "He was in Scotland when the telegram reached him yesterday. His home's at Stirling—or just near it. He came down by the night train from Edinburgh and reached King's Cross early this morning. You can tell that he didn't lose any time getting here."

"Is he—feeling it?" asked Russell.

Jean's eyes clouded sympathetically.

"I'm afraid he is. I caught a glimpse of him. Poor lad…" She hesitated. "He's hardly that, of course—he's a grown man, nearly forty. But he looks so young that you think of him as being so. He was here with Lydia less than a fortnight ago, and he seemed full of high spirits, just like a boy. It was obvious that he was head over heels in love with her. Now—I don't think I would have known him. He's changed so much."

"It's a tragedy for him," said Tremaine quietly. "I can understand how he must be feeling."

During his reflections of the morning, he had been considering the murder dispassionately, in the light of an abstract problem to be solved according to certain rules. Mention of

Farrant had suddenly recalled him to the other side of it—the side that had to be computed in terms of human agony and suffering. All his sentimentalism had been called into play.

Jean Russell saw the look on his face and did not say what she had been on the point of saying—that she hoped that for Gerald Farrant's sake the murderer would be brought to justice. The resolve was already there—in Mordecai Tremaine's taut features, in the haunted depths of his eyes.

After lunch Tremaine did not return to his chair in the garden. It was hot now—almost too hot. The sun was overhead, pouring down upon the village. Little ripples of heat were rising shimmeringly from the slowly melting tar on the roads. But nevertheless he settled his battered old panama upon his head and set out from the house.

He had to walk; had to walk quickly, though the perspiration might run from him; had to walk so that his thoughts would go faster, faster…so that he could begin to see things more clearly.

He did not walk in the direction of the village. He did not want to meet people. He did not want to talk idly, to make conversation while his real thoughts were wandering tortured through space and time.

Something of horror had come upon him. Something of the secret horror of Dalmering was lying heavily over his soul, enveloping it, blanketing it, like some monstrous evil shadow.

He knew that it was his imagination. He knew that it was because Jean Russell had spoken of Gerald Farrant and the tragedy that had swept so suddenly down upon him and because the revulsion against the monstrous villainy that had taken place had come flooding upon the tide of romantic sentiment that had its source within him.

But although he knew—or thought he knew—the mechanics of his psychology, his will was not enough to stifle his instinctive reactions. Always he could see a still, pitiful figure lying murdered in the darkness and could see the ruin of high hopes. Always he could see ruin and destruction and human sorrow.

White for a wedding his thoughts ran, incoherently and yet with a painful, throbbing significance. White for a wedding—white all besmirched and bedraggled with black...

He walked faster. The perspiration was glistening down from the rim of his panama where it lay against his forehead. His pince-nez, always seemingly precarious, became so in earnest; he felt them slipping and put them back into position with a shaking hand.

The sun was a molten fury. It was glaring in the sky and beating fiercely down upon him. And it was indescribably evil. He could feel unmentionable horror all about him, suffusing the atmosphere, gradually, inevitably, submerging him...

An arm came urgently around him as he staggered.

"What's wrong, Mordecai? Aren't you well?"

He knew that it was Boyce. Inspector Boyce of Scotland Yard. Solid Boyce. Dependable Boyce.

The other's voice beat slowly through the fog of evil that was encompassing him. He stood swaying, trying to understand what the words meant. And then the horror had gone and he was standing in the sunshine and the world was normal again.

"What's wrong, man?" repeated Boyce in concern. "You look as though you've come back from the dead!"

"I think I have," said Mordecai Tremaine.

Boyce regarded him curiously—saw the unhealthy pallor of his face, unnaturally taut skin stretched tight over prominent bones and oddly streaked with perspiration; the pince-nez all askew; the still semifixed stare.

"You'd better sit down and rest for a moment," he said decisively. "You look just about finished."

Tremaine allowed himself to be seated on the grassy bank at the side of the road. He moved a little to allow his companion to join him.

"It's all right, Jonathan. It's over now."

"What happened? You look ghastly."

"Too much sun," said Tremaine, still shakily. "Too much thinking and too much sun." He gave Jonathan Boyce a long, intent stare, drew a deep breath. "Jonathan," he said, "do you find anything strange about this place—about Dalmering?"

"In what way?"

Tremaine searched for words.

"Do you feel evil in the air? Do you feel hate and horror and murder all around?"

Inspector Boyce uttered a sudden exclamation.

"Don't," he said, "tell me that now *you're* going to start!"

Mordecai Tremaine smiled. He looked apologetic.

"Sorry, Jonathan," he said. "It does sound a little fantastic. But just for a moment, coming along the road, I had the feeling that the whole place was running with evil—just as Vaughan told us that Lydia Dare said it was. There's something here that isn't normal—something *wicked*."

"I'll agree with you there," said Boyce practically. "It sounds a fair description of murder. But—"

"But you're only interested in facts and my psychiatric ravings haven't any value in a law court. I know." Tremaine eyed his friend quizzically. He had fully recovered now. "Did you know that Gerald Farrant was here?" he asked.

"Yes. I saw him this morning. I suppose he will be helping to clear up Miss Dare's affairs. It was a great shock to him—naturally."

"Naturally. Did he offer any theories as to who might have been responsible?"

Boyce shook his head. "No. He seemed stunned by it. He told me that he couldn't think of anyone who could have had any reason for killing her."

He was silent for a moment or two. And then he added, in a matter-of-fact voice: "You seem to have had a few social engagements after you left me last night."

"Oh—you mean Mrs. Hammond and the fellow who stopped me and asked for a light?"

"Is that what he wanted? I wasn't close enough to hear what was going on."

"That's what he *said* he wanted," returned Tremaine. "What he really wanted was to see what I looked like because he'd been following Mrs. Hammond and he'd just seen her speaking to me. I've been wondering whether you saw what happened."

"I wasn't far behind you," said Boyce. "But I kept out of sight when Mrs. Hammond stopped you. What did she want?"

"She wanted me to find out who killed Lydia Dare."

"Just like that?"

"Just like that," agreed Tremaine. "She wanted me to find out quickly."

He told his companion of Karen Hammond's agitation; told him how she had left him with those few broken words and hurried into the darkness.

"I agree," said Boyce, as he finished. "It doesn't make sense. If her husband was with her she knows that he couldn't have had anything to do with it, and so there's no reason for her to be alarmed."

"Precisely," said Tremaine. "*If* he was with her."

The Yard man pulled idly at a tuft of long grass growing near the spot where his left hand had been resting.

"I saw Sandra Borne today," he announced. "Had quite a chat with her."

"What's your opinion?"

"You're quite right. She's hiding something. Her story won't stand up to hard questioning. *Why* didn't she become alarmed when Miss Dare didn't return? *Why* didn't she at least ring up Vaughan's house and find out whether her friend was all right? Her cottage and Vaughan's house are both on the telephone. Did you know that?"

"No. I hadn't noticed."

"She's only telling part of the truth. There's more to come—perhaps the most important part. She didn't just go unconcernedly to bed without bothering about Lydia Dare and leaving her to let herself in. But I think I've scared her. I let her see that I didn't believe her. I've a feeling that before very long it will produce results."

"Well, you certainly haven't been wasting your time, Jonathan."

"We've been plodding," said Boyce. "Just like policemen do." He added, "We've found the weapon."

He spoke so casually and so quietly that at first Mordecai Tremaine did not realize what he had said. And then he sat up suddenly.

"Where was it?" he demanded eagerly. "And what was it?"

"It was lying hidden in the undergrowth not many yards from the spot where the murder was committed. The killer seems to have kept it long enough to wipe off any fingerprints and then just dumped it in the bushes. Naturally, I've been having the copse thoroughly searched and my men found it early this morning. It's a long-bladed, very sharp knife—just the sort of thing we were expecting. It appears to be some sort of curio."

"Now you *are* getting somewhere," said Tremaine, the excitement plain in his voice. "Find the owner and you can say that you're practically there!"

"We have found the owner."

Mordecai Tremaine sat up even straighter. He gave his companion a prolonged, searching look.

"You know something. I should have guessed it before. The symptoms are plain enough now. Who *does* own that knife?"

"It belongs to Martin Vaughan," said Jonathan Boyce dispassionately.

1

There was no doubt that Martin Vaughan had taken a dangerous leap into the position of Suspect Number One. Mordecai Tremaine found himself weighing the evidence against him as he walked back toward the village after having left Inspector Boyce.

Opportunity Vaughan had undoubtedly possessed. The weapon had now been proved to be his. There remained the motive.

The motive. Tremaine pursed his lips. Somewhere, in the heart of the darkness, there *was* a motive. Even if not for Vaughan, then for someone. Lydia Dare had not died without a reason.

He had been walking slowly along, engrossed in his thoughts, his head down and his hands clasped behind his back. He looked up for an instant and saw two people approaching him.

One of them was Pauline Conroy. She wore a flowered summer dress of some thin material that emphasized her seductive grace. Her companion he did not recognize, but it was clear from the way in which she was looking up into his face that the whole of her overelaborate charm was being turned upon him.

Tremaine studied him curiously as they drew nearer. Tall, dark, and handsome was the description that came into his mind. So he thought at first and then began to revise his opinion as his long-distance view merged into a close-up.

It was certainly true that the other was tall, but the remaining two adjectives hardly applied. If he was dark he was untidily so. He had the appearance of a man who did not shave with enough care: his chin was rough and black-looking. His hair, thick and badly in need of cutting, was straggling down toward his collar. And the somewhat coarse outlines of his face, which became evident upon a closer inspection, spoke of a man of flashily good looks a little past their prime rather than of a handsome one.

A sullenly resentful expression had come into Pauline Conroy's face. It said that she did not wish to stop and speak. But it was plain that having been placed in a position in which an encounter was inevitable, she lacked the courage to walk past without a sign of recognition, and Mordecai Tremaine, for his part, was in no mood to make matters easier for her.

"Good afternoon, Miss Conroy," he said pleasantly and

stood directly in her path so that she could not go on without making her action obvious.

"Good afternoon," she said unwillingly.

Tremaine was covertly studying her companion. This, he was saying to himself, is Galeski.

It was.

"This is Mr. Tremaine, Serge," Pauline was saying. "He's a friend of Dr. Russell and his wife. We met last night. Mr. Tremaine—Mr. Galeski."

The two men exchanged the conventional handshake. Galeski's hand was flabby, with no greeting in it. Tremaine was glad when it slipped limply out of his palm.

"I've heard a lot about you, Mr. Galeski," he lied hopefully. "I've been looking forward to meeting you."

"Who's been talking?"

Pauline Conroy snapped the question out so quickly that it was obvious that she had been on her guard and was reacting with the hypersensitivity of a person who sees enemies everywhere.

Serge Galeski waved a hand with a carelessly lordly gesture.

"My dear Pauline, who cares for the gossip of the rabble?"

Tremaine blinked. He told himself that he did not like the theatrical pose of Mr. Galeski.

But it did not betray his feelings.

"I assure you that no one has been—er—talking," he explained diffidently. "Not in any derogatory sense."

It seemed that Serge Galeski's opinion of Serge Galeski was a very high one. He brushed the explanation aside as one who was unconcerned with such minor matters.

"Don't speak of it, my dear fellow," he said airily. "A man in my position is used to being talked about. It's part of the price we have to pay."

"Serge is a film producer," put in Pauline Conroy hastily, as if she was afraid that Mordecai Tremaine might find some different reason. "But, of course, you know that."

She laughed, as though it was absurd to suppose that he had not known, and Mordecai Tremaine laughed too, as though he had not just been given the information for the first time.

"Of course," he replied. "Of course. Mr. Galeski's name is almost as familiar as that of Hitchcock or—or—René Clair."

The other ran his fingers through his unruly, overlong hair. He had the manner of one who hesitated to criticize but who considered it to be a painful duty. He shrugged meaningfully.

"Triflers," he said. "Mere amateurs, groping on the fringe of the camera."

Pauline Conroy slipped her arm through his.

"Come along, Serge. We must be going. Otherwise we won't have time to run over that scene together before tea.

Serge is helping me with my part in the play we're doing," she added. "You'll excuse us, Mr. Tremaine?"

Since he had no reasonable alternative, Mr. Tremaine said that certainly he would. He stood aside and allowed them to pass by.

As he continued slowly on his own way he added the untidy-looking man in the loosely fitting clothes to the collection of village personalities he had already amassed in his mind. Artist, Bohemian, *poseur*…all seemed to fit him. So Serge Galeski was a film producer. And Pauline Conroy, who was an actress, was quite evidently on very intimate terms with him.

It hung together understandably enough. The dark, voluptuous, and alluring Pauline was ambitious. Before her eyes the bright lights of stardom were beckoning. Serge Galeski represented the magic world of the film industry. Did Galeski have a future? That was no doubt in the lap of the gods. Perhaps more important was the question, were there influential people in the film business who thought that he did and who were prepared to back their judgment? The shrewdly determined Pauline had probably decided that Galeski's foot could—at the very least—hold open the door of the studios far enough to enable her to slip through. After that either she could make further use of him if he proved to possess a career in his own right, or she could promptly forget him and look for someone of greater promise to further her own.

Mordecai Tremaine realized that his thoughts had taken a decidedly cynical trend. He smiled wryly. He was losing his illusions.

There was, though, one other point upon which he might profitably reflect before dismissing Pauline Conroy and Serge Galeski from his mind.

That brief duel at "Roseland," when Karen Hammond had mentioned Galeski's name as though she had known that it must surely bring about a clash—just why had Philip Hammond's wife said what she had said? Just what significance had lain behind her remark? It seemed to be a matter in which Jonathan Boyce, with his ability to set in motion careful, persistent, and thorough if tedious investigations, might be of service.

He was drawing level with the wooden gate at the entrance to the path through the copse where Lydia Dare had died. There was no visible sign of activity, but he could hear someone moving about in the undergrowth. The police were still apparently searching for clues in their prosaic, uninspiring, relentless way.

Tremaine thought of the vast machinery of the law that had begun to move when Lydia Dare's body had been found. It was cumbersome. It was wearisome. It was overladen with rules and regulations. It was unimaginative. But it was deadly. It might take a long while to catch up with you, but once it had done so there was no escaping it.

He stood by the gate for a few moments. He was thinking over the exact location of Martin Vaughan's house and the most direct route to it that did not involve traversing the copse and going across the common. Then he looked at his watch and began to walk—briskly but not at any undue speed.

It took him nine minutes to reach "Home Lodge." He estimated that had he exerted himself he could have taken two or three minutes from his time quite easily.

At the side of the house was a path leading to the common that lay directly behind it. He walked to the edge of the common itself and followed with his eyes the well-worn track that pursued an uneven way across the open land, traversed the winding stream by means of the rustic bridge, and went on to be lost in the copse.

It was an attractive picture upon which he gazed. The roofs of the houses surrounding the common projected here and there into the landscape, the sun glinting on colored tiles; beyond them he could see the silver of the water, for the ground upon which he was standing was high enough to enable him to overlook the thin border of sea. Seeing it now, bathed in warmth and light, it was difficult to imagine that this scene had been overshadowed by murder.

He brought his mind back to the business upon which
he had come and tried to estimate how long it would take
him, walking without haste, to reach the cluster of trees.
About seven or eight minutes, he thought. He looked
down at his pocket watch, replaced it carefully, and took a
step forward.

"You needn't trouble. It could be done all right."

Tremaine swung around. On the other side of the neatly
trimmed privet hedge that separated the garden of "Home
Lodge" from the open land, Martin Vaughan was standing. He had evidently been there for some seconds, quietly
watching—and waiting. Mordecai Tremaine experienced an
odd fluttering in his stomach as he faced the cold stare of the
big man's gray eyes.

"I'm afraid I don't understand."

"You understand all right," said Vaughan harshly. "Don't
think that all of us believe that you're as harmless as you
look. Those pince-nez and that helpless air of yours don't
deceive everybody."

"Are you quite sure," said Tremaine, endeavoring to look
bewildered, "that you're speaking to the right person?"

"Quite sure." Vaughan's voice was quieter, but it was filled
with a vibrant menace. "I watched you coming up from the
village. I've been watching you since you've been standing
there. You're trying to decide whether a person going by the

road could reach that copse"—he gestured with his right arm—"before a person walking across the common."

It was disconcerting to hear his thoughts being flung back into his face, challengingly, as though he had spoken them aloud. Tremaine searched desperately for the right words.

"Why on earth," he said, still maintaining his pose, "should I want to do that?"

"Maybe your friend Inspector Boyce knows the answers."

The big man had taken a step forward so that now only the width of the privet separated them. "If I were you," he said unpleasantly, "I'd be very careful not to interfere in other people's affairs. It's unhealthy. We don't like officious meddling busybodies down here."

The look on Vaughan's face said plainly that it would be futile to attempt to argue with him. It would also be futile to attempt to continue with the pretense that he did not know what the other meant. Mordecai Tremaine took off his pince-nez and polished them unnecessarily.

"I don't know what's in your mind, Mr. Vaughan," he said slowly, "but I'm sorry that you're adopting this attitude. It makes things so much more difficult."

"That," said Vaughan, "is a matter of opinion."

He turned on his heel and went into the house. Tremaine stared after him until the door had banged angrily shut and then walked slowly back to the road.

Certainly Martin Vaughan was on the defensive. He was behaving like a man who was expecting trouble—behaving, in fact, like a man who knew himself to be guilty and was trying to hide it beneath a blustering manner.

Why? Was he actually guilty? Did he really have something to hide?

Tremaine took off his panama and fanned himself gently as he walked. It was still very hot, and he was not anxious to undergo a repetition of the experience he had had in the afternoon, and yet it was necessary that he should think— and think hard.

He was back where he had been when he had left Inspector Boyce. Martin Vaughan *could* have killed Lydia Dare. But if he *had* done so then it had been for a reason. Murder was not a casual affair, to be embarked upon lightly in the spirit of a moment. It was dark, sinister, heavy with penalties. It required a deadly purpose. It required a motive.

That Vaughan was aware of his own connection with Jonathan Boyce was no longer of significance. From the moment when Karen Hammond had stopped him in the darkness of the road by the village hall it had been obvious that there could no longer be any question of secrecy. Tremaine knew that he had not given sufficient heed to the inevitable village grapevine; he had not stayed to think that in a community so small as Dalmering there could be nothing hidden for long.

Fortunately, the Inspector had taken it philosophically. No doubt when he had observed Karen Hammond talking in the roadway he had guessed what it portended. He had merely shrugged, like a man who was used to the sudden sweeping away of the plans.

"It was bound to come sooner or later," he had said cheerfully. "We haven't lost anything by it."

"But the chief constable?" Tremaine had asked. "Won't he have something to say when the story reaches him? Civilians interfering in official matters and so on. He's sure to hear about it. You know how people talk."

"When we come to our fences, Mordecai, we'll think about jumping them." And Boyce had put an arm around his shoulder. "Don't worry. Nothing's going to happen, and you don't want to be afraid you're going to be warned off. You're a tower of strength, and I wouldn't be without you."

Tremaine smiled at the recollection. Lies, of course. But pleasant, friendly lies. They told him that Jonathan Boyce trusted him; that the stocky, bullet-headed Yard man who sometimes seemed so brusque had received him into his heart.

He was still immersed in his thoughts when he arrived back at "Roseland." Jean came down the path to meet him, as though she had been watching for his arrival.

"Sandra's here," she said, and something in her manner made him wake from his reverie.

"What is it, Jean?" he asked.

"She wants to see you," she told him. "It's—it's important, Mordecai."

He followed her into the house. Sandra Borne was waiting for him in the drawing room. With a faint feeling of surprise he saw that Paul Russell was also there.

"Off duty, Paul?" he said, with a smile.

The doctor smiled back, but it was a half-hearted smile, and it did not last.

"Sandy wants to see you, Mordecai," he said. "She asked me to stay while she talked to you."

Tremaine looked from his friend's weather-beaten face, holding now a trace of anxiety, to Sandra Borne's peaked features. Her hands were twisting nervously. She had lost her gay perkiness, her birdlike quickness of movement. She looked a little pitiful, a little bedraggled. And she had been crying.

There was no mistaking the atmosphere of brooding strain that was heavy in the room. They had been waiting for him for some time. Tremaine sat down in the chair that had been drawn up for him. He waited.

"Inspector Boyce has been to see Sandy," said Russell quietly.

"Just a routine call," said Tremaine. "To ask routine questions."

"He didn't receive routine answers."

Tremaine looked up quickly.

"What do you mean?"

"I mean," said Russell, "that he wasn't told the truth."

There was a silence. A painful, pulsating silence. Through a gap between the drawn blinds a vivid bar of sunlight reached down to the carpet. It was as though the myriad particles of dust swirling in the bar were the only living things in the darkened room.

And then Mordecai Tremaine cleared his throat.

"Perhaps," he said, "Miss Borne will tell me what happened."

Sandra Borne stared at the mild-looking man facing her. The brown eyes behind her spectacles held an expression of uncertainty. It was as though she was searching for assurance and could not find it. She made a movement toward Russell, and the doctor read her expression.

"It's all right, Sandy," he said gently. "It's as I told you. If you tell him everything I'm sure Mordecai will be able to help you." He gave an apologetic glance in Tremaine's direction. "We haven't mentioned this before because we didn't want to embarrass you," he told him, "but there's been quite a lot of local gossip since it became known that Inspector Boyce was here. I'm afraid that everybody in the village seems to know that you're a friend of his. That's why, when Sandy came to me a little while ago, I suggested that she should wait and see you. I hope you don't mind?"

He finished on a hesitant, questioning note, and Tremaine smiled wryly.

"That's all right, Paul. I've already discovered that my slight acquaintance with Inspector Boyce has become common knowledge."

There was no doubt in his mind now that it was this knowledge that had lain behind Pauline Conroy's attitude when he had encountered her with Serge Galeski. It was the reason for her obvious unwillingness to talk and for her aggressively defensive attitude.

She had not wished to meet him because she had not wished to answer questions or to be trapped into a statement that might later prove damaging. She had been anxious to avoid him because she knew that anything she said might—in fact, probably would—reach the ears of Scotland Yard. It followed, therefore, that the glamorous Pauline had something to hide. The whole of Dalmering, thought Mordecai Tremaine ruefully, seemed to have something to hide.

He looked over his pince-nez at Sandra Borne with a friendly, disarming air.

"I believe I know why you're worried, Miss Borne—and why you're here. You told Inspector Boyce that when Miss Dare hadn't returned at a late hour you went unconcernedly to bed, expecting her to let herself in with her key when she eventually got back. That statement wasn't—well, it wasn't quite correct. Isn't that so?"

The brown eyes had widened. There was surprise in them now. But Mordecai Tremaine's calm implication that he already knew a good deal of the story had broken through her frozen reserve, given her the courage to say what she had come to say.

"It's true that I went to bed," she said, in a low voice. "But the rest isn't true."

"You mean that you *were* anxious about Miss Dare?"

She nodded.

"Yes. I—I was more than anxious. I was afraid."

"Because she had told you before going out that she expected to be back by eleven o'clock?"

"You know that?"

The question seemed to be startled out of her.

"Yes," said Tremaine, "I know that. What I do *not* know," he added, "is why you didn't at least ring up Mr. Vaughan's house when Miss Dare hadn't returned at the time she'd given you."

"That's why I've come," she said. "To—to tell you that."

Her words were forced. She was like a person speaking against her will but speaking because she knew that she must.

"I—I knew that the inspector didn't believe me. It must

have been because he knew that Lydia had told me when she expected to be back. When she didn't return, I didn't telephone—I didn't raise any alarm because—because I thought she was still with Martin."

She brought the last phrase out with a little gasp. It had cost her an effort to say it. She leaned back. Her eyes were glistening, on the verge of tears.

Tremaine tried to hide his bewilderment.

"You thought that she was still with Mr. Vaughan? But I don't quite see…"

It was as though she realized his difficulty and was nerving herself to speak more plainly.

"Martin—" she said, "Martin was in love with Lydia."

And now there was tragedy in the room. Tragedy forbidding and terrible, brooding in the dark corners, closing in oppressively from all sides.

No one spoke. No one until Paul Russell forced an odd sound between his lips and then managed to articulate his words.

"Are you *sure*?" he said, and his voice was an unnatural, harsh whisper.

"It's true," she said. "I've known it for a long time."

"You thought that Lydia—that she was staying with him *voluntarily*?"

Russell's eyes, incredulous, doubting, were turned upon her. Sandra Borne nodded her understanding of his question and her answer to it with a movement that had an air of fatalism. The doctor looked toward his wife, as if seeking solace from her.

"Lydia—I can't believe it. I just can't believe it."

"Miss Borne has told us that she *thought* Miss Dare was staying with Mr. Vaughan," put in Mordecai Tremaine. "But we know that she *didn't* stay with him. So we really haven't explained anything yet."

Sandra Borne sat up very straight.

"I know what you mean," she said. "It was my fault. I—I doubted Lydia. I allowed myself to think that she might be staying with Martin. I was disloyal to her."

"Sandy—don't!"

But she had made up her mind to speak, and she took no heed of Jean Russell's interjection.

"I first realized that Martin was in love with Lydia some months ago, but I think he's really been in love with her all the time—ever since we came here. At first I was glad. I was glad for Lydia's sake. All three of us had always been such friends. It seemed natural to think of Martin and Lydia being married. And then I learned about Gerald—"

She stopped. There was an elusive expression of sadness in her eyes.

"It's strange," she went on, after her brief pause, "how you can live with people and be on intimate terms with them and think you know all about their lives—and then suddenly find out that you really don't know the most important things about them after all. It was like that with us. I thought I knew everything there was to know about Lydia—what she liked to eat, what she liked to read, what she liked to wear; we'd always been such friends. But it was a long time before I knew about Gerald. She met him in Scotland when she was on holiday. She used to write to him and meet him sometimes in London. She used to say that she was going up on business or to see some of her old school friends. He never came to Dalmering. That's why I didn't suspect that it wasn't—that it wasn't all right for Martin—that Lydia was falling in love with someone else."

"But Mr. Vaughan *did* find out, didn't he?" said Tremaine. "I understand that the fact that Miss Dare was marrying Mr. Farrant was well known in the village."

"Oh yes. Their engagement was announced two or three months ago."

"What was Mr. Vaughan's attitude?"

"He took it very well. I don't think many people knew that he was in love with Lydia himself."

Paul Russell nodded agreement.

"I had no idea it was like that with him. He certainly didn't give any sign of it. He seemed genuinely pleased when the news was given out—as I told you this morning," he added.

"I knew," said Jean quietly. "Martin is very good at hiding his feelings, but he doesn't hide them successfully all the time."

Mordecai Tremaine was regarding Sandra Borne thoughtfully.

"It seems to me," he observed, "that you weren't altogether satisfied in your mind, Miss Borne. I mean that you weren't satisfied that Miss Dare was doing the right thing."

"No," she told him, "I wasn't satisfied. Perhaps it was because I'd always connected Lydia with Martin in my mind and was always imagining that I could see signs that she was beginning to return his feelings—little things, like the way she spoke and the way she sometimes looked at him. Even after the engagement was announced I kept feeling that Lydia wasn't sure of herself and that Martin was very often in her mind."

"Did she ever say anything to you on the subject?"

"She never actually discussed it—not directly. But it seemed to me that taking the definite step of becoming engaged to Gerald had caused her to think more seriously about Martin. I know it sounds illogical, but that was my impression; and when she said that she was going to have dinner with Martin, alone, I wondered whether she really was beginning to change her mind after all. That was why I didn't do anything when she didn't come back. I thought something had happened between them. I thought—I thought she was staying the night with Martin."

She broke off again. She glanced half fearfully at each of them in turn, as if she was afraid that she had repelled them by her confession.

And then: "Of course I was wrong," she went on quickly. "Dreadfully, horribly wrong. I shouldn't have thought like that—it was mean and disloyal. In the morning, when I heard that Lydia was dead, I knew how terribly I'd misjudged her. And I—I was ashamed. I didn't want anyone to know how little I'd trusted her and how much I'd wronged her. That's why I said that I'd gone to bed leaving Lydia to let herself in with her latchkey and that she hadn't told me what time she expected to be back. I didn't want her memory to be dragged through the mud because of my unjust suspicions.

"I knew that the inspector didn't believe me. I could see from his manner that he knew I was hiding something. But I *had* to keep to what I'd said. I felt trapped—desperate. I had to make amends to Lydia. Besides—besides…"

She faltered. Her eyes dropped.

"Besides," said Mordecai Tremaine, "if you had told the truth it would have incriminated Mr. Vaughan."

She looked up at him quickly—so quickly that it was as though his words had induced an involuntary nervous reaction.

"Yes," she said, a frightened look haunting her brown eyes, "yes, it would have incriminated Martin. At first I couldn't think of anything except that I'd misjudged Lydia and that all the time I'd imagined she'd been with Martin she'd really been lying dead out in the darkness. And then I realized what else it might mean. I realized that if I told the truth about why I hadn't done anything when Lydia hadn't come back it would mean telling the police that I knew that Martin had been in love with her. I knew what they would say. They would say that he'd killed her in jealousy; that he'd made up his mind that if *he* couldn't marry her no one else would!"

The frightened look had been replaced by horror now. She was sitting upright, her slim little figure taut and strained.

"You see how it was!" she said desperately. "I couldn't tell the truth! I had to go on pretending that I hadn't cared. And now the police have started asking questions, and I'm afraid—I'm afraid…"

She buried her face in her hands. Paul Russell rose to his feet and, crossing to her side, placed a comforting arm about her.

"It's all right, Sandy," he told her. "You've nothing to reproach yourself with."

"I had to come to you, Paul," she said, and clung to him.

"I couldn't keep silent any longer. And I couldn't go to the police. I couldn't tell them about Martin—"

"The police will have to know the truth," said Russell gravely, "no matter what it may involve. If Martin is innocent he will be able to tell them so."

She had relaxed a little when he had gone to her, but now his tone caused her to stiffen again in his grasp. She raised a tearstained face.

"You don't mean—you can't mean that Martin might have…"

He did not reply, and her hand went to her mouth.

"Oh, no—*no!*" she whispered. "Not *Martin!*"

For a long while after Sandra Borne had gone, Mordecai Tremaine remained in his chair, staring into the darkened room, staring at the dust particles still dancing a mad gavotte in that solitary beam of sunlight.

Martin Vaughan had been the last known person to see Lydia Dare alive. He could quite easily have followed her and killed her in the shadows of that fatal copse. The weapon with which the crime had been committed was known to be his.

He had been in love with Lydia Dare. He was a man of strong passions who had once lived a wild, primitive life; Paul Russell had spoken of Vaughan's earlier career, of the grim conditions under which he had founded his fortunes.

He could be expected to revert to type under the stress of great emotion.

He had immersed himself in the study of ancient peoples. His mind must have assimilated many strange and terrible items of knowledge, must be colored by fierce, disturbing pictures of revenge and blood sacrifice and primeval hate. And Lydia Dare had been about to marry another man.

It fitted. How damnably it fitted!

8

From his inconspicuous seat at the back of the village hall, Mordecai Tremaine was watching the rehearsal of *Murder Has a Motive*. He caught Paul Russell's inquiring eye and nodded. He was well satisfied. For a man who wished to meet and to study the members of Dalmering's "colony" there was no doubt that it was an ideal place.

Several people who had already been there on his arrival had recognized him and had spoken to him. Geoffrey Manning, Phyllis Galway, Edith Lorrington, and Howard Shannon had all greeted him, but only Shannon had revealed more than a passing interest. Tremaine had caught the plump man glancing at him nervously, as though the other could not make up his mind as to the reason for his presence and was worried by the fact.

Edith Lorrington had given him a smile once or twice, but it had been a vague, indeterminate smile, bestowed upon him as she had passed him upon some equally vague and indeterminate errand.

Geoffrey Manning, Mordecai Tremaine was pleased to note, had no eyes for him at all. His attention was centered upon Phyllis Galway. It seemed that Manning was not so oblivious of the girl's charms as he had appeared to be at "Roseland," and Tremaine felt a warm sense of pleasure within him. It had been a source of dismay to his sentimental soul that two young people so obviously fitted for each other should apparently have chosen to ignore each other's existence.

Watching them as they had stood talking by the side of the wooden stage, observing the way in which Manning's pleasantly rugged features had become animated as he had looked at her, seeing the expression in the girl's eyes, Tremaine had nodded approvingly. The romance seemed to be in the making after all.

He had been compelled to take himself sternly to task. This was no way in which to be reasoning. He knew nothing of either Geoffrey Manning or of Phyllis Galway. He was engaged upon a stern business in which sentiment was not only out of place but dangerous to his judgment. Murder was loose in Dalmering; until it had been conclusively bound by the chains of the law, even romance was suspect.

Duly chastened, he had settled back in his seat to await events.

The remainder of the company had arrived almost together, and in the bustle of their coming and the preparations for the rehearsal, Mordecai Tremaine had been practically unnoticed. Apart from the stage, over which an electric light bulb was burning, the hall was a gloomy place full of shadows. A long building, with a low, dark-beamed ceiling and with narrow, many-paned leaded windows, it was never brightly lit, even in full daylight, and now, with the evening sun already at an angle at which its rays were screened by neighboring trees, it was heavy with patchy semidarkness.

Soon the rehearsal had begun, and with everyone's interest centered upon the stage, no one had remarked upon his presence, although he was aware that several of the latecomers had managed to distinguish his diffident form seated in the shadows and had recognized him with varying degrees of interest. Karen Hammond had been one of them. He had observed her blond head turn in his direction and then had seen her nudge the man at her side, who had thereupon—although not ostentatiously—followed her example and turned also.

He had guessed that it must be her husband. The intimacy of their relationship was obvious—far more so than would have been the case in such a public place and among so tightly knit a community if it had not been legalized in the eyes of the said community by the bonds of matrimony.

Philip Hammond, although no longer a young man, was still a presentable one. His fair hair was thinning but in a manner that gave him a distinguished appearance. It revealed a wide forehead, the brow of a man of intelligence and of a man who could accept responsibilities. His features were strong and firm, even if the mouth was perhaps a shade too sensual, the lips a trifle too full. He was slightly built, almost frail in fact, but he was well proportioned and despite his frailty he had an air of confident strength. He was, Tremaine decided, the sort of man who could appeal to women. He was the sort of man whom they would both respect and want to mother. He was the sort of man who would excite both their maternal instincts and their secret desire to be treated as the weaker partner.

Hammond was apparently taking no part in the production, although his wife was playing quite an important role. He was seated in a chair near the stage but was paying very little attention to what was going on, seemingly far more concerned with his own thoughts.

It was clear that the rehearsals were well advanced. The play was being taken straight through, and there was very little "fluffing" of the lines. The prompter—Jean Russell was performing that unsung but essential duty—was seldom required.

Tremaine found himself becoming more and more engrossed as the play developed. At first his interest had been desultory; he had been more concerned with the players than with the play. But gradually his attention was gripped by what was passing on the stage.

One reason for it was Martin Vaughan. The big man was giving a powerful performance. When he was on the stage his big form seemed to dominate the rest of the cast. He spoke his lines with an intensity that gave them the mark of truth. He was not merely playing but living his part.

As the piece moved toward its climax it became more and more evident that Vaughan was overshadowing everyone else; that he was becoming the dominant figure, assuming an importance the author had never intended. Perhaps it was because as his own part grew in stature as he built it up inexorably upon his lines, so those of the other characters gradually diminished, as though his brilliance was causing theirs to fade and as though the strength was being drawn out of them to flow into him, leaving them the appearance of puppet figures moving spiritlessly in the shadow of a juggernaut.

"...*He doth bestride the narrow world like a Colossus*..."

Uninvited the fragment came into Mordecai Tremaine's mind. It was evident to him that he was not the victim of his always active imagination. Others besides himself were aware of the phenomenon. That was clear from the expressions on the faces he could see around him—faces white and fixed in the gloom or yellowish and staring under the electric light; the faces not only of those who were watching from their places in front of the stage but of the players themselves. It was clear, too, from the questioning glances that were being exchanged, and plain in the brittle, tension-filled atmosphere that was being slowly created.

Sandra Borne was watching from the wings. Tremaine could just make out the piled mass of her hair and could see the occasional glint of the light on her tortoiseshell spectacles as she peered around the corner of the scenery. She was too far off, and the light was too poor for him to be able to tell whether she had recovered from the emotions that had ravaged her when she had been telling her story that afternoon, but he fancied that she would have done her utmost to hide all traces of the strain she had undergone before coming to the rehearsal.

From what Paul Russell had told him, he had previously gained the impression that Sandra Borne had been responsible for a good deal of the work which had gone into the production of *Murder Has a Motive*. Although she was acting no part in the play, Tremaine guessed that without her industry and without her patience and quiet determination, it would not have flourished so vigorously. It would have perished of apathy long since.

"Loyal, painstaking little Sandy," Russell had described her, "always doing more work than anybody else and making less fuss about it."

He had added, "For Heaven's sake don't tell her I said so, otherwise she'll turn and rend me! She hates anything that looks like publicity."

And then he had voiced his concern for her. The murder had been a tremendous shock. She had been wrapped up in Lydia. Their two lives had been almost completely interwoven. Not quite utterly identified each in the other—as the matter of Gerald Farrant had shown—but certainly in the small things, the little intimacies of daily life. The doctor had been worried as a medical man; he had been worried about the effect upon her nervous system of the abrupt, the brutally abrupt, cessation of the close companionship and the exchanges of confidences that had become so integral a part of her being.

In addition there was the question of Vaughan. Hard upon the shock of Lydia's death had come the numbing horror of the suspicion that Martin Vaughan might have been responsible for what had happened.

What secret struggle had been going on in her mind? What torment of doubt and fear had she lived through before she had made her way to "Roseland" to seek relief by telling her story—the age-old relief of confession? Paul Russell had shaken his head gravely. There was no doubt that she had been cruelly torn by conflicting thoughts. Loyalty to Lydia, loyalty to Martin Vaughan, fierce desire to see the truth laid bare and murder avenged, and yet with it a desperate anxiety not to lose another of her friends in the accomplishment—there had been war within her.

Her sudden collapse and the stormy sobbing that had followed her recital of her story had been in the nature of a safety valve. It had driven her turbulent emotions outward instead of inward; it had given her relief, saved her from what might have been a longer delayed but far more harmful nervous prostration.

Tremaine found himself wondering what she was thinking as she stood in the wings watching Martin Vaughan's performance. Was she laboring under the same sense of strain as all the others so obviously were? He knew that even if the big man had not himself added to it by the very force of the manner in which he was playing his part, there would have been that about him which would have drawn attention upon him tonight. Suspicion had swept through Dalmering. It was as evident as though the placard hung upon Vaughan's chest, bearing the design of the accusing finger pointing inward.

There were no secrets in a village. Without any definite words having been spoken or any definite accusation having been framed, the big man had been indicted.

The atmosphere in the hall was an accusing atmosphere, an atmosphere charged with a belief of guilt. Tremaine knew it now. He wondered that he had not sensed it earlier, he who judged himself to be quick to feel and assimilate such things.

Only Vaughan seemed unconscious of it. He was striding through his part like a man who lived only for what he was now engaged upon.

And then, as though one half of his mind had, until that moment, been blacked out by a shutter that had suddenly been lifted, Mordecai Tremaine realized what was happening. He realized just why that dreadful, tense, unspoken accusation lay in the air. He realized why it was that Vaughan's performance was so compelling and so laden with drama.

The part the big man played was that of Robert Barnett, a solicitor who had fallen in love with a girl much younger than himself. Phyllis Galway played the girl. The sight of her trim loveliness on the stage had earlier caused Tremaine to remark mentally that it was not surprising that the middle-aged bachelor whom Vaughan was supposed to be had fallen in love with her. Strike thirty years from his age, he had ruminated unprofitably, and he would have been delighted to do the same thing himself.

In the play, the situation, after having promised favorably for Barnett, had taken a turn decidedly against him. An opponent (Geoffrey Manning) younger than himself had begun to challenge the issue. The girl, from being acquiescent if not really in love with him, had become uncertain.

She had begun to realize that she was not at all sure that she wanted to tie herself for life to a man so much older, so set in his ways.

The drama had surged toward a climax. Jealousy had eaten its insidious way into Barnett's soul until now it was consuming him, turning him from a reasoning human being into a cunning madman, thirsting to destroy.

Tremaine knew the next step. Robert Barnett was going to kill the girl. Martin Vaughan was going to kill Phyllis Galway. Martin Vaughan was going to kill Lydia Dare. Martin Vaughan *had* killed Lydia Dare…

That was the thought sequence that was running through the hall. The reason for his inability to see until now what the others had seen so long before him was clear at last to Mordecai Tremaine. He had been suffering from the disadvantage that he had not seen the play before; he had not known from the beginning, as all the others had known, that Vaughan was going to act the murderer.

And among those who had known, of course, was Martin Vaughan himself. That was why the big man had dominated the performance and why he was still dominating it. He was behaving as he had behaved to Inspector Boyce and as he had behaved that afternoon. He was being deliberately aggressive. He was flaunting the parallel between his actions on the stage and what he knew might be regarded as his actions in reality; he was flaunting it as a bullfighter might flaunt the red cloak in the ring, daring the beast to charge. Only in this case the beast was that unspoken accusation of guilt.

The murder, when it came, was an act of defiance. Martin Vaughan thundered his lines and drove home the killer's knife with a savagery that betrayed him. Under other circumstances it would have been a remarkable piece of acting. As it was, real tragedy was too near for there to be any abstract appreciation of the way in which he had played the scene. It was too obviously a gage flung at the feet of those who watched.

The crime did not mark the end of the play. There were, in fact, two other violent deaths before the final curtain. *Murder Has a Motive* certainly provided its quota of bodies.

Nevertheless, it was Vaughan who stole the thunder—on this occasion at least. Before the violence of his jealousy—or, rather, his portrayal of it and of the bloody climax of his passion—the other crimes became of minor significance. They were mere sidepieces supporting the central drama; there was no virility in them compared with that fierce realism Vaughan had infused into his own act.

Tremaine subjected the play to a critical mental examination. What effect had the author been striving to obtain? It was a thriller, of course, devised as a vehicle for giving entertainment, but there seemed to be another aspect. Murder had been analyzed. An attempt had been made to study the underlying psychology of murder and to dissect the several minds of the guilty.

Karen Hammond played the part of a murderess. Her "victim" was Howard Shannon. Tremaine felt rather sorry for the plump man. The plot required that one of the scenes should end with the discovery of his "dead" body in a trunk occupying a prominent position on the stage. No wonder, he thought, that Shannon's suit invariably looked so crumpled! He must spend an uncomfortable period at each rehearsal cramped inside the trunk waiting to be "discovered." There seemed to be a faithful attempt at reproducing all details; Shannon *was* found in the trunk.

The motive behind this "killing" was also a familiar one. Shannon played the part of the unfaithful husband, murdered by his tormented, desperate wife. The "other woman" did not make any actual appearance, but the dialogue suggested her presence so well and so cleverly that the atmosphere of the wronged wife, finding the situation becoming more and more intolerable, was dramatically developed. In its creation by inference of events and persons not shown upon the stage, it reminded Tremaine of the play *Jealousy* by the French author Louis Verneuil, that powerful *tour de force* in which only two characters appeared and all the rest were created by the dialogue.

The third victim was Pauline Conroy. Tremaine—secretly

a little ashamed of his callousness—experienced no concern for her. Perhaps it was an unconscious reaction. He was afraid of women as overpowering as Pauline; confronted with them he always felt like a small boy in need of protection despite his attempts to appear blasé.

It amused him to see that her murderer was Paul Russell. Tolerant, friendly old Paul, playing the killer! The sheep in wolf's clothing!

This crime was a somewhat more complicated one, involving a considerable emphasis upon psychology and the interplay of emotions. Pauline Conroy played Margot Forester, a young, ambitious actress—not a difficult part for her since it came so close to the truth. The doctor was her evil genius— also a doctor, incidentally, in the play. Tremaine guessed that these chance resemblances had influenced the casting.

Under the guidance and inspiration of Karl Loudon—the doctor—Margot Forester was shown as achieving the success for which she craved. But success at a price; success that monopolized her life and bound her—body and soul—to the man who had created her.

And, of course, it could not last. A vague hunger to be free hardened into a fierce hatred of the possessive doctor who had given her all she had desired but who, in doing so, had become the dominant force in her life. Karl was always there in the background, suggesting, ordering, framing her existence. It was Karl who said do this, Karl who said you must not do that. Karl, Karl…

So she decided that she must break with him—and learned that he had no intention of allowing her to be free; that he would never release her from her bondage. She pleaded with him, stormed at him, reviled him, and, at last, told him that there was another man and that she was going away with him.

It was untrue. There was no other man. But Karl, the doctor, believed it.

And he killed her. Not in passion, after a furious, emotional scene. But coldly, deliberately, with the poison that he as a doctor knew so well, with a deadly, implacable purpose rendered all the more dreadful by his apparent impassivity.

Tremaine thought that Paul was uneasy in the part. He did his best, but it was obvious that Karl Loudon, the scientific, self-centered killer, was far removed from the easygoing humanitarian Paul Russell whom Dalmering knew and loved. He was struggling to portray a sadistic, dominating character completely alien to his own way of life, and the contrast too often became evident.

Pauline Conroy, on the other hand, was excellent. Ungrudgingly, although he did not like her, Mordecai Tremaine admitted that she could act. Her Margot Forester was a clever, understanding character study. But for Martin

Vaughan's overwhelming dominance of the play, she would have attracted considerably more attention.

Inevitably, as there were three separate plots, although each was linked to the others, the piece was inclined to be a little sketchy in treatment. Its construction was not always faultless, but there was no doubt that it possessed a compelling quality. It left one with a sense of horror and explosive force. Tremaine could imagine it being well received.

When the final curtain fell there was no attempt to study the evening's performance. As if by common consent, players and audience drifted into detached little groups, talking idly but with an obviously artificial inconsequent gaiety that belied their attempts to appear at ease. This latest rehearsal of *Murder Has a Motive* had been too raw a thing, too much an exposure of a painful, open wound to permit of any discussion.

Martin Vaughan had seated himself in a chair just below the stage. He was seemingly immersed in a notebook he had produced. No one had made any attempt to speak to him, and Tremaine guessed that he had taken refuge in the pretense of consulting the book in an endeavor to render less obvious the fact that he was being avoided by the others.

The big man's attitude was not easy to explain. Despite his apparent preoccupation, his expression still held the challenge that had been evident in him all through the evening. Was he behaving with such truculence because he was guilty and knew the net to be closing about him? Or because he was guilty and was trying to create an exaggerated impression of guilt in order that, paradoxically, it would be thought that he was giving himself away so utterly that he must be innocent? Or because he *was* innocent?

Tremaine was not given the opportunity of pursuing his thoughts along what would, in any case, merely have been a circular road leading him back to his starting point. Paul Russell was trying to attract his attention. The doctor was talking to Karen Hammond and her husband, and evidently he was mindful of his friend's request to meet Philip Hammond.

The introductions were made. Tremaine knew that he was being subjected to a close scrutiny; as their hands met, Philip Hammond's eyes searched his face with more than a conventional curiosity. It was as though the other was weighing him up, making a shrewd if necessarily quick estimate of his capabilities.

He fancied that the man was disappointed. Was there a faint trace of dismay in his attitude? Tremaine thought that it was quite possible, although he could not see why Philip Hammond should react in such a manner. People very often did experience an initial sense of disappointment when they came face-to-face with an elderly, benevolent-looking ex-tobacconist with an old-fashioned pair of pince-nez balancing, by no more than the mercy of Providence, on the end of his nose, instead of with a strong-jawed, obvious sleuth with man hunter stamped on his lean and hungry features.

However, Hammond said nothing to produce the suspicion that such were his particular thoughts. The conversation followed routine lines.

"What did you think of the play, Mordecai?" asked Russell.

"Strong meat, Paul," he returned. "But it should be a big success. I thought the production was excellent."

"Thanks to Sandy," said Karen Hammond. "She's worked harder than any of us to get things going."

"I thought Mr. Vaughan played his part very well," observed Tremaine.

He expected that there would be a sudden silence, and he was justified. There was.

"Er—yes," said the doctor hastily, before the silence could become too painful. "Martin is usually pretty good."

Neither Karen Hammond nor her husband made any attempt to elaborate Russell's remark. Tremaine saw that his seed had fallen upon stony ground. He said: "I thought you were very good, too, Mrs. Hammond. Have you done much acting?"

"No," she said, with a smile. "This is the first time on any stage—except for small parts at school when I was dragooned into making an appearance. I'm afraid you're trying to flatter me."

"On the contrary, I thought you played extremely well," he told her. He added questioningly, "Mr. Hammond isn't taking any part then?"

Philip Hammond started to make a reply, but his wife broke in quickly before he could do more than shape the first words.

"No—Philip's business engagements make it awkward for him to attend rehearsals," she said, "so he decided that it wouldn't be fair to the others to take a definite part. He did try, but he found it so difficult to get away on several occasions that he had to give up the idea. That was when we were just reading the play," she explained. "Before we had the cast arranged."

"Let me see," said Russell, "wasn't it suggested that you should take Shannon's part, Philip? Opposite your wife? I've an idea you weren't keen on it, though."

Karen Hammond revealed a momentary agitation, but her husband was unmoved.

"That's right, Paul," he returned calmly. "It *was* suggested. But I turned it down for the reason Karen gave—it's so infernally difficult sometimes to get away from the office. That's part of the price I have to pay for the pleasure of living in Dalmering," he said to Tremaine.

That gentleman nodded understandingly.

"It's a pleasure that is certainly well worth paying for."

In a moment or two the group was broken up—Geoffrey Manning called across to Karen Hammond with a question about a tennis party that had apparently been arranged some while before and was now likely to be canceled—and Tremaine took advantage of his release to explore the hall more thoroughly. He had had ample opportunity of studying the main part of the building while the rehearsal had been in progress, but he was curious to see of what the rest of it consisted.

The stage, although not elaborate, was a workmanlike affair, with double curtains. They appeared, most unusually for amateur properties, to work smoothly and reliably. Behind the stage were several small rooms. There was one on either side, each used as a dressing room, and these two were connected by a third, somewhat larger, so that it was possible to leave the stage on one side and reappear on the other without having to go out of the building in order to avoid being seen by the audience when the play required a change of entrance.

This center room contained a big porcelain sink provided with two taps, a gas ring, and a fair-sized gas stove. Upon a plain kitchen table there was a neat pile of cups and saucers, a jug still containing a little milk, and canisters of tea and sugar. This, apparently, was the nerve center of the production; no doubt innumerable cups of tea had been brewed here during rehearsals, although tonight—probably by virtue of the atmosphere created by Martin Vaughan—looked like being a departure from precedent.

"They tell me," said a quiet voice, "that you're a detective."

Tremaine had heard the sound of light footsteps on the bare boards. He turned without haste. It was Philip Hammond who had followed him inside.

"It's a little—exaggerated," he said deprecatingly.

"Maybe," said Hammond. He seemed quite cool, entirely self-possessed. His eyes were still appraising, judging. "You know, of course, who killed Lydia."

His level statement brought a look of surprise to Tremaine's face. Hammond saw it and smiled.

"Naturally, you aren't going to commit yourself. But we don't need to beat about the bush. It was Vaughan. When are you going to arrest him?"

"But I've no power to arrest people, Mr. Hammond. And isn't that rather a grave accusation to make against Mr. Vaughan?"

"Murder is rather a grave business," replied Hammond, and Tremaine was not quite sure whether he was being mocked. "You may not be able to arrest anyone, but your friend Inspector Boyce isn't in the same category." He took a step closer. He lowered his voice. "We all know that Vaughan is the man you want. Why don't you get it over with? Arrest him and finish the whole wretched affair. Every miserable little reporter in the country will be coming down here poking and prying. Dalmering is being turned into a peep show for every morbid-minded sensation-seeking busybody for miles around. There'll be no privacy for any of us soon. Put Vaughan behind bars, give him what he deserves, and let's forget this thing ever happened."

Tremaine tried to think of something adequate to say and failed. Hammond misconstrued his silence.

"Is it proof you want?" he asked. "Is that what's holding you back? I'll get your proof for you. Proof enough to convince twelve good men and true and to hang him as high as Haman. Only when you've got it see that you act quickly."

A footstep sounded outside. Hammond stopped.

"We don't want the world to hear us," he said. "I hope we understand each other."

He gave Mordecai Tremaine one final, comprehensive stare and then turned on his heel. Tremaine stared after him. His mouth opened, but he closed it again without producing any words. It had been Philip Hammond's manner that had overwhelmed him. It had been his matter-of-fact efficiency, his calm announcement of Martin Vaughan's guilt that had bereft him of speech.

Mechanically he walked toward the door. Because of Karen Hammond's agitation, because of the way in which she had followed him from "Roseland," he had expected developments from the direction of her husband. But not quite such a development as that which had just occurred.

As he reached the outer dressing room someone came through the doorway from the main hall. It was Howard Shannon. The plump man saw him and halted in his stride. A look of fear leaped to his eyes.

"I'm not going to answer any questions," he said breathlessly. "You can't make me! You're not anybody official. You've no right to go asking people questions. I'm not going to say anything, d'you hear?"

He regained control over his limbs. He lurched forward. He fumbled vainly with the handle for a second and then pulled open the door leading to the open air at the rear of the building. His plump figure pushed unsteadily through. The door banged behind him.

Mordecai Tremaine adjusted his pince-nez. He drew a deep breath. Undoubtedly it had been a night of surprises.

9

The hour was 6:30 a.m. Mordecai Euripides Tremaine, clad in his pajama trousers and baring his chest to the morning air, was performing his exercises in front of the open window. It had been his practice for many years to indulge in a ten-minute course of exercises, winter and summer, on waking in the morning. He would have been the first to admit that the physical effect was very small, but the psychological value was enormous.

This morning, however, he was aware that he was losing some of the benefits attendant upon this daily ritual. He was not concentrating as he should upon the fact that he was drawing fresh, health-giving air into his lungs. His mind was wandering. He was not in his bedroom at all. He was in Dalmering village hall, reliving the events of the previous night.

He shaved and dressed in a preoccupied manner. Until he had classified Philip Hammond and Howard Shannon and had placed them, duly labeled, in their respective compartments, he knew that he was unlikely to be allowed much mental peace. He was certain that those two gentlemen were men of mystery.

What he was not certain of was the precise nature of the mystery in each case and whether it had any direct bearing upon the murder of Lydia Dare.

Jean Russell gave him a curious glance when he sat down at the breakfast-table.

"You've cut yourself, Mordecai…"

He fingered his chin self-consciously.

"Yes. It was my own fault. I was too busy thinking—not paying sufficient attention to what I was doing."

"You look as though you're still deep in thought," observed Russell banteringly. "It seems to me that our rehearsal last night gave you plenty to think about."

"The rehearsal—and other things," returned Tremaine.

It was obvious that the doctor would have liked to ask questions, but having succeeded in his object of persuading his visitor to take an active interest in the murder he had adopted the policy of not attempting to press him for information and he did not make any comment.

"Paul told me that you were impressed with the play," said Jean, pouring his tea.

"Yes." Tremaine nodded. "Yes, I found it very"—he searched for a word—"very compelling. I'd like to read it—study it more closely. I wonder if you have a copy I could borrow?"

"Certainly," Russell told him. "Jean and I both have a copy. When we decided to do the play we had a number typed."

"Typed? It hasn't been printed?"

"Apparently not. According to Vaughan we couldn't get it in book form, so we had it typed by some people in Kingshampton—friends of Edith Lorrington, as a matter of fact. If you remember, she mentioned them yesterday morning. They have a bookshop and typing agency in the town."

"Yes, I remember. You must have been very keen to do this particular play."

"Well, Vaughan was. And as it seemed to be the sort of thing that could be put over fairly easily, we decided to make our own arrangements about obtaining enough copies."

Tremaine nodded and relapsed into silence for a while, busying himself with his bacon and egg. And then: "How long has Howard Shannon been in Dalmering?" he asked.

The doctor looked surprised at his change of topic.

"About five or six years, I should think," he said. "I wouldn't be dogmatic about it though. I'm speaking from a rather hazy memory."

"I believe you said that nothing very much is known about him. Does he work for a living?"

Russell laid down his knife and fork. He shrugged.

"Sorry, Mordecai," he said, "I just don't know. If he does he spends quite a lot of time here in the village, so obviously he doesn't work very hard. He seems well supplied with money. At least, I've never heard of his refusing a subscription to any of the local charities or claiming to be hard up. Wasn't he on the same train when you came down? I believe we mentioned then that he was our man of mystery."

"Yes," said Tremaine, "he was. And so you did."

After breakfast he smoked his routine cigarette—he decided against risking a pipe—and settled down to read the copy of *Romantic Stories* he had brought with him. It was a sign that he was restless, unable to think clearly. He turned to *Romantic Stories* as another man might turn to whiskey. In its sentimental, harmless pages he invariably tried to find solace when he was troubled.

Only this morning the solace was not there. The magic would not work. After half an hour he gave up, and with a brief explanation to Jean that he was going out for a stroll, he walked slowly down the road.

His destination was the Admiral. He had not seen Jonathan Boyce since their meeting on the previous afternoon, and he was aware that the time for a talk with the Yard man was long overdue. Boyce had said that he knew that the weapon with which the crime had been committed belonged to Martin Vaughan, but no steps appeared to have been taken to arrest him.

Why was Boyce holding back? Tremaine had an

uncomfortable suspicion that he knew the answer and that
he had certain responsibilities in the matter.

The Yard man was still searching for a motive. It was
probable that as yet he did not know that Martin Vaughan
had been in love with Lydia Dare. It was certain that he had
not had the fact put to him as plainly as Sandra Borne had
put it, even if he had begun to suspect.

Tremaine tried to find excuses, but he did not succeed in hiding from himself the knowledge that he should have told Boyce
what had passed at "Roseland." He should have made known
what Sandra Borne had told him. In itself it might not be evidence, but Boyce would know what to do in order to make it so.

The side door of the Admiral was open. There seemed
to be no one from whom to ask permission, so Tremaine
stepped inside and, pushing open another nearby door that
stood invitingly ajar, he found himself in a pleasant, sun-filled
room provided with armchairs and having the comfortable
air of a lounge.

The only occupant was standing with his back toward
him, gazing out through a deep bay window fitted with the
small, leaded panes that were typical of Dalmering and that
gave the village its attractively old-fashioned appearance. He
did not hear Tremaine's approach, for he did not turn, and his
unsuspected visitor, as he drew nearer, was able to see what it
was that was holding the other's attention.

The bay window overlooked the fields at the back of the inn, and walking at a brisk pace along a public footpath that traversed them was a figure Tremaine recognized. It was that of the ferrety gentleman who seemed to be displaying such an interest in Karen Hammond.

A moment or two longer Tremaine stood without speaking, until a turn in the path took the man from sight. And: "A rather curious person, don't you think?" he observed gently.

The man at the window spun around. He was in the thirties—a well-built, keen-faced individual with questing eyes. Those eyes surveyed Mordecai Tremaine searchingly.

"What makes you think so?" he asked.

"You're Mr. Barry Anston, aren't you?" said Mordecai Tremaine, sidestepping the question. "Barry Anston, of the *Daily Record*."

"Suppose," said the other, "that I am?"

"You're down here to cover the story of the murder," went on Tremaine, ignoring the unfriendly note in his tone. "I know who you are because I saw you yesterday, and I made inquiries about you."

"Indeed?" Anston moved away from the window and came into the center of the room. He said pointedly: "Did you wish to see me?"

"I didn't exactly call to see you," said Tremaine carefully, "but it's possible that you may be able to help me. You seemed to be very interested in the man who went across the fields just now, and as it happens *I'm* interested in him, too."

Anston gave him an intent, prolonged stare, but before he could make any reply the door opened again and Boyce came into the room.

"Hullo, Anston," he said cheerfully and then saw Mordecai Tremaine. "Hullo, Mordecai—do you two know each other?"

"Not yet," returned Tremaine. "But I have hopes."

The newspaper reporter looked inquiringly from one to the other of them.

"A friend of yours, Inspector?"

Boyce did not betray himself by any hesitation.

"Yes," he replied easily. "He's staying in Dalmering—by a coincidence. He has friends in the village."

"The name is Tremaine," remarked that gentleman. "Mordecai Tremaine."

"Sorry," interjected the Yard man. "I thought you'd both introduced yourselves."

"We were just leading up to it when you came in, Jonathan." Tremaine glanced in the newspaperman's direction. "I saw Mr. Anston looking out of the window," he went on. "He was watching someone walk along a footpath across the fields. I must confess I felt rather curious about it because it was a man who stopped me and spoke to me the other night. He's a stranger to the village, but he's been seen in the neighborhood several times lately. People have been wondering just who he is."

The inspector caught, as he was intended to, the significance in Mordecai Tremaine's tone. He looked at Anston and raised an eyebrow.

"Do you know him?"

The other nodded. If he had been cautious in his attitude to the mild-looking man with the pince-nez, whom he did not know, he certainly had no objection to talking to Jonathan Boyce, of Scotland Yard, who might prove a useful source of information.

"His name's Hornsby. He runs a private-inquiry agency. That side of it's aboveboard, but I've an idea that he hasn't any objection to combining a little blackmail with his normal business."

"Hornsby?" Boyce reflected, his brow crinkled. "The name's familiar, although I've not met him before."

"I ran across him when I was covering a story several months ago," explained Anston. "That's how I came to suspect the possibility of a sideline in blackmail."

"It *is* only a suspicion?"

"So far, anyway," said the reporter. "I imagine that if it was any more than that it would have come into your province, Inspector."

"Anston has a remarkable memory for criminal facts

and faces," said Boyce, by way of explanation to Mordecai Tremaine. "They call him the Criminal Record Office of Fleet Street."

"It isn't quite as wonderful as the inspector is making it sound," said Anston deprecatingly, also addressing himself to Tremaine. "It's a matter of habit. I've been crime reporting for so long that it's second nature to remember odd scraps of knowledge."

Tremaine regarded him with respect—not untinged with envy.

"It must be a very useful attribute," he observed. He glanced at the Yard man. "I really came to see you, Jonathan," he said. "It's a glorious morning. I was thinking that if you weren't too tied down by your investigations you might like a stroll."

It was necessary to explain his presence at the Admiral since Anston was there, and for the same reason he did not wish to say anything that would compromise Boyce. He hoped he did not sound as lame to the other two men as he sounded to himself as he made his statement.

"I think I can spare an hour," said the inspector cheerfully, showing no sign of having been disconcerted. "It will probably do me good to get away from thinking about the murder for a while, anyway—it may help to get rid of some of the cobwebs."

Despite the Yard man's easy manner, however, the reporter did not look as though he had been convinced. There was a slightly puzzled expression in his eyes.

"Anything—new, Inspector?" he asked.

"Not yet."

"Are there likely to be any surprises at the inquest?" Anston persisted quietly.

Boyce shook his head.

"No—it'll be just routine. But don't lose heart. I may have something for you very soon that will enable you to satisfy your thirsting public."

He spoke lightly, but there was an undercurrent of seriousness in his voice. Anston seemed to appreciate what he meant, for he smiled.

"I think I may have something for *you*," he said.

The inspector gave him a questioning look, but the other would not be drawn further.

"I'm not sure about it yet, so I won't go making any rash statements," he remarked.

"Is the inquest definitely being held today?" queried Tremaine. "It's at Kingshampton, isn't it?"

"The answer is yes to both questions," said Boyce. And added, "If you want that walk, Mordecai, let's make a start before work begins to rear its ugly head and prevents my going."

When they were in the roadway and out of the reporter's

range of hearing: "Sorry I butted in at the wrong moment, Jonathan," said Tremaine. "I hope I didn't make it awkward for you."

"Of course not. Everybody in Dalmering is aware by now that we know each other, and Anston would have found it out sooner or later."

"But he's a reporter. Won't he make things difficult for you if he starts linking you up with me and starts dropping hints about it in his newspaper?"

"Barry Anston and I know each other," said Boyce confidently. "He won't do a thing to embarrass me. Reporting the murder is his job, and I'm handling the case. He knows that if he keeps on good terms with me I can make things a good deal easier for him."

"Oh, I see," said Mordecai Tremaine. "A quid pro quo."

"Call it live and let live," said Boyce.

They walked on up the roadway. It was very pleasant in the morning sunshine. Tremaine felt that it was all wrong that they should be discussing murder and its attendant horror and guilty fear in such an atmosphere. But: "Why haven't you arrested Vaughan?" he asked.

Boyce did not look at him. He kept up his unhurried stride.

"Why should I arrest him?"

"Don't you think he *is* guilty?"

"I think he might be," said Boyce carefully.

Tremaine had the depressing feeling that he was battering at a brick wall, but he persisted in his efforts.

"You told me yesterday that you'd found the weapon and that you knew that it belonged to Vaughan. What makes you certain of that?"

"Because," the inspector stated calmly, "I showed it to him and he admitted that it was his."

Tremaine assimilated this somewhat startling item of information.

"What made you show it to him?"

"I thought," remarked Boyce, "that the purpose of coming upon this stroll was to take my mind off such questions."

"Oh, no," said Mordecai Tremaine frankly. "That was obviously merely an excuse for Anston. I came along to see you because there are several things I want to talk to you about."

Boyce gave a chuckle.

"All right," he said, "I give in. Vaughan's an archaeologist. His house is full of curios of various kinds. The knife was obviously an unusual one, and Vaughan seemed to me to be the most likely man in the neighborhood to know something about it, so I decided to get straight to the point. I took it to him and asked him whether he'd ever seen it before. He recognized it at once."

"And told you it was his?"

"And told me it was his," agreed Boyce.

"Did he seem surprised?"

"Very," said the Yard man drily. "In fact, for a moment at least, stunned would be the more suitable word to describe it."

"But you're not going to arrest him?"

"No, I'm not going to arrest him—yet." Boyce's tone became more serious. "He didn't admit that he knew any more than that the knife was his, of course. He said that he hadn't realized that it was missing and that he had no idea how it had come to be in the murderer's hands. I know it's pretty feeble and that the case is building up against him, but I'm not anxious to commit myself too soon.

"There's no reason why I should. He'll be here when—and if—I want him. If he should be foolish enough to try to make a break for it he won't get far. My men are keeping a watchful eye on him. You see, Mordecai," he finished, "when you arrest a man you take a drastic step, and I'm not satisfied that such a step would be justified."

"Meaning that you haven't yet established a motive sufficiently strong?"

"Perhaps."

"Suppose," said Tremaine slowly, "that I could give you such a motive?"

"You mean that Vaughan was in love with Lydia Dare?"

Mordecai Tremaine stopped in the roadway. Over the top of his pince-nez he eyed his friend reprovingly.

"You know then?"

"I suspect," corrected Boyce carefully. "It isn't quite the same thing as knowing—or proving."

The time had obviously arrived for confession.

"I'm sorry, Jonathan," said Tremaine haltingly. "I know that I should have told you this sooner, but I've been trying to make up my mind which would be the best way to do it and be fair to all the people concerned. Sandra Borne called at 'Roseland' yesterday afternoon. You were right when you said that you thought you'd scared her and that it would produce results."

He told his companion exactly what he himself had been told, omitting nothing. They had reached a convenient stile and Boyce leaned against it, apparently staring into vacancy but missing no detail of the recital.

"Interesting," he commented. "Very interesting. D'you think she'd tell the same story in court?"

Tremaine nodded.

"I think she would."

"H'm. It's all circumstantial, of course. If only we could find someone who actually saw Vaughan out that night."

The inspector relapsed into a thoughtful silence. Tremaine waited for what he considered to be a suitable interval. And then: "I was at the rehearsal last night," he observed.

"Rehearsal? Oh, you mean that play they're doing. Anything happen worth noting?"

"Well, our friend Vaughan was in the limelight."

Tremaine described what had transpired. He mentioned the plot of the play insofar as it explained Vaughan's part in it, but the Yard man appeared more interested in the attitude of the various people concerned rather than in the characters they were portraying.

"It looks as though relations are getting rather strained," he observed. "There doesn't seem much doubt that they think he's guilty. Of course, if he really was in love with Lydia Dare someone in the village must have had a suspicion of it. There must have been some whisper or other about them."

"I rather imagine that there was," agreed Tremaine. He hesitated. "By the way, Jonathan, what's your impression of Geoffrey Manning?"

"Seems a nice young fellow—from what little I've seen of him."

"And Phyllis Galway?"

"Seems a nice girl," said Boyce, with slightly more enthusiasm.

"You don't think—you don't suspect that they're mixed up in the murder in any way?"

"Just what are you getting at?" said Boyce. And then his face cleared. "Oh! Old man Cupid's been at work again. Is that it?"

Mordecai Tremaine had the grace to look embarrassed.

"Well, they're a well-matched young couple. I wouldn't like to think that anything was going to interfere with the—er— with the wedding bells." In an attempt to save himself from further questions—he could see the wicked gleam in the inspector's eye—he changed the subject hurriedly. "There's something decidedly odd about both Howard Shannon and Philip Hammond," he said. "I saw them both at the rehearsal. Shannon went into a panic when I happened to bump into him on his own. Said that he wasn't going to answer any questions and that I couldn't make him. It was pretty obvious that he was afraid of me because he'd learned about my knowing you."

"What about Hammond? Was *he* jittery too?"

Tremaine shook his head.

"No. As a matter of fact he seemed cold-bloodedly sure of himself. He said that Vaughan was the killer and that we knew it. He wanted to know why we didn't arrest him. He said that if it was proof we wanted he'd see that we got it."

"Did he?"

There was no disputing the undercurrent of excitement in Boyce's tone. Tremaine gave him a sharp glance.

"You sound as though you're on to something, Jonathan. What is it?"

"I'm not sure," said the inspector slowly. "I'm not sure. I saw Mrs. Hammond this morning. I asked her if her husband was here, and she said that she thought he'd gone to London."

"She said she *thought* he'd gone?" queried Tremaine, accenting in his turn the word his companion had emphasized.

"Yes. I couldn't quite make her out. She seemed in a near panic about something, and yet as though she was afraid to tell me what was on her mind."

Inspector Boyce lifted himself from the stile. He thrust his hands deep into his trousers pockets and faced Mordecai Tremaine squarely.

"Where was Philip Hammond on the night Lydia Dare was murdered?" he asked.

"At home—with his wife."

"That's where he said he was," observed Boyce. "And where his wife said he was. But he wasn't anywhere near Dalmering. I've been making a few inquiries about Mr. Philip Hammond. I can produce two people from his London office who are prepared to swear that he spent the night in town."

Tremaine stared at him.

"Are you sure?"

"I've had a report from one of my most reliable men. He isn't likely to have made a mistake—not that sort of mistake, anyway."

"But it's absurd! If he was in London why doesn't he say so? It would clear him of all suspicion of the murder."

"Precisely. But if he admits that he was in London," said Boyce, "then it's obvious that he can't swear that his wife didn't leave the house. Which means that Karen Hammond will no longer have an alibi. Had that occurred to you?"

Mordecai Tremaine's eyes widened. He shook his head.

"No," he said. "No. It hadn't."

10

As Jonathan Boyce had forecast, the inquest on Lydia Dare did not produce any surprises. The evidence taken was purely formal, and the expected verdict of willful murder against some person or persons unknown was returned with due celerity by a jury quite satisfied that their conclusions were incontestable.

It was obvious that it was merely a routine operation that necessarily had to be performed in order to allow the development of something far greater. There was an air of subdued drama in the little room in which the inquest was held. There was a subtle suggestion in the atmosphere that the police had not told all they knew and that important events were being shaped behind the scenes.

The coroner hinted delicately that such was the case. It was very possible, he said, that in the near future the authorities would be in possession of valuable evidence. He had every faith in the abilities of the police. Investigations were proceeding. Very soon, no doubt, the guilty person or persons would be arrested and brought to trial.

No suspicion was directed against Martin Vaughan. He gave evidence, but the cross-examination touched no vital matters, and there was no attempt made to fasten an accusation of guilt upon him.

Mordecai Tremaine thought that the big man was surprised by the apparent lack of interest in him. His attitude when he had begun to give his evidence had been his usual truculent one, but in the almost friendly atmosphere of the courtroom and before the sympathetic manner in which the questions had been put to him, he had lost his defensiveness. He had become more responsive, more like a sociable human being than Tremaine had so far known him. He had returned to his seat like a man who was puzzled but from whose mind a weight had been lifted.

Tremaine watched him as he sat with folded arms, listening to the proceedings. He tried to read the expressions on Vaughan's face and fancied that he saw strained expectancy change gradually to relief and then to confidence—or something very near it.

A number of the colony were present. Tremaine saw Karen Hammond—although not her husband. She was leaning forward most of the time, her blond head resting upon her hand, following closely all that took place. Sandra Borne was there. And the Russells—Paul had managed to snatch a few hours from his busy day—and behind them Geoffrey Manning and Phyllis Galway.

At the back of the room Gerald Farrant was sitting. There were black shadows under his eyes. He looked like a man who had not slept and who was tortured by his thoughts. Tremaine could understand what those thoughts were.

Several times he observed Farrant studying Martin Vaughan. Studying him not casually but with a terrible intentness and with hate in his drawn features. There was no doubt that in his mind he had accepted the other's guilt, even if, as it seemed, the coroner and the police had not.

When the inquest was over and he stood outside on the pavement in the sunlight, Mordecai Tremaine felt unreality flooding his soul. It couldn't be true that he had been listening to a calm, official explanation of the violent death of a human being and that it was very probable that among his companions there had been another human being whose conscience was heavy with guilty knowledge.

All murderers were tormented by conscience. Tremaine was sure of that. No matter how callously unmoved a man—or a woman—might appear, at some time, in the secret places of their hearts, they knew the agony of self-judgment.

He looked around him. The Russells had followed him from the courtroom. Paul had turned to speak to Sandra Borne.

"How about a cup of tea, Sandy?" he had asked her. "Would you care to come along to the Pier? We could give you a lift back afterward—we brought the car over."

She gave him a grateful smile but shook her head.

"No, thanks, Paul," she told him. "It's very nice of you and Jean, but I've promised to have tea with Edith and her friends."

The doctor nodded understandingly.

"That reminds me," he observed. "I didn't see Edith inside."

Sandra Borne hesitated.

"No—she told me that she didn't think she would be going to the inquest. She said she thought she would find it too—too painful. Edith doesn't say a great deal, but she's taken it to heart. She—she was very fond of Lydia."

"It's natural enough that she should want to stay away," agreed Russell. He said it as though he realized that it was the conventional reply but was not entirely convinced that it was true. "We'll see you later then, Sandy."

Sandra Borne gave a nod that was both agreement and parting and that included Mordecai Tremaine, and they saw her trim, businesslike little figure go quickly along the pavement. Russell turned inquiringly.

"What about you, Mordecai? Does a cup of tea appeal to you?"

"Don't worry about me, Paul," he returned. "I'm staying over here for a little while. I've arranged to meet Jonathan. I know you're a busy man, so don't trouble to wait about for me. I'll be going back on the bus."

"I am rather rushed," admitted the doctor. "I only suggested taking Sandy along to the Pier because I thought it might cheer her up."

"In that case then," said Tremaine, "you and Jean go along back. I don't suppose I'll be more than a couple of hours behind you, but don't be alarmed if I should happen to be a little late."

When his friends had driven off in the hardworking saloon that had carried them all to Kingshampton, Tremaine made his way toward the promenade and the Pier pavilion. It was at the Pier that he had promised to meet Inspector Boyce.

He enjoyed his unhurried stroll. Kingshampton was not one of the bigger and more popular seaside resorts; it seemed to have been sandwiched in between its more prosperous—and more flamboyant—neighbors and had become somewhat overlooked in the process. Not, thought Tremaine, that it was any the worse for that. On the contrary, it had escaped some of the more unpleasant manifestations of a trippers paradise. Its long promenade was sedate without being forbidding. It commanded an uninterrupted view of a beach that did not suffer from a rash of ice cream stalls and abandoned bottles and newspapers. The hotels that lined it were invitingly gay with colored awnings and yet possessed of a calm dignity.

It must be confessed that deep in Mordecai Tremaine's

soul there dwelt a streak of good honest vulgarity. He enjoyed noisy crowds, and children with buckets and spades, and cockle-stalls and all the carnival atmosphere of a slightly rowdy bank holiday. But there were also times when he realized that he was growing older and that it was pleasant to sit back in the sunshine and watch the glimmer of the water and hear it swishing musically upon the pebbles and to be undisturbed by the virile gaiety of the multitude. Kingshampton, he told himself, would be an ideal place in which to spend his leisure hours.

He was within a hundred yards of the Pier Pavilion—the "pier" was hardly big enough to justify that proud description, being no more than a bulge in the promenade upon which was located a combined restaurant and concert hall—when, leaning over the railings and gazing down at the beach, he saw a figure he recognized. It was Anston. He took up a position at the reporter's side.

"A penny for your thoughts," he said, without originality but hopefully.

Anston glanced in the direction from which the voice had come.

"Oh, hullo," he said, recognizing the mild-looking man with the pince-nez whom he had met at the Admiral and who seemed to be on good terms with Inspector Boyce, of Scotland Yard. "Been to the inquest?"

"Would that be termed a leading question?" asked Tremaine. Anston smiled.

"Not really. I was just making conversation. As a matter of fact I saw you there."

"In that case," said Tremaine, "I *was* there."

He looked curiously over the railings, searching for the reason for the absorption that had been so evident in the other's attitude when he had approached him. Anston saw the action. He reflected for a moment or two, and then, as if he had come to a decision: "I was doing what I was doing when we met at the Admiral this morning," he said. "Watching our mutual acquaintance Hornsby."

He pointed. Tremaine followed the direction of his finger, and for the first time he noticed that two men were standing on the sands between the steel supports upon which the pavilion was erected. They were close under the wall, which was why he had not observed them before. One of them was the ferrety Mr. Hornsby. And the other was Howard Shannon.

They were deep in conversation. They were too far away for it to be possible to hear what they were saying, but whatever it was there was no doubt that it was engrossing the plump man's attention. He was in an intent attitude, leaning rigidly toward his companion.

"Do you know who the fellow with Hornsby is?" asked Tremaine.

The reporter nodded.

"Yes. His name's Shannon. He lives in Dalmering, doesn't he?"

"That's right." Tremaine was looking over the wall of the promenade, apparently staring at the water. "When you told Inspector Boyce that you might have something for him," he went on, in the same impassive tone, "was it Shannon who was on your mind?"

"When I told Inspector Boyce that," said Anston, "I also told him that I didn't wish to make any statement until I was sure of my facts."

"But it *was* Shannon?" persisted Tremaine gently.

Anston gave him a sharp glance.

"Perhaps."

At that moment, their conversation over, the two men on the sands drew apart. As they moved away from each other Shannon glanced up. They saw him start as he recognized them. He hesitated, and then, making an obvious effort to appear unconcerned and as though he had changed his mind for a reason that had nothing to do with their presence, he turned and walked off along the sands in the opposite direction.

"Frightened," observed Tremaine pleasantly. "Definitely frightened. I wonder why?" He moved away from the wall and took out his big pocket watch. "I'm late," he announced. "I'm supposed to be having tea with Inspector Boyce.

Goodbye, Mr. Anston. No doubt we'll be seeing each other again very soon."

He nodded and strolled away along the promenade toward the Pier Pavilion, leaving Anston staring after him.

The newspaperman's face bore a puzzled expression. Mordecai Tremaine was inclined to have a somewhat exasperating effect upon people at times. With his benevolent appearance, his undisciplined pince-nez, and his general air of needing someone to look after him, he gave the impression that he was a harmless, even a somewhat simple soul, of whom no one need be in any dread. But sometimes his voice would become firmer, his whole manner more assured, and his eyes would hold a steady, probing quality that would give the lie to the facade of ineffectiveness and would leave the person who witnessed the phenomenon with the uncertain—and often slightly resentful—feeling of having walked suddenly and without warning into deep water.

Tremaine, of course, was well aware of the minor sensations he caused. It must be confessed, indeed, that inwardly he delighted in them. He was chuckling now as he walked along the promenade. He could imagine some of the questions Barry Anston must be asking himself.

He was still chuckling as he entered the Pier Pavilion. The restaurant was crowded, but a glance around revealed the stocky figure of Jonathan Boyce beckoning to him from a table for two in a moderately secluded corner overlooking the sea.

"Hullo, Jonathan. Sorry I'm late. This is very nice." Tremaine looked approvingly through the window at the long stretch of beach it commanded and at the waves washing lazily in against the pebbles. "I like having my tea in a place like this where you can overlook the sea."

"You sound very pleased with yourself," observed the Yard man. "What've you been up to?"

"The worst of being a policeman," said Mordecai Tremaine, helping himself to the bread and butter and cakes that his companion had already ordered, "is that you develop such a suspicious nature. Haven't I mentioned that to you before? I've merely been talking to the press in the person of Mr. Barry Anston. As a matter of fact, that's why I'm a little late."

"What have you been telling him?"

"Not a great deal, Jonathan, not a great deal. But I've hopes of his telling *you* something before long."

"You sound," said Boyce, "as though you're in one of your cryptic moods again. Well, I'm listening. What's it all about?"

"Howard Shannon and the mysterious Hornsby have been holding a conference on the sands. Shannon saw us watching him, and it obviously upset him."

"Did he speak to you?"

"No. On the contrary, he did his best to get away from

us before there was any danger of our being able to have a word or two with him. There's something very odd about Mr. Howard Shannon. Have you verified his alibi?"

The inspector consulted a small notebook.

"He left Dalmering on the 3:45 p.m. London train on the afternoon before the murder. The ticket examiner and the stationmaster both remember seeing him. He came back the following afternoon by the 3:30 p.m. from Victoria. You're a witness to that yourself."

Tremaine abstractedly took another cake.

"So far so good. But what about the time in between? Are you sure he *was* in London?"

"Why?" demanded Boyce bluntly.

"Because," said Tremaine, "I don't believe he was there."

"What makes you think so?"

"When Martin Vaughan asked him whether he'd been caught in a heavy storm in London that day he said that he'd managed to escape it as he'd taken a taxi from the station. I dare say you were in town yourself that day and you know that there was no storm—not even a slight shower, in fact. If Shannon had really been in London he would have denied all knowledge of a storm. At the very least he would have looked puzzled and asked a question or two about it. But if he hadn't been there it would have placed him in an awkward position. He would have been forced to ask himself quickly what answer he should give and he would most probably have done exactly what he did do—taken the fact that there had been a storm for granted and given some explanation or other of his whereabouts at the time. Obviously, for a man who hadn't been on the spot at all and didn't know what had happened it was the safest course to follow—*provided Vaughan wasn't trying to trap him.*"

The inspector was interested now.

"What's your opinion?" he asked. "Do you think Vaughan *was* after him?"

"I'm not sure," said Tremaine slowly. "At the time he seemed casual enough. The fact of Shannon's having been in London had come up, and Vaughan remarked that a friend of his in Kingshampton had been caught in one of the unexpected summer storms that go with our uncertain climate. He said that he hoped Shannon hadn't been so unlucky. It all seemed perfectly innocent and conversational, but now I'm beginning to wonder whether there was anything more behind it. I'm beginning to wonder just what is wrong with Shannon and how much Vaughan knows about it."

He sipped his tea reflectively and then looked questioningly across the table at the inspector.

"What account of his London visit did Shannon give you?" he asked. "His story when I heard it was that he'd made the trip in order to see someone—a business associate

I believe—who was going to be there but who wouldn't be available for more than a limited period and whom he was anxious to meet."

Boyce consulted his notebook again.

"His statement was that he'd gone up to see a man named Millward, who is a partner in a firm of shipping agents. Millward was staying overnight at the Regency Hotel. Shannon says that they didn't meet at the hotel but arranged a rendezvous at the Corner House at the Marble Arch."

"Did he say why he wanted to meet this Millward?"

"Yes—he was quite frank about it. Shannon has an interest in a small firm of furniture manufacturers just outside London. Millward's ships do a good deal of coastal traffic, and Shannon wanted to talk over the possibilities of a contract to bring occasional consignments of timber down from Liverpool on one of the coasters making a regular run. The stuff is coming into Liverpool because it's being carried along with bigger cargoes and the rates are much cheaper than charting a special freighter. He hinted that the firm was only just keeping its head above water and that it was essential to limit expenses wherever possible. He wanted to see Millward personally because he knows him slightly, and he thought he might be able to obtain better terms than by merely writing to the firm."

"Has Millward corroborated all this?"

Boyce shook his head.

"No. Not by word of mouth, anyway. We've checked up on him at the Regency hotel. He certainly stayed there on that particular night. He left for Holland on one of his own line's ships the next morning. He isn't expected back until next week."

"That supports Shannon's statement that he had only a limited opportunity of meeting him, anyway," observed Tremaine. "The whole thing fits together so well on the face of it," he added, "that I don't suppose you've troubled to take any steps to locate Millward?"

"No," agreed Boyce, "we haven't. There was no definite suspicion against Shannon, and what we were able to check against his story seemed to confirm what he'd told us. But if your belief that he didn't go to London is justified then the situation is very different. We've witnesses who saw him go, we've witnesses who saw him come back, and we've proof that the man he said he went to meet did stay at the Regency. But we've no proof that the meeting actually did take place. The Corner House, of course, is hopeless. So many people make use of it that it's highly unlikely that we'd be able to get any worthwhile evidence as to whether two men answering to the descriptions of Shannon and Millward were there on that particular day."

There was a pause. And then: "I've a feeling," said

Mordecai Tremaine, "that Barry Anston is going to ask you a few questions about me."

"What do you mean?" asked Boyce, a little sharply.

"When I was talking to him just now I let him see that I was interested in Hornsby and Shannon. I think he'll be asking you who I am and why I seem to be so curious about those two gentlemen." He leaned forward, lowering his voice to what was almost a conspiratorial whisper. "There's a link between Shannon and Hornsby, Jonathan, and if Anston doesn't exactly know what that link is I think he could make a pretty shrewd guess. I'd like to know what he suspects."

"I see. And I'm to use my authority to prevail upon Anston to tell me so that *I* can tell *you*."

Boyce stirred his tea in order to absorb the last grains of sugar, drank appreciatively, and then leaned back to survey his companion, his dark eyes speculative beneath his wiry eyebrows.

"You know, Mordecai," he said shrewdly, "I believe you're beginning to take the bit between your teeth. So far you've been wandering around giving everyone the impression that you're quite helpless and the last person in the world to start solving a murder problem, but now you're showing every symptom of preparing to leap into action."

"I wouldn't put it quite like that," said Tremaine deprecatingly. "You can't go straight into an investigation and lay your hand on the guilty person without hesitation. You have to look about you for a while. You have to sort things out and try to put people in their right places. That's what I've been doing—I've been absorbing the atmosphere, trying to get the feel of things. And now it's beginning to sort itself out. It's as though when you want something to tie up a parcel you pick up a handful of pieces of string all jumbled together. At first it's just a chaotic tangle, and then, gradually, you sort out the different pieces and take away all those you don't need one by one until you've got the particular piece you're looking for which suits your parcel."

"Only in this case," said Boyce, "the piece of string is a stout rope, and the parcel is someone's neck."

"Yes," said Tremaine quietly. "It's someone's neck." He looked across the table at his companion. He asked: "Have I seemed to be fumbling a good deal just lately? I mean have I acted like a—like a—well, like a doddering old fool who didn't seem to be able to grasp things?"

"You haven't," said Boyce carefully, "appeared to make a great deal of progress."

"There's no need to break it gently, Jonathan," said Tremaine ruefully. He added, after a moment or two: "Do you remember what Vaughan said when we first met him? He said that there was something wrong with Dalmering— that something evil and corrupt had crept in. He said that Lydia Dare had felt it, too. I've heard the same thing from other people—from Sandra Borne and from Jean and Paul. There is something wrong with Dalmering. I've felt it myself. It's hard to explain. It's a sort of cloying, suffocating evil in the very air. You're a policeman, Jonathan. As you told me the other day, you have to stick to hard facts. You can't allow yourself to be influenced by atmosphere. But I'm not bound by the same rules, and I've sensed the evil in the place."

"I wouldn't," said Boyce drily, "care to have to offer your psychic reactions as proof in court."

"Of course not. But you might be able to use them as a basis upon which to build up the facts you *could* produce. The trouble with me is that I've rather allowed myself to be overwhelmed by the atmosphere. I've gone too much the other way. But I'm getting over the anesthetic now, and I'm not certain that it wasn't a good thing, after all. It's like coming out of a fog into a brightly lit room. Perhaps it's the effect of listening to the formal account at the inquest, but I feel now that the whole thing is clear."

"Do you mean that you know who killed her?" demanded Boyce.

"Not," said Tremaine, "exactly that. But I can see which are the available roads. And at the end of one of them I shall find the murderer. More tea?" he asked.

The inspector nodded mechanically and allowed his companion to pour him out another cup.

"Now," said Tremaine, replacing the teapot, "let's get down to business. It was obvious from the inquest that all you wanted was a nice tidy verdict so that you could go ahead and produce the murderer in due course without having your hand forced beforehand, so I didn't learn anything from that. But what about the will? You've seen Lydia Dare's solicitors, of course. Dereford and Something, wasn't it? These fellows always seem to operate in twos or threes. Perhaps they think there's safety in numbers!"

"Dereford, Burgess, and Dereford," said Boyce. "The funeral is tomorrow morning—there was a slight delay in arranging things—and the will is to be made public afterward."

"But you know its provisions?"

"Yes. She had quite a comfortable little sum—apparently she had a legacy from an uncle some years ago. She left somewhere in the region of three thousand pounds in shares of various kinds—that's after allowing for duty—together with a half share in the cottage in which she lived with Miss Borne and various personal effects. Her share in the cottage and all her personal things go to Miss Borne, together with five hundred pounds. Another five hundred pounds goes to Miss Edith Lorrington."

"Edith Lorrington?" Tremaine raised his eyebrows. "They must have been on fairly close terms then. Who are the other legatees?"

The inspector did not reply for a moment or two. He regarded Mordecai Tremaine from eyes that had narrowed a trifle warily.

"There's only one other," he said slowly. "All the remainder, amounting to about two thousand pounds, goes to Dr. Russell."

"Paul!" Mordecai Tremaine sat up very straight in his chair. "Are you certain?"

"I don't think Dereford, Burgess, and Dereford were making any mistake," said Boyce levelly. "'All the residue of my estate I leave to my dear friend Paul Russell, in recognition of the many kindnesses he and his wife have shown to me and in order to give him some little opportunity of devoting himself to the work of medical research upon which I know he has set his heart'—that's more or less how it goes."

"I'm sure that Paul had no idea—he'll be amazed when he hears of it." Tremaine was looking as though he was even more surprised than he expected his friend to be. "He didn't dream of anything like this. He's always been keen on research work, of course, but he's been so generous and open-handed all through his career—giving his services for nothing on so many occasions—that he's had to abandon all hope of being able to spend any more than a very little spare time on any medical work outside his practice. He's never given me the idea that he and Lydia Dare were so well acquainted.

I thought they were merely village neighbors—certainly he never hinted that there was any prospect of her leaving him a substantial legacy."

"It's possible," said Boyce, "that he didn't think that there was such a prospect. But I imagine that Dr. Russell is a man who has done a great deal of good without saying very much about it and it's surprising how often people take notice of such things and remember them."

But despite his words there was a strange note in his voice—a note that found its echo in Mordecai Tremaine's mind. He tried to dismiss it from his thoughts.

"Is there any mention of Farrant?" he asked.

"No. The solicitors told me that Miss Dare mentioned to them a couple of months ago that she intended to make a new will, but she never actually did so. She probably intended to include Gerald Farrant in it, but she delayed matters too long. Fortunately," added Boyce, "for your friend the doctor. He would most likely have lost his two thousand."

"It isn't really a large sum," said Tremaine, searching for a straw to which to cling.

"No, but it's a very useful one," said Boyce. He pushed back his chair and rose to his feet. "You'll have to excuse me, Mordecai, I've got to get away. I arranged to have a word or two with the coroner before going back to Dalmering." He hesitated, and then his hand dropped to his companion's shoulder.

"I know that Dr. Russell is a friend of yours," he said quietly. "But my job still has to go on—no matter who may become involved. You will understand that, Mordecai—won't you?"

His fingers gave a slight pressure and then he was gone, leaving Mordecai Tremaine sitting in his chair, oblivious of the hum of conversation and the rattle of crockery in the busy restaurant.

When he had told Jonathan Boyce that the problem of the murder seemed to be spread before him, clearly illuminated and with the various roads that might lead to a solution plainly marked, he had been speaking the truth. But he had not visualized the name of Paul Russell as a signpost pointing along one of those roads.

Lydia Dare had left Paul two thousand pounds in a will that she had expressed her intention of altering—almost undoubtedly to his disfavor. But she had died before she could carry out that intention, so that Paul would still receive the legacy.

Lucky Paul. Even a few more days might have made all the difference to him. And what if he had known what was in that will?

Mordecai Tremaine fought against the deductions the reason he had trained was making for him. He was being disloyal. He was being false to his friend. He could not—must not—think that way of Paul.

11

The silence, which seemed to have been intensified rather than interrupted by the busy click of Edith Lorrington's knitting needles, was sharply broken by the shrill sound of the doorbell. With a mock gesture of resignation Paul Russell lowered the copy of the *British Medical Journal* at which he had been glancing.

"Don't," he said, "tell me that someone has decided to get born tonight!"

"You can relax, Paul," said his wife consolingly, ruffling his thick if graying hair fondly as she passed him. "It wasn't the surgery bell. And anyway it wasn't agitated enough to be that sort of ring. It's a visitor, not a customer."

They heard her voice in greeting in the hall, and in a few moments she was back with Karen Hammond.

"Paul thought you were an anxious would-be parent come to drag him away from his comfortable armchair, Karen," Jean was saying as they came in.

"I wasn't expecting a call until next week," put in

Russell, with a smile, "but in these uncertain times you can't rely on things."

Mordecai Tremaine thought, as he studied her, that an ethereal quality had crept into Karen Hammond's beauty. Her blond loveliness had acquired an appearance of fragility and a hint of poignancy lay in her blue eyes. It was as though some strange sorrow had placed gently insistent fingers upon her charms and had molded them into a form that possessed the illusion of belonging to the realm of the insubstantial.

"I hope I'm not interrupting, Paul," she said diffidently.

"Of course you're not," he told her. "You're always a welcome visitor, Karen. Come along and sit down."

"I—I was lonely," she said, and Tremaine thought that her voice held the echo both of loneliness and of fear. "I felt that I had to come out and talk to someone."

"You did the wisest thing by coming over," said Russell cheerfully. "There are very few nights when you won't find anyone here. Jean and I like to keep an open house."

The drawing room of "Roseland" was radiating its usual inviting air of comfort and friendliness. On a settee next to the easy chair in which Edith Lorrington's prim figure was sitting, her knitting needles steadily evolving a gay winter jumper from the supply of wool on her lap, Sandra Borne's trim little form was cozily curled up in a ball as she turned the pages of a fashion magazine. Paul Russell scanning his *Medical*

Journal, Mordecai Tremaine pretending to play patience at a side table, and Jean presiding over them all like a benevolent hen proudly watching her brood, completed the picture.

Karen Hammond seated herself gratefully.

"Philip not down tonight?" asked Russell.

"No," she said. "Not tonight."

"I suppose he rang you up this afternoon and told you that he'd be busy working on the firm's accounts or something! You'll have to watch that husband of yours, Karen. He's probably running around with a red-haired siren. You know what deceivers we men are!"

That Karen and Philip Hammond were very much in love with each other was well known in the village, and it was obvious that Russell was speaking jokingly, in an attempt to bring a smile to her face. But no smile came. Tremaine saw her wince, in fact, at the remark, as though it had pained her.

"No," she said hesitantly. "No, he didn't telephone."

She appeared reluctant to talk about her husband. The doctor gave her a curious glance, but he did not try to press her. He changed the subject with a complimentary observation on the knitted coatee she was wearing—the sun had gone down, and there was a cool breeze rising from the sea—and in a few moments the ladies were deep in a discussion on patterns in which Edith Lorrington's partially completed jumper came in for its share of attention.

"Anyone like the wireless on?" asked Russell, still playing the tactful host.

"I don't think so, dear," returned his wife. "There's probably a swing program on, anyway, and Sandy hates swing."

"At the first sound I either have to scream or switch off," agreed Sandra Borne. "And I think it's more cozy just to sit and chat, don't you?"

"I'm on your side, Miss Borne," said Mordecai Tremaine.

He did not speak without his reasons. He knew that it was inevitable that sooner or later any conversation would turn upon the inquest or upon the murder.

In a few moments it did—under the spur of a question from Edith Lorrington as to whether Gerald Farrant had been present at the inquest.

"Yes, he was there," said Jean.

Edith Lorrington sighed.

"Poor man! It's dreadful for him. He was very much in love with Lydia."

"I've been wondering whether we oughtn't to ask him along," said Russell, "but it's a difficult situation. He isn't easy to talk to, and I hardly like to approach him."

"He's changed," said Jean. "Terribly changed. He seems to be suspicious of everyone. He hardly speaks—just glares at people as though he thinks they might be guilty."

"He probably does think so," observed Mordecai Tremaine

quietly, and they all turned to stare at him. "What I mean," he explained, "is that he's suffered a tremendous shock. He was looking forward to being married—I dare say all their plans had been made—and then, suddenly, he learned that everything had been in vain. It must have been as though some wanton giant had taken up his life and dashed it to pieces against the rocks. If Miss Dare had died a natural death it wouldn't have been so hard—tragedy though it would still have been. But to know that she had been murdered, that there was no need for her to have died at all—it must have been almost unbearable for him. He hates Dalmering—hates the village and everyone in it. Because"—he finished—"he believes that the murderer is here; that one of the people around him killed the woman he was going to marry."

"Just a moment, Mordecai," broke in Paul Russell protestingly. "It isn't certain that the murderer lives here. The crime might have been committed by someone who knew Lydia outside."

"I didn't say it was certain. I'm merely suggesting the lines along which I think Gerald Farrant is reasoning."

"It's the truth," said Sandra Borne suddenly. She swung her legs down from the settee and sat facing them, her hands tightly clenched. "I think you're quite right—the murderer is someone in Dalmering. Lydia didn't know many people outside. If there had been anyone at all who might have wanted to kill her she would have spoken about them. I'm sure she would have said something when we were talking together. It's this place—this horrible place. It's full of evil."

"Yes," said Mordecai Tremaine soberly, "it's full of evil."

She stared at him, surprise and a strange relief in her eyes.

"*You've* noticed it, too?"

He nodded.

"Yes, I've noticed it."

Paul Russell was looking blankly from one to the other of them.

"Are you two talking in riddles?"

"It's all right, Paul," said Tremaine, turning to him. "Just a little secret between the two of us. I suppose," he added, making an obvious effort to sidetrack the doctor, "the will is to be read after the funeral?"

"The will?" Russell looked puzzled for a moment. "Oh, Lydia's? Yes, I suppose it will be. As a matter of fact, I hadn't given it a thought, but now you mention it Lydia must have left quite a nice little sum."

Tremaine was regarding him carefully. The doctor's air of unconcern appeared genuine enough.

"I wonder who will benefit?" he said casually.

"Farrant, perhaps," said Russell. "Although I dare say," he added, turning and half addressing his remarks to Sandra Borne, "Sandy will be included as Lydia's greatest friend."

"It was agreed between us that each of us should leave the other her share in the cottage," she returned. "We bought it jointly. But I don't think there will be any more than that. Lydia knew that I'm quite comfortably off. I've more than enough for my needs. In fact, I told her once that she wasn't to make any other provision for me."

So far Paul Russell had not betrayed any exceptional interest in the question of the will, nor did he appear to be acting a part. Tremaine found himself breathing a little more easily, and he realized then just how much the information that Jonathan Boyce had given him about the legacy had been weighing upon his mind.

He was able to divert his attention from Russell to the other people in the room. Karen Hammond had so far taken little part in the conversation. She had barely moved from her original position. She was sitting upright in her chair, her slim fingers playing nervously and abstractedly with her wedding ring. Although she was endeavoring to give the impression of listening to what was being said, Tremaine suspected that her thoughts were on other things.

Her attitude reminded him of his first close study of her when she had been in this same room on the night of his arrival in Dalmering. There was the same involuntary twitching at the side of her mouth, the same shadow of fear in the blue eyes, the same tense expectancy in her graceful figure.

"Has Hornsby been bothering you at all, Mrs. Hammond?" he asked.

"Hornsby?"

Her puzzled repetition of the name revealed that it conveyed nothing to her.

"Yes," he told her. "He's the fellow who was asking after you and your husband. We were talking about him the last time you were here. I've seen him in the neighborhood myself since then, and I was wondering if you'd had a visit from him."

She stiffened at that; he had pierced her guard.

"He hasn't been to the house," she said quickly, and he knew from her manner that it was an evasion. "I don't know him. I can't understand why he should have been asking for us." She seemed to make an effort to gather her courage. "Mr. Tremaine," she asked him, "has the inspector found—does he know who killed Lydia?"

"I can tell you that he's making good progress," he returned carefully. "I'm afraid that I can't say any more at the moment, but you appreciate that the police don't like to reveal all they know until they think that the time has come for it."

Momentarily he was back in the shadowed roadway with Karen Hammond looking up to him, beseeching him to help her in that only half-expressed appeal of hers that she had made when she had met him just after he had left Jonathan Boyce. There was the same agonized pleading in her eyes now.

"I wanted it to be quick," she said piteously. "It mustn't be too late."

It was Edith Lorrington who saved the situation. In the midst of the somewhat uncomfortable silence that followed Karen Hammond's remark she looked up suddenly, and in her inconsequential manner of bringing up some entirely new topic she announced, "I don't know what's come over Martin."

"Mr. Vaughan?" said Tremaine. "Why? What has he been doing?"

"He's going about asking questions," she said. "He came up this evening asking all sorts of things about what I was doing when Lydia was killed—almost as if he thought I'd killed her."

"That's odd," said Russell thoughtfully. "As a matter of fact, he made one or two remarks to me this morning. I thought at the time that it was strange, but I didn't pay much attention. He was asking me what I knew about Galeski."

"Pauline Conroy's boyfriend?" queried Tremaine, and when the doctor nodded, "*Is* that their relationship?" he asked.

"Well, it's rather a forbidden subject," remarked Russell. "Most of the village thinks the worst. Pauline is ambitious, and Galeski has some sort of pull with the film people. It's popularly supposed that Pauline—well, that she's in the habit of going over to his cottage at unconventional hours."

"But nobody says anything openly?"

"No. Pauline takes good care not to let them. You see, she usually plays the virtuous woman on the stage. She seems to be trying to build herself a reputation as an actress in sympathetic parts, and she probably thinks that it wouldn't do her professional reputation any good to have her private life dragged into disrepute. She may be right, of course. Stage and film folk seem to lead lives more in the limelight than we common mortals."

"From what little I've seen of her," observed Tremaine, "Miss Conroy appears to be a determined lady who is bent upon a career, so I can understand that attitude. Nothing is so important in her eyes as preserving her shining glory. She needs Galeski to help her on her way, but she doesn't want her association with him to be in the minds of the audience when they see her playing the Wronged Woman."

He turned to glance at Karen Hammond. His sentimental soul shrank from the thought that he might be inflicting fresh hurt upon her, but murder could not be solved by a refusal to face up to unpleasant tasks.

"Forgive my appearing personal, Mrs. Hammond," he told her, "but when you were all here several nights ago there seemed to be a certain amount of antagonism, shall we say, between Miss Conroy and yourself. Isn't that so?"

A deep blush became slowly visible beneath her tan.

"Yes," she said nervously, "we have been rather at

loggerheads. There's really nothing behind it. It's just that—well, just that women do get to dislike each other sometimes. Pauline seemed to be resentful in some way of Philip, and perhaps I haven't been as tolerant as I might have been. Things have become strained between us—you know how these little village quarrels start. One of you says something cutting and the other throws it back, and before you realize what's happened you're in the middle of a feud."

Tremaine recalled that mention of Galeski when the question of police investigations had arisen and Pauline had appeared to be hinting against Karen Hammond all the time. Serge Galeski was Pauline's blind spot, and Karen Hammond had retaliated by taking advantage of it.

"I understand," he said. "Life's a thorny business sometimes, isn't it."

After that the conversation became more noncommittal. Tremaine had caught a glance from Jean that had been both a warning and a plea. He guessed that she was becoming a little alarmed at the manner in which personalities were being mentioned, and he promptly steered the discussion into safer channels.

The little group broke up not long afterward. Paul Russell insisted professionally that Sandra Borne should go to bed.

"You're done in, Sandy," he told her. "If you don't get some rest we'll be having you on our hands as an invalid."

"I am tired, Paul," she confessed. "It's been a difficult week."

"You've been trying to do too much, Sandy," said Jean. "You should have let us help you out with some of the arrangements."

"You've been awfully good, Jean—both you and Paul. But I had to do what I could. After all, it was my duty, not yours. You know that Lydia and I—that we—" She showed signs of breaking down at that, and it was a moment or two before she could go on. "It's almost over now," she said, with a forced brightness. "After the funeral tomorrow I'll be able to take things more easily."

She was undoubtedly revealing signs of the strain she had undergone and was still undergoing. Tremaine had noticed her drawn, peaked features and the hard stare in her eyes—the stare of a person whose nerves were reaching the limit of her endurance. Sandra Borne was one of those people who, even normally, drove themselves without respite, aiding, planning, getting others out of difficulties, doing the lion's share of any social organizing that came along. And in addition she had now been carrying all the burden of the police inquiries and the funeral arrangements for her murdered friend.

When Edith Lorrington and Sandra Borne left, Karen Hammond left with them. She contrived to drop behind in the hallway as the others went out. She spoke in a low voice to Paul Russell as she held out her hand to him, but Tremaine was near enough to hear the whispered, tremulous words.

"Good night, Paul. Thank you for tonight and for all you've done since we've been here. Whatever happens, please don't—please don't think too hardly of me."

Before the doctor could make any reply she had gone and was hurrying down the path in the moonlight after her companions.

Mordecai Tremaine went to bed twenty minutes later in a thoughtful mood. He took with him a typewritten copy of *Murder Has a Motive* by Alexis Kent. Evidently it engrossed his attention, for it was two o'clock in the morning before his bedroom light went out and he settled down to sleep.

Over the breakfast table he caught Paul Russell regarding him speculatively. He raised his eyebrows, and the doctor admitted that he had been detected.

"I was thinking that you were awake late last night, Mordecai," he said, a note of inquiry in his voice. "I saw a light under your door just before two o'clock. As a matter of fact, I didn't sleep too well myself."

"I don't remember Paul being so restless," remarked Jean. "I told him it must be a bad case of conscience."

Tremaine fancied that he saw a faint trace of annoyance cross the other's face, but Russell passed it over easily enough.

"I was beginning to think that I must have given one of my patients the wrong drug in error and that my subconscious was choosing that way of getting back at me. However, I did manage to drop off to sleep eventually, so perhaps it isn't as bad as that after all."

"I was rather late turning out the light," admitted Tremaine, "but it wasn't a case of insomnia. I was reading your play. It's a very interesting piece of work. Have you ever met the author?"

Russell shook his head.

"I don't recollect even having heard of an author called Alexis Kent before we began the rehearsals. I don't know whether he's written any other plays. If he'd been down to the village at any time I'd be certain to have heard about it even if I hadn't actually met him. But why don't you tackle Vaughan? I believe I mentioned that it was through his recommendation that we decided to do *Murder Has a Motive* when we were looking around for a play."

"Yes, you did tell me."

Tremaine busied himself with his breakfast for a few moments. And then: "What do you think Karen Hammond meant by that last remark of hers, Paul?" he asked.

"So you *did* hear it?" said Russell. "I've been wondering whether you did. Jean and I have been talking it over. Neither of us can think what she could have had in her mind."

"It seemed to me that she was expecting something to happen."

"She's been on edge ever since Lydia's death," said Jean thoughtfully. "Didn't you notice last night how tensed and worried she looked?"

"Yes, I noticed it," returned Tremaine noncommittally.

The morning's most important event in Dalmering was the funeral of Lydia Dare. Nearly all the village was present to watch the procession make its way from the cottage where she had lived to the ancient church where her last service was read and from thence to the little churchyard adjoining it where the coffin containing all that remained of her mortal body was to be lowered into the cleanly cut grave, banked with flowers, that had been made ready to receive it.

The dead woman's father was the chief mourner. Tremaine learned that he had only arrived in the village that morning, having traveled down from Yorkshire and spent the preceding night in London. He was a very frail old man, obviously suffering badly from the shock of his daughter's tragic end. His wife was an invalid, which was why she was not present. Tremaine could imagine how bitterly the news must have fallen upon the fabric of their restricted lives, and pity for the old couple the twilight of whose years had been so cruelly blighted brought anger against the murderer rising again within him.

It was evident that the old man was incapable of having done much to handle any of the arrangements that had had to be made. Sandra Borne's air of worried tiredness on the previous night was explained. She had carried the whole burden on her shoulders.

Pale but visibly determined not to give way, she bore herself unflinchingly through the ordeal of the funeral service. Only the whiteness of her features and that unnatural fixed stare of her brown eyes betrayed the strain under which she was laboring.

Gerald Farrant was among the mourners. He was grim and stern looking, his face gray and his grief heavy upon him. Once, at the graveside, as the coffin was about to be lowered, Tremaine thought that he was on the point of breaking down, but he managed to bring himself under control.

Martin Vaughan was not there. Tremaine had thought that it was unlikely that he would appear among the chief mourners, but he had subconsciously expected to find him somewhere in the vicinity. He glanced around at the quiet crowd gathered about the graveside, but he did not see the other's bulky form, nor had he seen him in the church. Others, too, had noticed the big man's absence. Tremaine heard Vaughan's name mentioned in a whisper behind him, and it was easy to guess what was being said.

Was it fear that had kept the other away? Was it his

awareness of the fact that he was under suspicion that accounted for his absence? Had he shrunk from running the gauntlet of all the accusing eyes that would have been turned upon him if he had been present?

Tremaine looked across the still-open grave into which the earth was about to fall, and what he saw in Gerald Farrant's face was sufficient explanation of why Vaughan had kept away. Confronted with the man whom he must suspect most of all, Farrant's tortured, hate-filled mind might have driven him to some sudden uncontrolled act of revenge.

Mordecai Tremaine sighed. The day was beautiful. The sky was again blue and cloudless, and the slight breeze of the night before had had the effect of tempering what might have been an over-fierce sun, so that it was pleasantly warm. It was a bitter reflection that beneath the fragrance and the sunshine there lurked hate and fear and lustful murder.

He saw tears glistening in Edith Lorrington's eyes, saw a tiny, only partially opened rose fall from her hand into the grave. She was displaying far more emotion than he had so far observed in her. Did she know about that five hundred pounds in Lydia Dare's will, and was this public exhibition of grief intended for the eyes of the village?

The thought was fully formed in Mordecai Tremaine's mind before he knew that it was on its way. He recoiled from it. Because he had taken it upon himself to investigate murder, did it mean that he had to become cynically suspicious; that he had to find a base motive behind every human appearance and action?

He knew the answer. Knew it instinctively, without a prolonged mental searching of his soul. He had only reacted as he had trained himself to react and as he had done when Jonathan Boyce had given him the news that Paul was the chief beneficiary under the will. Murderers did not shriek their guilt aloud to the world. They betrayed themselves in little things. That was why he had to be critical. That was why he had to watch for every detail and take nothing for granted but be constantly on the alert for the tiniest slip that might be an indication of guilt.

Coming away from the churchyard he caught sight of Pauline Conroy and Serge Galeski. Upon Galeski's face there was an expression of polite boredom, but Pauline bore herself with the conscious dignity of a leading figure in the tragedy. Tremaine guessed that the dark tie Galeski was wearing with his sports jacket was a gesture to convention that Pauline had prevailed upon him to make. As he passed them he fancied that Pauline gave him a half-smile of recognition. She said something quickly to Galeski and that untidily dressed gentleman gave him a definite if somewhat brief nod.

Tremaine smiled back and went on his way a little puzzled. He had not expected such gracious acknowledgment from Pauline Conroy. Her dark ladyship appeared to be developing a manner that was almost friendly.

The corpulent but indubitably important-looking and confidence-inspiring Mr. Burgess, who was the middle portion of Dereford, Burgess, and Dereford, paid a visit to what was now Sandra Borne's cottage during the afternoon and made public the contents of the will. Only a handful of people who had been requested to be present—Sandra Borne herself, Edith Lorrington, Gerald Farrant, the Russells, and Lydia Dare's father—were there to hear the terms read out, but it was not long before the news of the legacies was common knowledge.

Tongues were soon wagging all over the village, and the most favored topic of conversation was the fact that Dr. Russell had been left the bulk of Lydia Dare's monetary estate.

The doctor himself had seemed genuinely surprised—and a trifle disconcerted. He had turned to his companions and to the solicitor, expressing doubts as to whether the will really represented Lydia's feelings. He had drawn attention to the date; insisted that her father, Sandra, or Farrant should accept some or all of the sum that had been left to him.

But Burgess had assured him of the will's validity. There was no doubt that it was perfectly legal, and the others had refused to listen to any suggestion that some sort of compromise should be worked out.

"If Lydia said that you were t'have t' money, doctor," the old man Dare had stated in his blunt Yorkshire manner, "then have it you shall. Lydia always knew what she was doing, and I'm standing by what she wanted. She knew that her mother and I weren't wanting for owt. We've all we need for all t' days we've left. Take it, doctor, and good luck in t' researches."

"I agree with Mr. Dare," said Farrant. "It was obviously Lydia's wish."

"You know the way I feel, Paul," said Sandra Borne. "Lydia and I understood each other. I know that she admired you and wanted to help you. It would have made her happy to know that she'd done something to help you do what you've always hoped to do."

Somehow the legacy had seemed to exercise a dampening effect upon the atmosphere at "Roseland." Russell had appeared ill at ease, and even Jean had developed a strangeness of manner. It was as though both of them felt that they had to guard their tongues; that they had to weigh their words before they spoke lest one of them should make a fatal error.

Sensing the constraint, Tremaine tried to probe gently into his friend's mind.

"Will the legacy make much difference to you, Paul?" he asked. "Will it be enough to enable you to give up your practice here?"

"Not immediately," the other replied, "but it will certainly make it possible for me to get away much more quickly than I'd imagined, I can start making plans—start looking around for the right instruments and a decent laboratory, for instance. Normally it would have taken me a few more years to reach that stage and by that time my ambition might have died on me."

"Yes, I suppose there was that danger," said Tremaine slowly. "Ambition is inclined to die off as the years slip by. It tends to make one impatient of achieving one's goal."

Jean rattled a teacup nervously against its saucer. Russell, too, seemed momentarily at a loss, and Tremaine did not pursue the subject. Obviously it was not likely to make for his enjoyment of his tea.

A rehearsal of *Murder Has a Motive* had been fixed for that evening. It had been arranged before the time of the funeral had been known, and it had not been canceled through some general lack of coordination. The fact caused the proceedings to start off at a disadvantage, and they never recovered from it but plunged progressively deeper into gloom.

The atmosphere engendered by the funeral seemed to have produced a state of nervous tension. Tempers were short, and Tremaine observed several little outbursts that were patently due solely to the general unhappy air of suspicion and depression. He had made his way to the village hall for a variety of reasons when he had learned of the rehearsal. Paul, of course,

as one of the principal players, had been under an obligation to attend, and it had been natural for him to extend an
invitation to his friend to accompany him. Secondly, he had
wanted a further opportunity of studying the various actors
in the real-life drama that was being played around him and
had wanted to observe their latest reactions. And thirdly, he
had developed a considerable interest in *Murder Has a Motive*
and was anxious to see it performed again.

Martin Vaughan, uncommunicative, inclined, in fact, to be
more than offhand with anyone who approached him, but at
the same time watching his colleagues with a darting, watchful intentness, his eyes alive with a curious probing quality,
was one of the early arrivals. He just missed Gerald Farrant,
who arrived some five minutes afterward and took a seat in
the gloom at the back of the hall, where he sat unmoving, his
attention fixed upon the stage.

From the beginning the performance was ragged and
uninspired. Sandra Borne was taking Jean's place as prompter
(Jean had been prevented by various urgent domestic duties
from attending) and was doubling that task with her others as producer and stage manager. She was kept fully occupied, for this time, unlike the previous rehearsal where most
of them had appeared to be almost word-perfect, there were
many painful halts when lines were forgotten or missed cues
when they were wrongly spoken. It was possible to see the

production heading for inevitable disaster; each scene was a little less well played, a little more out of control.

Vaughan was revealing none of his old fire. No longer did he tower above the rest of the company. He had sunk into mediocrity and worse. He spoke his lines mechanically and without feeling.

Tremaine had to admit that the only performance worth applauding was Pauline Conroy's. There was no disputing her talent as an actress. At the side of her dark vitality, Paul Russell as her controlling genius was a clumsy wooden puppet who deceived no one.

Phyllis Galway and Geoffrey Manning did their best to infuse life into the play, but appealing though the girl's youthful beauty was and enthusiastic though Manning tried to be, their abilities were not enough to defeat the prevailing lack of spirit, and they too were not altogether free from the depression and were in consequence guilty of occasional lapses.

Howard Shannon was unable to concentrate or to remember his lines for more than a few moments at a time. Again and again Sandra Borne was compelled to correct him, and Tremaine could see that she was gradually losing her patience. Her own nerves had not remained unaffected, and although she was making obvious efforts to remain calm it was clear that she would not be able to hold in her temper much longer.

The situation had degenerated to a point where the simplest incident, and one that would normally have been laughed aside, was sufficient to awake a storm, and very shortly one such incident arose. During the course of the play, as Tremaine now knew, Howard Shannon as the unfaithful husband was murdered (offstage) by his outraged and jealous wife. The plot required that the wife should effect to "discover" his body, in the presence of witnesses, inside a large tin trunk, and since the trunk occupied a position on the stage for some ten minutes of the scene in question before the discovery was made, it was therefore necessary for Shannon to spend some while in cramped confinement.

At the previous rehearsal Tremaine had remarked upon the passion for detail that had been displayed, inasmuch as Shannon's "body" had actually been "discovered" in the trunk although there had been no need to convince an audience. But tonight the plump man displayed a violent reluctance to perform the duty. He made the point that it was merely a rehearsal and that there was no necessity for him to undergo the discomfort. He acted, in fact, like a petulant small boy stubbornly refusing to play as his companions wanted.

He made quite a scene, and Tremaine saw Sandra Borne bite her lip in annoyance.

"What's the matter with you, Howard? You've never made this fuss before."

"I don't see why I should have to stay in that confounded trunk," he persisted sulkily. "We're only rehearsing, aren't we?"

"I know, but we've always made a point of playing it as much like the real thing as possible."

"I'm not doing it, anyway. The whole thing's a stupid waste of time."

"All right," she said hastily, recognizing the danger sign in his voice, "we'll leave it for tonight. But you might put the trunk in position, Howard, so that we can at least make some pretense at it. You'll find it over there behind the scenery."

Still protesting and grumbling, the plump man began to drag the trunk from its place in the darkness of the wings into the position in which it was required on the stage for the ensuing scene.

"It's darned heavy," he said petulantly. "Why can't we let it go for once?"

"If we're going to play the scene at all," snapped Sandra Borne, "we've got to play it properly."

It was the first time Mordecai Tremaine had seen her control really go, and the ragged note of anger made itself evident to Shannon and sobered him, for he completed his task without any further argument.

The scene was mainly carried by Karen Hammond, the climax being her pretense of surprise and horror as she "discovered" the body of her husband. She was shown as cleverly trying to build up an alibi; it was not until the last act of the play that her guilt was revealed.

She began haltingly. Like Vaughan, she seemed to have her mind centered upon something else and to have no interest in what she was saying.

Tremaine looked around the gloomy hall. Philip Hammond was not there. He glanced back to the beautiful woman on the stage and tried to read the haunted expression in her eyes. What lay behind her strange evasiveness where her husband was concerned? What was she attempting to conceal?

The drama limped on, approached its climax. Karen Hammond spoke the lines, apparently casual but in reality premeditated, which were intended to give her the opportunity of opening the trunk in front of Paul Russell and Geoffrey Manning, with whom she was playing the scene.

She walked toward the trunk. She threw back the lid. She screamed.

The scream was part of her performance. It was a very realistic scream.

But suddenly Mordecai Tremaine was aware that something was wrong. Karen Hammond was no longer keeping to her part.

She was still screaming—wildly, hysterically, as though she would never stop.

He heard Sandra Borne's voice, sharp with panic and anxiety.

"Karen—what is it?"

Tremaine came out of his seat and ran for the stage. He did not trouble to use the steps at the side but clambered hastily over the footlights. He made straight for the open trunk at the side of which Karen Hammond was standing like a woman demented.

And then, in an incredible moment of horrified comprehension, he understood why the screams had not stopped. Staring up at him from the interior of the trunk was the queerly pink and distorted face of Philip Hammond. But the wide-open eyes that were meeting his own with such a frightful intensity could see nothing, for Philip Hammond was undoubtedly dead.

12

The newspapers had made the most of their opportunity. Horror Comes to Dalmering, said the two-inch headlines of the *Daily View*, over photographs of the village hall and of the entrance to the copse bearing a prominent *X*: Unknown Killer Claims Second Victim. And, adding its voice to the chorus: Beautiful Widow's Ghastly Ordeal, said the *Morning Globe*. Finds Husband's Body in Trunk: Who Is the Mystery Murderer?

The headlines were the model for the accounts that followed. The circumstances in which Philip Hammond's body had been discovered would have been dramatic enough had they only been recounted in a plain, matter-of-fact manner; under the exuberant pens of some of Fleet Street's most colorful writers they formed the foundation for columns of vivid prose that were not lacking in adjectives.

The murder of Lydia Dare had already focused attention upon the village. The second murder, therefore, fell upon fruitful soil that had already been well prepared. Enough information had been gleaned by the journalists who had been dispatched to cover the original story to enable a firm background to be provided, and the provision had been lavish.

It was perhaps a natural development that the macabre element should have been stressed. Its news value was too great for it to be passed over. The scene in the village hall had been reconstructed, not without a certain freedom of description, and Karen Hammond had been featured as a tragic figure of beauty occupying the central place in a drama terrifying in its grotesqueness.

Mordecai Tremaine read Barry Anston's report in the *Daily Record* several times. The journalist had written what was perhaps the most detailed account of all. It was evident that his time in Dalmering had been well spent. He revealed a knowledge of the village and its inhabitants that was a proof of a great deal of painstaking investigation.

In addition to his recital of the facts, which although both accurate and arresting, contained nothing that Mordecai Tremaine did not know, Anston had also written a general article on the two murders in which he had allowed himself the luxury of some highly imaginative passages. Tremaine could tell that he had enjoyed himself when he had been setting them down.

What is the secret of Dalmering? What strange, grim truth lies behind the horror that has fallen like a malevolent shadow across this beautiful and once quietly peaceful village?

It is impossible to live here, as I have done during these past few days, and not sense the tragedy that seems to permeate all its beauty. There is evil in the air. Does that seem a fantastic statement for a hardened crime reporter to make? Nevertheless it is true. The foul presence of murder can be detected in the atmosphere. It is as though the neighborhood is being haunted by some unspeakable fiend that has been conjured up from the depths of the inferno and needs to be exorcised before peace can come back again.

One looks out upon some of the loveliest scenes to be found anywhere in this English garden of ours. But there is no pleasure in them. For one's mind whispers that there it was that Lydia Dare was struck down. In that place Philip Hammond died. And the horror of their deaths has caused fragrance to perish and beauty to wither away.

Twice already has the evil been unleashed. Will there be a third time? Will there be a third dreadful manifestation and a third victim?

That question dominates life in this little community. That is why, as I write, people's voices are hushed and no children play in the sunlit roadway outside my window. That is the reason for the unspoken terror that at this moment lies paralyzingly over the village of Dalmering.

Mordecai Tremaine folded the newspaper carefully and, leaning back in his deck chair, gazed reflectively up at the blue sky. He found the article interesting. It tended to support the theory that had been slowly developing in his mind.

He had not been openly expecting the murder of Philip Hammond. Which is to say that when it had come it had shocked and horrified him. But he had gradually become aware of a strange belief in his mind that he had known about it all along and that it had not come as such a surprise to him as it should have been.

He had tried to tell himself that it was a mere trick of his brain—a sensation, for instance, such as people often experienced when they went into a room that they knew was strange to them and yet in which they had a suddenly odd feeling that they had been before. It was something to do with the relativity of time and the subconscious mind receiving an impression the tiniest fraction of a second before the conscious mind also received it.

And yet, somehow, his reasoning had not been convincing. He had not been able to rid himself of the persistent idea that he had known that the murder must come. It was absurd, of course. He could not have known. Had he even suspected that such a thing was possible he would have gone at once to Jonathan Boyce and laid what facts he had before him. The tear-streaked, haunted face of Karen Hammond had come into his mind. Never again did he want to see such utter misery and despair in the eyes of a human being. It was not true that he could have known that tragedy so devastating was stalking her and yet have remained inactive. He would have accounted himself a criminal as black as the murderer himself.

But now his chaotic thoughts had begun to settle. As yet it was only half-formed; as yet he was still groping in the darkness toward a coherent entity to which he could point with the confidence of knowledge. Nevertheless, fantastic though the solution seemed, the truth was slowly being revealed to him.

He rose to his feet and strolled slowly down the garden path, admiring, even as his mind worked busily in other directions, the neat orderliness of Paul Russell's flowerbeds. He came up to the little potting shed and he stood for a moment or two eyeing it thoughtfully. Yes—that, too, was possible.

He went into the house and collected his panama. Paul, as he knew, was busy with his morning surgery, and Jean had her hands full with the affairs of the household. Tremaine poked his head into the kitchenette where she was busy superintending the cooking preparations and at the same time trying to keep an eye on the maid of all work who hailed from the village and was willing but unpredictable in her actions. He announced his intention of going out for an hour or so. Jean tried to give him a friendly smile but succeeded only in managing a harassed look. She had, Tremaine reflected, been very far from her usual placidly efficient self since the news of Paul's legacy.

He strolled slowly down the road. He did not expect to meet Jonathan Boyce, or, if he did meet him, he did not expect that the inspector would have any time to spare in conversation. A second murder before the first one had been solved was not the best of publicity for a Scotland Yard detective. Boyce was unlikely to be in the happiest of moods.

The one bright glow amid the prevailing gloom was the fact that he had been in the village when Philip Hammond's body had been discovered and that no time had been lost in setting the machinery of investigation in motion. The hall had been subjected to an intensive examination. Photographers and fingerprint experts had been at work in a matter of minutes. Boyce had recognized the crisis, and he had risen fighting to meet it. He had turned the full powers of the complex organization at his command on to the task of measuring, searching, questioning, recording. He had left nothing to fate.

The routine facts of the murder had been quickly unearthed. Philip Hammond had died nearly forty-eight hours before his body had been discovered. The murderer had struck him a violent blow on the back of the head with a hammer that had been used for minor repair work in the hall and that had been kept in one of the rooms behind the stage, where, incidentally, free of fingerprints, it had been found. The blow, in the opinion of the police surgeon, had been sufficient to stun but not to kill. Hammond's unconscious body had then been dragged into the largest of the three rooms, his head and shoulders lifted into the gas oven and the taps turned on. Carbon monoxide poisoning, said the surgeon, had undoubtedly been the cause of death. The pink discoloration of the skin, he had pointed out, with a certain macabre if professional relish, was typical of such cases.

Suicide, he had gone on to state, *was* possible. Hammond *could*, after having recovered from a decidedly heavy blow on the head that must have been delivered by a second party, have then made up his mind to kill himself and thereupon turned on the gas taps and placed himself in the stove. But on the other hand it didn't seem reasonable to suppose that, being dead, he had then turned the gas taps off again and settled down in the trunk to await discovery.

Seeing the look upon Inspector Boyce's face, the surgeon had added hastily that he was merely endeavoring to bring out all the possibilities. Of course, as a second person had clearly been necessary to deliver the hammer blow and a second person had obviously been equally necessary to turn off the taps and deposit the dead man in the trunk upon the stage, it was practically a certainty that this same person had also turned the taps on. Suicide was really so improbable that he had only raised the subject so that it could be dismissed once and for all.

What was left was cold-blooded murder. It had been no heat-of-the-moment crime. The killer had stood callously by, waiting for his unconscious victim to die under the gas fumes.

A little way ahead of him Tremaine saw the tall figure of Barry Anston. He increased his pace, and in a few moments he had overtaken the other.

"Hullo," he said slyly. "Listening to the hushed voices?"

The journalist turned toward him with a puzzled expression.

"Hushed voices?"

"You remember—no children playing in the sunlit roadway and everybody going around waiting for the Day of Judgment!"

Anston gave him a dubious glance, and then he saw the twinkle in Tremaine's eyes and his face cleared.

"Oh, you've read it? I suppose it was a bit lurid in places, but the public likes a certain amount of color now and then."

"It was the touch about the sunlit roadway that amused me," remarked Tremaine. "Since the murder was only discovered last night it must have been dark when you wrote that because you obviously had to telephone it straight away in order to get it in this morning's edition."

"Call it intelligent anticipation," said Anston. "After all, the sun's shining now, and I haven't seen carefree youth disporting itself in the village street so far. As a matter of fact, the place seems to have become full of policemen."

"I gathered from your account," observed Tremaine, "that you've been out collecting impressions from the local inhabitants."

"I've been around," agreed the journalist. "After all, that's my job." He hesitated for a moment or two, looking at his companion a little uncertainly. And then: "You know, Tremaine," he added, "I didn't write all that with my tongue in my cheek. There really is something queer about this place. Maybe it isn't quite so spooky as I made out—I'll admit that I deliberately played up that stuff about the atmosphere of terror and so on—but I'm convinced that all of it isn't moonshine."

"You mean," said Tremaine, "that you've discovered that there's a feeling of…well, of fear, terror, foreboding, what you will…which has communicated itself to people living in the village. A feeling that Lydia Dare experienced before she died. Is that what you've found?"

Anston looked at him strangely.

"Yes," he said, "that's it." He added, "You seem to know what I mean."

"*I've* been around, too," returned Tremaine evasively. "What," he said, changing the subject in an obvious manner, "do you think of Hammond's murder?"

"If you mean do I know who did it, the answer is that I don't but that I can give you a number one suspect."

"Vaughan, of course?"

"Vaughan, of course," agreed Anston. "Our friend Boyce is grilling him now. If he doesn't possess an alibi for last night things are going to look pretty grim as far as he's concerned."

"It will look like an open and shut case," said Tremaine. "Hammond said publicly that he knew that it was Vaughan who had killed Lydia Dare. He told me that if it was proof we needed he'd see that we got it. I suppose you knew that?"

The reporter nodded.

"The inspector told me. It sounds bad. Vaughan killed Lydia Dare. Hammond got hold of proof that would have hanged him, so Vaughan killed him too in order to keep his mouth shut."

"That," said Mordecai Tremaine, "is the obvious answer." He glanced inquiringly at his companion. "Have you seen Karen Hammond today?"

"No—poor kid, she's taking it badly," said Anston slowly.

"She and her husband were devoted to each other. I don't envy Boyce his job in questioning her." He gave Tremaine a curious, expectant look. "I was wondering whether you'd seen her," he remarked, and added: "Hammond was killed forty-eight hours before his body was discovered. It seems rather a long time for him to be missing without any inquiries being made about his absence."

"It does," agreed Tremaine.

He knew that Anston was waiting for him to discuss the point, but for some reason that he could not explain, he was not willing to discuss it. In a few moments he parted from Anston and walked on down toward the village square. Karen Hammond was represented in his mind by a vague feeling of doubt. She fitted into her place in his theory, and yet somehow she didn't fit. There was something wrong, something missing.

He worried at the problem as he walked. Was he on the wrong track, after all? He had already admitted to himself that the solution he had been building up in his mind was a fantastic one. Was it too fantastic? Was it, in fact, utterly false?

There was an air of activity over the village square. A number of the occupants of the surrounding houses were standing in groups of twos and threes, apparently engaged in casual conversation but in reality eagerly watching for any signs of the latest developments. Plenty of strangers were also in evidence.

The newspapermen could be picked out by their manner of joining the village gatherings, evidently in search of local information with which to embellish the reports they would be sending back to their insistent editors; the police officials were equally distinguishable by the way in which, whenever they appeared, they moved purposefully, like men who were engaged upon grim business and had no time to lose.

Outside the village hall, which Boyce seemed to have turned into his headquarters, Tremaine caught several glimpses of the inspector as he conferred with his colleagues. He did not attempt to interrupt him. For the moment Boyce had his hands fully occupied.

As he turned away again and came back down the roadway toward the center of the village, he saw Pauline Conroy. He had a suddenly instinctive feeling that she had followed him, and as he drew nearer, his suspicion was partially confirmed for she smiled at him and made it quite clear that she intended to speak to him.

Tremaine slackened his step.

"Good morning, Miss Conroy."

She returned his greeting and, turning, began to walk along at his side, thereby completely confirming his suspicion that she had been following him.

"Your friend the inspector is very busy this morning," she observed. "He's been at it ever since it was light, poor man."

"Inspector Boyce doesn't waste any time," replied Tremaine, wondering what was in her mind. "In a case of murder it's important to begin the search for the murderer immediately. Vital clues are sometimes lost through delay in looking for them."

"Yes, I can see that must be so," she said.

Her face was puckered into a tiny frown, as though she was giving his words very careful thought. Her always slightly overemphasized dark beauty was wearing a mood of appeal. Tremaine caught a whiff of some heady yet subtle perfume that stirred his senses even as his reason subjected it to a critical examination. Molyneux? Chanel? Guerlain? He allowed himself a mental smile. Pauline was putting on an act for his benefit.

"It's a terrible tragedy," she was saying. "Poor Philip—who would have dreamed that such a thing could have happened! And the newspapers taking it up as they have done and all those reporters coming down. I seem to have done nothing but answer questions since last night. I suppose it's publicity, and an actress is supposed to live for that, but I'd rather have no publicity at all, ever, than have it this way."

Tremaine gave her a cautious, sideways glance.

"I dare say you'll find yourself worried by reporters and photographers for a few days. Particularly by the *Daily View*'s men."

She looked at him sharply, and for an instant he thought that her pose disintegrated. Touché, Miss Pauline, he told himself. So the *Daily View*, alert to serve its readers, had already taken advantage of the alluring Miss Conroy's photogenic qualities. And the lady's apparent reluctance to reap the benefits of the publicity attendant upon her appearance in a murder play in which the corpse had been a real one was merely an assumption demanded by convention.

However, his reasoning did not show in his face, which retained an expression best described as one of benevolent blankness.

"I feel so dreadfully sorry for Karen," she went on. She gave an appearance of half-ashamed hesitancy and said slowly, "Perhaps you knew that she and I—that we haven't been on very friendly terms just lately?"

"I had heard something of the sort," admitted Tremaine, deprecatingly, as if to imply that he had paid scant attention to whatever it was he had heard.

"It was just a stupid quarrel," she told him. "Both of us were equally to blame. Of course, I didn't have any idea that anything like this was going to happen, otherwise I would have forgotten all about pride and tried to make things up between us. I wouldn't like to feel that Karen still wanted to carry on that silly feud. She has enough to contend with. All this must be terrible for her. She and Philip were so much in love…"

She broke off suddenly. She looked at her companion. Mordecai Tremaine realized that it was his cue and duly obliged.

"Yes?" he prompted.

"I hardly like to say this," said Pauline Conroy slowly. "Of course, I wouldn't dream of saying anything about it to the newspapers. But I think perhaps that you—that the inspector ought to know. They *seemed* such a devoted couple. But there were—things…"

"Things?" said Tremaine, responding like an actor with a lifetime's experience.

"Philip was away so often. He seemed to be working in London so many times. You could never be certain when he would be home. And he never took Karen up to town; in fact, he hardly took her out at all, considering he was supposed to be so devoted to her. Then there was the night Lydia was murdered—I couldn't help thinking that it was strange. Karen said that Philip was with her all the time and that the reason why no one saw him the next morning was because he'd gone back to London very early. But I didn't hear his car going off, and I nearly always did."

"*Nearly* always? You could have missed it that one morning, you know, especially if he went off earlier than usual."

"Somehow I don't think I did," she said, perhaps with just a shade too much certainty in her tone. "I feel sure I would have heard the car if he had used it—I'm a very light sleeper and I would have heard him taking it out of the garage. I've been wondering, Mr. Tremaine—wondering whether there was some mystery about Philip, whether he had any enemies, for example, and was leading a sort of— well, a life in semihiding."

"Have you anything definite in mind that makes you think he might have had enemies? Do you know if he had any trouble with anyone?"

She shook her head.

"I don't really *know* anything. There's that man who's been hanging about the village for some days, of course—Karen seemed to be frightened of him in some way."

Evidently it was Hornsby whom she meant. Tremaine had already pigeonholed the ferrety gentleman's name for future reference.

"Anyone else?" he asked.

"Well…"—again there was that well-acted hesitancy— "there was some trouble between Philip and Geoffrey Manning at one time. But it all passed over," she said hastily. "They became good friends again."

"What sort of trouble?"

"I don't know," she returned. "No one knew. It seemed to be serious. They almost came to blows over it. But then it all seemed to be forgotten."

"How long ago was this?"

"Oh, it must have been two or three months ago," she told him. "I really don't think it can be of any importance now."

They had reached the square again, and two or three hundred yards away, coming down the road that led into it from the opposite side, Tremaine saw the shambling, flannelled figure of Serge Galeski. Pauline Conroy saw him too. She made her excuses, and Tremaine watched her as she went to meet the other. Galeski looked in his direction and made a gesture of recognition.

Tremaine almost waved gaily back in reply. He was right. He was sure now that he was right. His theory was working itself out.

In the afternoon he caught the bus to Kingshampton, and his first task on reaching that pleasant seaside town was to seek out the bookshop and typing agency where Edith Lorrington's friends carried on their business. The shop itself was small, but it was well stocked, and it seemed to be prosperous for it was crowded with customers. The typewriting portion of the undertaking was apparently carried on in the rooms above. Standing near the stairs at the rear of the premises, Tremaine heard the busy clicking of the machines overhead.

He chose his moment and approached the elderly, gray-haired woman who seemed to be in charge when she was temporarily free of inquiries.

"Excuse me," he said quickly, "but I believe you are a friend of Miss Edith Lorrington who lives in Dalmering."

She looked at him suspiciously.

"Are you a newspaper reporter?"

"Oh no," returned Tremaine disarmingly. "I suppose you might describe me as a friend of Miss Lorrington's also. I'm staying in the village for a few days—with Dr. Russell."

His mention of the doctor's name proved to be the talisman.

"I'm so sorry," she told him. "Since those dreadful murders we've been expecting all sorts of persons here because we know Edith—you know what newspaper reporters are like. They ask everyone a dozen questions. Can I help you at all, Mr.—?"

"Tremaine," he replied. "Yes, I think you will be able to help me. I'm very interested in a play that they're producing in Dalmering."

"You mean *Murder Has a Motive*?" she said. "I was reading about it in the newspapers this morning. How dreadful that Mr. Hammond should have been found like that! It must be terrible for his wife, poor soul. I was struck by it because we did the typing of the play here. We run a typewriting business as well as a bookshop, you know."

"Yes." He nodded. "I know. As a matter of fact, that is the reason for my visit. I wonder if I could speak to the person who actually did the typing?"

"I think we could manage that." She gave him a glance of curiosity. "Would you come upstairs?"

Mordecai Tremaine followed her obediently, and in a few moments he was speaking to the typist whom he had made the journey to Kingshampton to see. He had a number of questions to ask concerning *Murder Has a Motive*, and apparently the answers he received were satisfactory, for he quitted the premises in a confident state of mind, albeit he left behind him several very puzzled ladies.

For the rest of the day, after his return to Dalmering, Tremaine appeared to be no more than an inactive spectator of the busy village scene, but when it was dark he made his way to the Admiral Inn. Here it was that he had arranged to see Jonathan Boyce. He entered the inn by the side door and went up to the low-ceilinged but pleasant room the other was occupying. The inspector was drinking thirstily but gloomily from a pint tankard.

"Hullo," he said morosely. "Find yourself a chair."

Tremaine accepted the invitation, and when he was comfortably seated in a wicker chair that allowed him to lie back at his ease: "Have the brickbats started to fly already?" he asked.

"Not yet," said Boyce, "but they'll be coming. I've been expecting a personal message from the commissioner all day."

"You can't do more than you have been doing," said his visitor consolingly.

"I could make an arrest."

Tremaine eyed the Yard man expectantly.

"What have you found out? That Martin Vaughan hasn't an alibi?"

"Correct," nodded the other. "He admitted himself that he was out of his house at the time when the medical opinion states that Hammond must have been killed. He didn't go back there for a long time after the rehearsal at the village hall. On the night of the first murder, if you remember, his man Blenkinson said that his master was in his study from the time Lydia Dare left until the time he went to bed. But as far as the night before last is concerned—the night of Hammond's murder—Blenkinson says quite definitely that Vaughan didn't come in until a very late hour."

"And Vaughan doesn't deny it?"

"In the face of Blenkinson's evidence he isn't in a position to."

"I suppose his explanation of his whereabouts is a thin one?"

"You've guessed it," said Boyce. "He was wandering around—didn't feel like going to bed and stayed out in search of fresh air."

"At the rehearsal last night," said Tremaine, "he looked pleased with himself—at least, he looked as confident as I've ever seen him. What did you make of his attitude toward Hammond's death?"

"Noncommittal," returned the inspector. "He didn't shed any tears, but at the same time he didn't act as though he was trying to hide anything. In fact, he seemed almost casual about it."

The wicker chair creaked as Mordecai Tremaine leaned even farther back in it so that he could stare at the ceiling.

"*If* Vaughan killed Lydia Dare… *If* Philip Hammond knew it and not only knew it but was in a position to prove it… *If* Vaughan knew that he knew and if he killed Hammond in order to safeguard himself…*then* it's very possible that he would be going around looking satisfied with himself—because he had removed a potential source of danger—and that he would display a casual, almost a callous attitude toward the murder."

"Vaughan would need to be a cold-blooded devil to make that true," observed Boyce. "A madman, in fact."

"Whoever killed Hammond *was* cold-blooded," said Tremaine. "And Vaughan's behavior hasn't exactly been consistently normal. But I agree that the case against him, although it all adds up, is largely theorizing. Is there any solid proof? Did you connect him with those footprints in the copse, for instance?"

"The prints were made by boots," returned the inspector, "and Vaughan habitually wears shoes. On the other hand, they were bigger than Vaughan's normal prints, so that if he had worn the right-sized boots on that one occasion he could quite easily have made them. Which brings us back to where we were."

He returned to his tankard and was inarticulate for a satisfying period. When he was once again able to carry on a conversation: "I'm still not satisfied, Mordecai," he announced. "Vaughan *could* be our man. He *could* have committed both murders. In fact, it looks as though he *did*, and yet I don't like it."

"You mean it's all too obvious?"

"Something like that. As a suspect he leaps to the eye too easily."

"Suppose," said Tremaine, "that a murderer knew that no matter how clever he was he couldn't hope to avoid coming under suspicion. Don't you think it would be a good idea to make himself *look* like a murderer?"

"My brain," said Boyce, "isn't working very well. I've had a hard day."

"If the murderer knew that it was inevitable that sooner or later the possibility of his being guilty would come under examination, he might deliberately draw attention upon himself from the very beginning. He might even set out to act like a guilty man—for instance, he might go out of his way to be unsociable and make it quite plain that he was under suspicion. It would be a dangerous game, of course, especially if there was any flaw in his plans, but it might lead the police to think that he was such an obvious murderer that he couldn't possibly be one in actual fact. Little points that they might regard as highly significant if he tried to gloss them over might come to be regarded as having no real importance."

"I see," said the Yard man, "what you're driving at. But I'm not anxious to bring a definite charge against Vaughan until I've cleared up several other points. There's that fellow Shannon, for example. After what you told me when we were having tea the other day, I set to work on that story of his again. Until I've had the latest reports in and until I've had a chance to tackle Anston and find out exactly what he knows, I'm not leaving Shannon out of my thoughts. Why did he refuse to get into that trunk last night? That's another thing we'll need to clear up."

"Everybody was in a bad state of nerves. They'd been gradually going to pieces all day. Shannon was feeling the strain just like all the others, and that happened to be his particular outburst."

"He'd never objected to getting into the trunk before," said Boyce, "and there must have been plenty of other rehearsals. Why did he choose last night for his refusal? Was it because he knew Hammond's body was there?"

He did not wait for any answer to his questions, which had, in any case, been plainly rhetorical.

"Then here's Mrs. Hammond," he went on, and Mordecai Tremaine gave a gentle sigh.

"I thought it was coming," he said. "You're not satisfied with her story."

"No," said Boyce, "I'm not. I'm beginning to get used to people telling me only half the truth in this village. Philip Hammond attended the rehearsal at the village hall and was seen to leave it with his wife. After that nobody saw him again until his body was discovered—*forty-eight hours* later. Why didn't Karen Hammond say that he was missing? Why didn't she at least tell *me*?"

"Any explanation?"

"She said," the inspector replied, "that her husband's business claimed a great deal of his time and that he often had to go to London at short notice. She said that there was a telephone message from his office just after they reached the house. She said that he left almost immediately and that she hadn't seen him again."

"Did she tell you that she herself took the message? Or that her husband answered the phone and told her that it was from his office asking him to go up?"

"She said that it was her husband who answered the phone," admitted Boyce. "But there wasn't a telephone call from London that night. I didn't believe there had been, of course, but I checked up with the local exchange to make certain. I also found out that Philip Hammond didn't leave for London by train—he was nowhere in the neighborhood of the station—and he didn't leave by road because his car is still in the garage at this moment."

"The conclusion being," murmured Mordecai Tremaine, "that Karen Hammond's story is full of holes."

He raised himself out of the protesting wicker chair. He stood looking down at his companion.

"Jonathan," he said quietly, "I don't suppose that you're anxious for there to be a *third* murder?"

The inspector started so violently that he was barely able to save his tankard from being swept to the floor.

"Have you gone crazy?" he demanded.

"I'm afraid, Jonathan—honestly and dreadfully afraid." Tremaine leaned over the table, and the note of seriousness in his voice was so genuine that Boyce's expression of protest died half-formed on his lips. "I'm telling you now—if you want to prevent more tragedy and more terror in this doomed village—*watch Pauline Conroy!*"

"Pauline Conroy?" The inspector's eyes widened incredulously. "You mean that she's—"

"I can't tell you what I mean. I'm not even certain exactly what I'm thinking. But watch her, Jonathan, watch her day and night. *Don't lose sight of her for one single moment!*"

Mordecai Tremaine straightened. He turned. Inspector

Boyce, his tankard still clutched in his right hand, heard his footsteps echo back from the bare oak stairs as he went out, heard him open the door of the inn, heard the sharp sound of it closing behind him.

13

The carriage wheels were drumming out the same phrase over and over again in a rhythmically soothing if oddly accented repetition. *Ka*-ren Ham-*mond*… *Ka*-ren Ham-*mond*…

And then the train rattled and swayed over multitudinous points, and Mordecai Tremaine came out of his doze with a start to find that they were running through the South London suburbs.

Karen Hammond had been on his mind ever since he had left Dalmering that morning. She had been on his mind because he was afraid. Because he was afraid of what he would very soon find out. Because he knew that a tangled twisted story lay behind her grief-stricken, tragic eyes and behind the death of Philip Hammond—and because he shrank from facing it although he knew that it was inescapable.

A dozen times during the journey he had thought over what little he already knew. He had recalled her hunted expression that night at "Roseland" and the pleading, desperate appeal in her face when she had stopped him later in the roadway. He had recalled the ferrety Hornsby and his interest in the Hammonds and the fear of him that Karen Hammond had tried to conceal. He had recalled that glaring fact with which Jonathan Boyce had found himself face-to-face—the fact that Philip Hammond had been murdered a full forty-eight hours before his death had been revealed and that in all that time his wife had not voiced any anxiety because she had had no news of him nor had she done anything to set inquiries on foot.

And he had recalled the obvious tension she had betrayed on the night after that upon which her husband was now known to have died and the strangeness of the expression she had used to Paul Russell when she had deliberately lingered in the hallway so that she could speak to him: "...*Whatever happens, please don't—please don't think too hardly of me.*"

What was it that had driven her to speak? Mordecai Tremaine had thought of the most likely reasons, and his sentimental soul had been agonized.

The train pulled into Victoria station. Tremaine took a taxi, and within thirty-five minutes he was enjoying a cup of coffee with Miss Anita Lane in her charming Kensington flat. Anita Lane was well-known to a great many people who had never met her. She had built up a reputation as one of the most reliable if sometimes slightly pungent critics in London, and her articles on stage and film matters were eagerly read and her judgment respected.

She was a softly spoken, graying-haired woman of fifty, charming in manner and able to talk intelligently upon many topics. Mordecai Tremaine had met her on one of his periodic visits to London to see Jonathan Boyce. The inspector had introduced them—it was surprising the number of people with whom he seemed to be acquainted and how varied were their interests—and they had taken a liking to each other on sight. They had met several times since and corresponded regularly, and Tremaine knew that he was always sure of a friendly reception at the artistically furnished little flat in which a portable typewriter was the only visible sign of Anita Lane's literary activities.

She allowed him to finish his coffee and the chocolate biscuit that went with it. And then: "Now, Mordecai, what's the reason for this unexpected visit? You don't usually arrive without letting me know of your intention in your letters beforehand, so I take it that it's something special."

"Yes, as a matter of fact it is," he admitted. "I'm staying in Dalmering at the moment, and—"

"Dalmering?" She drew her eyebrows together suddenly at the name and then made a gesture toward the newspapers she had evidently been reading before his arrival. "You mean *that* Dalmering? You've been detecting again!"

"Well, I suppose you could call it that," he told her. "Jonathan Boyce is there and I *have* been taking a sort of interest in the case. That's why I've come to see you, Nita." He held out the square, brown-paper parcel he had brought with him. "I'd like you to read this play for me."

"A play?" she said, amusedly. "Don't tell me *you've* started on the road to ruin!" And then her expression changed. "Oh—you mean the play they're producing in the village—the one they were rehearsing when the body was discovered on the stage! Let me see—*Murder Has a Motive*... Isn't that it?"

"That," said Tremaine, "is it." He unwrapped the parcel and handed her the bundle of manuscript it contained. "I'd like you to read it, Nita, and give me your opinion of it. Unless," he added, as an afterthought, "you've read it already."

"No," she said, "I haven't read it." She glanced down at the typescript. "Alexis Kent—I can't say I've heard the name."

Mordecai Tremaine looked at his watch.

"It's almost eleven o'clock. I'll call back for you in an hour and a half and you can come out to lunch with me. That is," he added hastily, "if you haven't a previous engagement."

"If I had one I'd cancel it," she told him. "This sounds exciting. Anyway, I'm not doing very much at the moment—that's why you found me in. Off you go, Mordecai. For the next hour and a half I'm not to be disturbed!"

Tremaine smiled. He did not wish to stay in the flat

because he was anxious that she should read through the play
he had brought without the distraction of having to look
after the comfort of a visitor. He knew that an hour and a
half free of interruption would be ample time for her to dissect it. Hers was a quick, agile brain, and it had been trained
in such tasks.

He himself found plenty to entertain him during the
time of waiting. London always fascinated him. Its huge gray
buildings, its air of having its roots immovably in the earth,
its busy traffic and its hurrying millions, its power and drive,
and its tremendous sense of life never failed to arouse the
small boy in him, never failed to send him through its streets
wide-eyed with the wonder of its high adventure.

When he returned to the flat Anita was waiting for him,
and over lunch a few streets away in a small but perfect
restaurant whose chef made of each dish a labor of love, she
gave him her opinion.

"It's immature, Mordecai. The construction could be
tightened, and the dialogue needs pruning. But it has something. There's life in it. You can sense that it was written
white-hot. The whole thing rushes along almost as though it
got out of control and the author couldn't do much about it."
She hesitated. "It's funny, but in places I found it almost—
almost terrible."

"That's interesting," remarked Tremaine. "Decidedly

interesting." His eyes were shining behind his pince-nez. "Thank you, Nita. I knew your opinion would be invaluable."

"The pleasure was mine," she said. "I feel I've made a discovery. I'd like to meet Alexis Kent. She must be an intriguing person."

"She?" he interjected sharply.

"Why, yes. It *is* a woman, isn't it?"

"I don't know," said Tremaine. "Yet."

He stayed talking with Anita Lane as long as she would allow him—conversation with her was always stimulating—but finally she told him with regret that she would have to leave.

"I'm not doing a great deal," she said, "but I *am* doing something. I've a column to finish for the *Stage Review*. A girl must live."

"I'm sorry," he said contritely. "I've been talking away like a selfish old man and completely forgetting that you must have work to do."

There was a frequent service to Dalmering—it was on one of the main Southern electric lines—and he had only ten minutes to wait at Victoria, for he arrived at an opportune time. He came out of the little station at the end of the journey with the pleasant feeling that his arrival at "Roseland" would coincide with tea.

He was walking down the roadway toward the house

when he saw Geoffrey Manning. The other nodded and would have passed on, but Tremaine beckoned to him.

"Just a moment, Manning, if you don't mind—I was hoping I might see you."

Manning came across to him. He looked a little apprehensive. His acquaintance with Inspector Boyce, thought Tremaine wryly, seemed to be inducing an increasing amount of apprehension in the local inhabitants. Pauline Conroy had revealed hers by a sudden display of friendship; Manning, not possessing such a well-developed talent for acting, was revealing his more obviously.

"Terrible business about Hammond," remarked Tremaine.

"It's hard for Karen," said the younger man. "She's prostrate, they say."

He was looking uncomfortable. He knew that these were merely the preliminaries and that the mildly speaking man with the pince-nez who was reported to be on such close terms with the Scotland Yard detective who was in charge of the murder investigations had not stopped him in order to indulge in banal remarks.

Tremaine did not keep him in suspense.

"I believe," he said quietly, "that you and Philip Hammond were on bad terms."

Manning started. For a brief instant there was alarm in his face.

"Who told you that?" he demanded.

"The source of my information doesn't matter," said Tremaine. "What I'm concerned with at the moment is whether or not it's true."

He looked Manning straight in the face. The other's eyes flickered uneasily away and then came back to his own.

"All right—you probably know, anyway, so I may as well admit it. We did have an argument. But I thought it had all been forgotten. Hammond didn't refer to it again, and *I* certainly didn't intend to."

"What was the subject of your…er…argument?"

"I've told you it was all over," said Manning.

There was a note of anger—and dismay—in his voice, and Mordecai Tremaine knew that he was trying to hide something.

"What was it about?" he persisted gently.

"Why should I answer your questions?" broke out Manning. "You've no right to cross-examine me!"

"Of course I haven't," agreed Tremaine. "But I think you would be wise to tell me all you can. I might be more sympathetic than some people—the police, for instance."

"I met Hammond several months ago in London," said Manning unwillingly.

"That doesn't seem important enough to start a quarrel between you."

"I didn't think so either. But when I mentioned it casually in the village just afterward he lost his temper over it—accused me of spying on him and threatened to knock my head off if I didn't stop. Of course, I wasn't going to stand for that. I told him what *I* thought."

"I take it that you hadn't seen Hammond in London on any other occasion?"

"No."

"Had anyone else in the village seen him?"

"I don't think so."

"Have you any idea why he seemed so put out because of your meeting him?"

"Yes," returned Manning. "I have. He was with a woman. It wasn't his wife."

Tremaine was silent. There was no doubt that the other was speaking the truth. He had the look of a man who knew that he had applied a spark to the gunpowder and was half-afraid of what he had done. After a moment or two Manning said: "Look, I don't think anyone else knows about it. I haven't breathed a word to a soul—not even to Phyllis. I don't think Mrs. Hammond knows."

His meaning was obvious. So patently obvious that it was almost pathetic.

Philip Hammond had very often been away from his home, and during those absences he had been having an affair with another woman. In itself the fact that he had been seen on one occasion with someone who was not his wife could not be classed as important. There might be a dozen quite simple explanations. But the damning factor was Hammond's reaction. He had behaved like a guilty man, a man who knew that he had something to hide.

That was what Manning meant. He meant that he knew that Hammond had been leading a double life. And he was desperately anxious that the police should believe that Karen Hammond had *not* known. Because if she had been aware of it, then something else became obvious—*she had had a motive for killing her husband.*

Tremaine found his voice.

"You can rely on me not to broadcast what you've told me," he said. "But you appreciate its importance, of course. You realize that Inspector Boyce must be informed?"

"Yes," said Manning, "I realize that."

Mordecai Tremaine was conscious as he walked on toward "Roseland" that Geoffrey Manning's troubled eyes were following him. It was not until he had turned into the gateway of the house that he ceased to be aware of the other's fixed stare.

It was Jean who let him in, and he greeted her cheerfully.

"I hope I'm in time for tea. I've a thirst like a camel who's exhausted his reservoirs. And none of the pubs are open yet."

"You'll be trying to make me believe you really like drinking beer next," she told him. "You know you've never been able to acquire a taste for it."

"You're quite right," he admitted. "As a practiced beer drinker holding a foaming tankard I'm a dismal failure. Is Paul in?"

"He's in the surgery—but he'll be out in a moment or two; he's only looking over some case notes."

"A busy day?" he asked.

"About the usual."

"Routine calls, I suppose? He hasn't been anywhere off the beaten track?"

Jean looked at him with a suddenly guarded expression.

"No. He's either been in the surgery here or making his normal round."

"Is he going out tonight?"

Tremaine's voice was casual, but there was a faint undercurrent of sharpness in her reply.

"No," she told him. "We're both staying home. It isn't often we go very far. What is it, Mordecai? Why are you asking these questions?"

"It's nothing," he said hastily. "Nothing at all. I was just wondering whether you had anything planned. It's only that I'm going along to have a chat with Boyce and I didn't want to put you out in any way."

All through the tea meal there was a feeling of constraint in the room. Several times Tremaine caught Jean's eyes upon him, and once he intercepted a significant glance between her and Paul. Neither of them made any reference to his visit to London. They seemed afraid of what they might hear, anxious to keep the conversation as innocuous as possible.

It was a relief when he was able to make his excuses and go down to the village again. Although he had said that he intended to see Jonathan Boyce, he was not at all certain that the inspector would be able to talk to him. His duties might be keeping him fully engaged.

However, his mind was soon reassured on that particular score, although he was given fresh cause for meditation. The Yard man was on the watch for him and came to meet him as he walked down the roadway toward the Admiral Inn.

"Glad I've seen you, Mordecai," he announced. "Anston wants you and me to meet him tonight. In his room at the pub."

"Anston?" Tremaine's voice revealed his surprise. "What's it all about?"

"I don't know," returned Boyce. "He wouldn't say anything except that it was important and that he'd tell me the whole story at the right time. He wants us to meet him there at nine o'clock."

"You're going?"

Boyce nodded. "Why not? We're both staying in the

same place, and anyway I know Anston. If he says it's important he means it. He wants you to come along, too—thinks you'll be interested. He seems to regard you as one of the family now," he added.

"All right, I'll be there," said Mordecai Tremaine. "Perhaps our friend Anston is going to surprise us."

He did not say anything to the inspector, but it was Howard Shannon who was on his mind.

At five minutes to nine he was on his way once again to the Admiral. Outside the main door he saw the tall figure of the journalist and next to it the stocky one of Jonathan Boyce. Anston gave him a nod of welcome that seemed to hold at the same time a hint of mingled amusement and triumph and led the way to the little bedroom he occupied at the back of the inn. He had obviously been making it ready to receive his visitors, for it had been crowded by the addition of three easy chairs and there were glasses standing upon a bedside table.

"Make yourself at home, gentlemen," said the newspaperman.

Tremaine sat down and produced his pipe. He proffered his pouch to Jonathan Boyce, knowing the other's love of his much-bitten briar, and the inspector stared at him.

"A pipe! So you've managed it at last, Mordecai."

Tremaine glanced up at Anston, who was watching the little scene with a puzzled smile.

"Jonathan here thought I'd never succeed in breaking myself in to a pipe," he explained. "It was always upsetting my stomach. But I've reached the stage now where I can even risk a smoke in public. And I thought," he added meaningfully, "that a pipe atmosphere would be the one most suitable for this little conference."

"It would," agreed the other. "If you don't mind, I'll dig into your tobacco myself."

In a few moments all three of them were leaning back comfortably in their chairs, and the smoke clouds were ascending toward the ancient, misshapen beams supporting the roof of the inn. Boyce looked expectantly at the journalist.

"It's your party, Anston. What's your big surprise?"

"Did I say it was a big surprise?" countered the other. "As a matter of fact I have got something to tell you that I think you will find was worth your visit, but first of all I thought we might have a general chat and swap ideas. After all, I'm a reporter, and my editor expects me to report."

"It wouldn't," said Boyce, "be blackmail, would it?"

"Now would it?" said Anston disarmingly. "You know me, Inspector. I believe in working with you and not against you. But at the same time I've a job to consider, and I'd like to know all that you think I can print. Let's see if we can induce the right social mood. Beer?"

"Yes, please," said the Yard man. "If I'm going to talk I'm going to get thirsty."

"For me," remarked Tremaine, "cider. If there is any."

"There is," said Anston. "I found out from the inspector that you'd prefer cider to the local beer."

Tremaine smiled.

"You're putting it tactfully."

Jonathan Boyce leaned forward. He took a long drink and then leaned back again. It was obvious that his verbal fencing had been merely camouflage. If he had been unwilling to discuss the case upon which he was engaged he would not have visited Barry Anston's room. He knew the journalist, and he knew that his confidences would be respected.

"Well," he remarked, "you're both waiting for it, so you may as well know. I'm still trying to make up my mind whether to plump for Vaughan or not."

"I imagine your case against him is pretty strong," said Anston.

"It's strong enough," agreed Boyce. "But there are too many loose ends lying around for my piece of mind. What I'd like to know, Mordecai," he said, addressing Tremaine, "is what motive you think Pauline Conroy could have had. My fellows are watching her, but so far she hasn't put a foot wrong."

"I didn't say that she did have a motive," returned Tremaine, "but if you like I'll suggest one. She's an actress. She's waiting for a chance to make her name and to break into the West End productions. In fact, she's more than just waiting. She's consumed by ambition. Have you ever considered to just what lengths a woman like that will go?"

"You mean that the murders are a publicity stunt—just to get her name in the headlines so that the London producers will go after her?" Boyce shook his head. "No, I can't swallow that. It's too far-fetched."

"There's Galeski as well, you know. He could be in on it, too."

"Even with Galeski it doesn't make sense. People get hanged for murder. You get the publicity all right, but it doesn't do you any good."

"I didn't say that it *was* like that," remarked Tremaine. "I was only pointing out that there *could* be such a motive for our glamorous Pauline."

"But you told me to watch her—"

"Yes," he agreed, "I told you to watch her."

Mordecai Tremaine leaned back. He puffed carefully at his pipe.

"'The play's the thing,'" he quoted softly, "'wherein I'll catch the conscience of the king.'"

"So we're going to amuse ourselves with riddles, are we?" said Boyce. "I know that it's Shakespeare. I know that it comes from *Hamlet*. We're not all illiterates because we happen to be policemen. But just what are you getting at?"

Tremaine sat up, and now his pipe was forgotten.

"I'm not telling you that this is what I think," he said. "I'm merely pointing it out to you because it seems to me to be an interesting theory. You're working on the possibility that Vaughan killed Philip Hammond because Hammond knew that he'd killed Lydia Dare. In other words, you're assuming that both murders are connected. But suppose they aren't connected, after all. Suppose, in fact, that they're two *entirely separate* crimes. Where do we stand then?"

Barry Anston was looking at him intently, his attention suddenly gripped.

"Go on," he said, "what are you suggesting?"

"I'm suggesting in the first place that it's possible that Martin Vaughan killed Lydia Dare because he was in love with her and she was going to marry another man. And I'm suggesting in the second place that *Karen Hammond killed her husband because he was having a love affair with another woman!*"

Jonathan Boyce did not display the sharp reaction Tremaine had been expecting.

"I've been trying not to think it," he said reluctantly. "But her story wouldn't stand up for five minutes in the witness box once the prosecution started working on it. The only straw I can cling to is that there's no evidence that she and her husband weren't a devoted couple."

"That's just the point," said Tremaine. "There is such

evidence. I've been speaking to Geoffrey Manning. Several months ago he saw Philip Hammond in London with a woman. Hammond didn't like being seen—accused Manning of spying on him and went so far as to threaten him. In short, he behaved like a man who had something to hide."

Now the inspector certainly was reacting. He was sitting forward in his chair, his pipe unheeded in his hand.

"Do you think Manning was speaking the truth?"

"I can see no reason why he should have lied," countered Tremaine.

"I can," said Boyce. "I've learned that Manning had what was a pretty violent quarrel with Hammond. The fact that there was a quarrel is well known, so Manning can hardly deny that it took place. But the cause of it doesn't seem to be such general knowledge. Manning now says that it was because he saw Hammond in London—so you've just told me—and that Hammond made a great fuss about it. It sounds credible, but suppose the quarrel wasn't over that at all and that the real explanation of the bad blood between them is one that gives Manning a motive for the killing. What of his story, then? It could be a clever fake, designed to bring suspicion on Karen Hammond and to take away the lime-light from himself."

"I suppose it could," admitted Tremaine. "Of course, I can't prove whether Manning was lying or not."

"I think," interjected Barry Anston, "that this is where I come in." For some moments he had been listening to his companions without offering any comment. He stood up and looked from one to the other of them. "The situation appears to be," he went on, "that Philip Hammond may have been a philanderer; that all the time he was supposed to be living as a happily married man here in Dalmering he had a mistress in London. Further, that Karen Hammond may have found him out and killed him in jealousy. Am I right?"

"What," said Boyce, "are you leading up to?"

"This," said Anston. "Mrs. Hammond is here. Perhaps she can help us. No—don't get up," he added quickly, as the inspector made a movement. "I asked you to come here because I knew that she was also going to be here. She's waiting in the next room."

He walked across to a door that had been concealed in the shadows of the far wall and pulled it open.

"Would you mind coming in now, Mrs. Hammond?" he said.

There was a moment's pause, and then a woman came into the room. Mordecai Tremaine looked up at her curiously and then found himself staring, for he had never seen her before. Certainly her dark hair and eyes and her rather tired-looking features bore no resemblance to Karen Hammond's blond loveliness.

Inspector Boyce had half risen from his seat.

"What game are you playing, Anston?" he demanded, a touch of anger in his voice. "I thought you said you had Mrs. Hammond here!"

The woman betrayed no resentment at his outburst. She might, indeed, have been expecting it. She came into the center of the room.

"I *am* Mrs. Hammond," she said. "The *real* Mrs. Hammond."

14

━━━━━━━━━

It was Anston who took command of the situation.

"Mrs. Hammond is my surprise, Inspector," he said. "I asked you to come here in order to meet her."

Boyce had recovered his self-possession. He was once more the impersonal police machine, ready to absorb new facts and fit them into place.

"So Philip Hammond was a bigamist," he said slowly.

The woman who had described herself as "Mrs. Hammond" shook her head.

"No," she said, "he wasn't a bigamist. He wasn't married to—to the other." Her voice trembled. She broke off. And then she added more firmly, "It isn't any good trying to hide anything—you'll have to know it all so I may as well be frank."

"I appreciate that this must be a very painful situation for you, Mrs. Hammond," said Boyce.

"It would have been painful—once," she told him. "Now—I'm not sure. Philip and I had been gradually drifting apart for a long time. We'd been married almost ten years when

I first realized that he was beginning to change. He began to stay away for longer periods; to make excuses about the amount of work he had to do. Then I became certain that there was someone else. You can't live with a man and not learn to know him—not—not if you love him."

She hesitated again, and none of the men who were listening to her story tried to press her to continue. They allowed her to choose her own time.

"We live—lived—at Harford Row. It's a village about ten miles north of London. To begin with Philip used to travel back and forth every day, and then, after his time for coming home had been getting more and more uncertain for some months, he said that the journey was becoming too much for him and that he thought it would be better if he stayed in London when his busy periods made it necessary for him to work late. At first it was only an occasional night—perhaps once a week—but gradually he stayed away more frequently. It reached the point where he was away far more often than he was at home."

"From what you said a few moments ago, Mrs. Hammond," said Boyce, "I gather that you didn't believe the excuses your husband gave you to explain his absences?"

"No," she said, "I didn't believe them."

"Did you take any action?"

It was several moments before she replied.

"Not for a long time," she said at last and went on: "I know that you're going to ask me why I didn't. I'm not certain. I suppose—I suppose it was partly because I was still in love with Philip. I—I was afraid of losing him completely. Besides, I thought that there was a hope that he might get over what I took to be his infatuation for someone else and that if I could hold out for long enough he might forget her and everything would go back as it was."

"But he didn't forget her," said Boyce quietly.

"No," she said in a low voice, "he didn't forget her. I realized that it was more serious than I'd imagined at first. I think that it was then my own attitude changed. I found that I'd stopped loving Philip—or, at least, that it didn't hurt anymore. I began to think about divorce…"

The inspector gave her a sudden glance of interrogation.

"Your husband had never asked you to consider giving him a divorce?"

"I knew that he wouldn't do that. He couldn't. The scandal would have done him too much harm. It might even have ruined him. He was in a position where he had to be above reproach." Her eyes traveled uncertainly to each of them in turn, as if she expected to see unbelief in their faces: "And I think—I think that there was another reason, too. We'd been happy in the early years, and I think he remembered that. He didn't want to hurt me. That was why he took such pains to deceive me. He didn't want me to know what was happening because he still cared a little."

"You don't think he suspected that you knew?" queried Boyce.

"I'm not sure of that, but I don't think he did. He would have betrayed it if he had guessed. Philip was a strange person," she said, and there was a sudden note of tenderness in her voice. "He was weak, but he could be very lovable. I don't think he could have had a very quiet mind torn between the two of us—between his new love and his old love for me. Perhaps it's just because I'm getting sentimental over him now that he's dead that I'm talking like this. If he was still alive I might still have been making preparations to divorce him—whatever happened to his career."

"You *were* making preparations then?" said the inspector.

"Yes. I went to a private inquiry agent. I told him that I was certain that my husband was being unfaithful and that I wanted evidence."

"Hornsby," interjected Mordecai Tremaine, and she turned toward him.

"You know?" she asked, and Tremaine looked a little embarrassed.

"I suspected," he said, "but please go on, Mrs. Hammond. I didn't mean to interrupt your story."

"I don't think there's anything else to say," she told him.

"I knew that Hornsby had traced Philip to a village named Dalmering, where he was living with a woman who called herself his wife. When I saw the report in the newspapers about a Philip Hammond having been murdered I was stunned. I—I didn't know quite what to do. I felt certain that it must be Philip, but I knew that if I came down here and announced myself as Mrs. Hammond the whole story would have to come out. There would be a scandal that would be printed in all the newspapers, and Philip's reputation would be torn to shreds. And then I had a message from Mr. Anston here." She indicated the journalist. "He told me that it was my duty to come forward and tell you everything. Of course, I knew that he was right. That was why I came."

"It was the wisest thing you could have done, Mrs. Hammond," said Boyce. "You've been exceedingly frank and helpful, and I know that it hasn't been easy for you."

She looked at him with an expression of appeal that reminded the watching Tremaine for a fleeting instant of Karen Hammond, although there was no physical resemblance.

"You won't rake everything up, Inspector?" she said pleadingly. "You won't let them make everything public?"

"I can't give you a promise to conceal anything," returned the inspector. "You see, what you've just told me may have an important bearing on your husband's murder, and you may be required to give it as evidence. But you have my assurance that everything possible will be done to spare you pain. No more facts than those that are essential to the case will be required."

"Thank you, Inspector," she said gratefully. "Is there anything else you wish me to tell you?"

"Not for the moment. I take it that we can easily get in touch with you should it be necessary?"

"I've arranged for her to stay in Mereham," said Anston. "There's a car waiting to take her over. I thought it would be better for her there than here in Dalmering under everybody's eyes."

Mereham was a village about five miles away. Boyce nodded his agreement with what the journalist had said and watched silently as Anston escorted Philip Hammond's widow from the room.

And when the door had closed behind them: "Well, Mordecai," he said soberly, "it's a bad business."

"You're right, Jonathan," agreed that gentleman. "I wonder if we know just how bad it is."

Jonathan Boyce gave him a shrewd glance.

"At least," he observed, "it removes Karen Hammond's motive. She isn't the wife who killed her unfaithful husband. She's the Other Woman."

"Does it mean that she didn't kill Philip Hammond?" said Tremaine. "Or does it merely mean that she didn't kill him for the reason we originally thought she might have had?"

"She had everything to lose by his death. A woman who lives with another woman's husband isn't in a very happy position if anything happens to him."

"On the other hand, a woman who has flouted convention to the extent of living with a man to whom she isn't married isn't likely to think along normal lines. She's liable to act first and ask questions afterward. Suppose she had reason to think that Philip Hammond was getting tired of her and was contemplating going back to his wife—do you think she might have killed him then?"

"There's no evidence to suggest that he intended to do that. In fact, all that we've heard tonight supports the theory that so far from leaving her he was actually seeing more of her."

"I didn't say that there was any evidence," remarked Tremaine. "I was just pointing out that we aren't in any position yet to clear Karen Hammond—I'll still call her that since we don't know her real name."

There was a touch of exasperation in the inspector's voice.

"All right," he said, "all right. So we still don't know where we are."

Mordecai Tremaine was in a sober mood as he walked back from the Admiral. He never liked to see romance shattered, and shattered irretrievably it had been tonight.

There was an explanation now for Karen Hammond's attitude during the past few days—an explanation for her appeal to him on that first night. She had wanted the mystery of Lydia Dare's death to be solved as quickly as possible because she had feared publicity. She had wanted the murderer found quickly so that inquiries would not proceed too far in other directions.

Explained, too, was her fear of the ferrety Hornsby. If his legal wife was to be believed, Philip Hammond had done his best to conceal from her the fact that he had a mistress, but had his mistress—Tremaine found himself using the word in spite of himself; there was, after all, no other he could use—known of the existence of a wife? If she had known, then in her knowledge lay the reason for her fear. She may not have been certain of Hornsby's intentions, but it was probable that she had suspected them.

There was even, now, a feasible explanation for her failure to notify Philip Hammond's nonappearance over a period of forty-eight hours. She had been used to his absences, and she had had no means of being certain that he had not gone back to his wife for some reason. She had been waiting hour by hour for some word from him.

Her position had been an unenviable one. Torn with anxiety regarding the whereabouts of the man she loved and at the same time shrinking from instituting any inquiries lest they should lead to a public scandal that would ruin him, she had not known which course it would be best to adopt.

It had to be admitted, of course, that there *was* another possibility—that Philip Hammond had deceived her just as he had deceived his wife. Suppose Karen Hammond had suddenly stumbled upon the truth? Suppose, in a storm of jealousy, she *had* killed the man who had wronged her? Her gradual realization of Hammond's duplicity could explain her nervous, her tense uncertainty before his murder, and her knowledge of her guilt could explain her strange attitude after it.

Mordecai Tremaine shook his head sadly. It was a tragic, unhappy situation, whatever might be the truth behind it. It was still weighing upon his mind when he reached the house and went up to his bedroom. There was no pleasure for him in *Romantic Stories* when he tried to read that sentiment-laden magazine before going to sleep. He turned off his light and lay for a long time in the darkness, his thoughts allowing him no peace.

The next morning the air of constraint that had crept into their relationship was still in evidence between Jean and Paul Russell and their guest. Tremaine sensed the suspicion in their eyes as he entered the dining room and sat down to breakfast. Their conversation was normal; outwardly nothing had changed in their attitude toward him. But he knew that they were on their guard.

"By the way, Paul," he said casually, as the meal was nearing its conclusion, "I wonder whether you'd have any objection to my going with you on your rounds today?"

The doctor gave him a look of surprise.

"Of course not," he said. "Come by all means. I'm afraid you'll find it rather boring though."

"I don't think so," said Tremaine. "I feel in the mood for being driven around somehow. And I don't suppose you'll spend a great deal of time over each call."

"That's true enough," admitted Russell. "I've the surgery to get through, of course, before we start."

"That's fine," said his guest, with every appearance of enthusiasm. "As a matter of fact, I'd like to slip down to the village first."

The doctor clearly did not know what to make of his attitude. Tremaine saw him glance at his wife, and he saw, too, the doubt in Jean's eyes.

His business in the village was merely the purchase of an ounce of tobacco. The session at the Admiral on the previous evening had made considerable inroads upon the contents of his pouch. As he came out of the little general store in the village square he caught sight of a feminine figure walking briskly up the road that led to Kingshampton. He recognized the trim back and somewhat ostentatiously swaying hips as those of Millicent Silwell. He had seen her once or twice in the neighborhood of the village and knew that she was

Pauline Conroy's maid. The girl was obviously influenced by her mistress. She was like a smaller, more subdued edition of the intense Pauline, a reproduction pictorially accurate but without quite the same vivid personality to back it.

Acting upon a sudden impulse Tremaine hurried after her. She heard the sound of his hasty footsteps and turned inquiringly. When she saw who he was a shadow crossed her face and she adopted the slightly defensive attitude to which he had grown accustomed.

"I believe you're Millicent Silwell, aren't you?" he said. "Miss Conroy's maid."

She looked him up and down.

"That's right," she said, a trace of defiance in her tone.

It was that note of antagonism that made Mordecai Tremaine decide to take the plunge. If she had smiled at him or appeared willing to talk, his resolve might have weakened. But he saw that she believed she had something to hide, and his feelings hardened. He adopted an air of sternness.

"I want to talk to you," he told her. "And I want the truth."

She could not hold his glance.

"The truth?" she said falteringly. "I don't know what you mean."

He pressed home his advantage.

"You told the police that on the night Lydia Dare was killed Miss Conroy never left her house. You lied—didn't you?"

The quick fear she could not hide from her eyes gave her away and made it impossible for her to maintain any pretense with him.

"You *did* lie," he said. "Don't you think you would be wiser to admit it? You may find yourself in a very dangerous position if you persist in your story. Obstructing the police is a very serious matter."

"All right," she told him. "I'll admit it. I don't want to get into any trouble. She wanted me to say it—she said it wouldn't do any harm. She wasn't in the house. She—she was with Mr. Galeski."

Mordecai Tremaine did not reveal whether or not the information had surprised him. He said: "Perhaps you hadn't realized that giving false evidence could render you liable to be classed as an accessory to a very grave crime?"

Her eyes dilated at that.

"You don't mean—you can't think that *she* did it?"

"I didn't say so."

"But that was what you meant. Oh, no—she couldn't have—"

"When you say that Miss Conroy was with Mr. Galeski, do you mean that she was at his cottage?"

She nodded, held by his gaze.

"Yes—she's often there."

"You may have seen her leave the house. She may have

told you that that was where she was going. But can you *prove* that she was there? Did you actually see her there?"

"No, but—"

"What you *think* she did or didn't do," said Tremaine, an echo of Jonathan Boyce in his mind, "isn't evidence. All that you really know is that she wasn't at the house with you that night. Isn't that correct?"

"I didn't mean to do anything wrong," she said, on the verge of tears, and he hastened to adopt a softer tone.

"Perhaps there won't be any serious harm done. You can go along now. But don't say anything to your mistress about what you've told me. Inspector Boyce may send for you or come to see you, but until then don't say a word to anyone. You understand?"

"I won't say anything," she said, and was obviously relieved at being allowed to go.

Tremaine watched her with a faint pang of remorse. Despite her appearance of sophistication, so evidently copied from her mistress, Millicent Silwell was a simple soul. He guessed that her conscience had already been worrying her. The two murders in the village had been preying upon her mind, and she had been troubled about her own position, which was, no doubt, the reason for her quick collapse. She would probably soon be feeling greatly relieved that she had been given an opportunity of confession. On his way back

Tremaine kept a watch for Jonathan Boyce's stocky figure, but the inspector did not appear to be anywhere in the neighborhood, and he could not afford the time to go in search of him. He knew that the surgery must be almost finished by now, and he did not wish to keep Paul waiting for him—nor did he wish the doctor to go without him.

As it happened he arrived with ten minutes to spare, and he spent the remainder of the morning in the hardworking saloon car in which Russell did his rounds. When they returned at lunchtime the doctor gave him a peculiar glance.

"Satisfied, Mordecai?" he asked.

"Completely," he returned, as though he had noticed nothing strange in the other's manner. "It's been a change—and I've enjoyed your items of local gossip on the way, Paul."

After lunch the doctor was once more engaged, and Tremaine took the opportunity of going into the village again in search of Inspector Boyce. This time he found him without difficulty, and the Yard man listened attentively to his story of his encounter with Millicent Silwell.

"Pauline Conroy seems to be coming into the front of the picture," he observed. "So she wasn't safely accounted for in her own house on the night of the first murder, after all. And whether she really was at Galeski's cottage isn't going to be easy to check. If they were in the killing together each of them will support the other's alibi."

"The job of the professional policeman," said Mordecai Tremaine, "is to break down false alibis. I leave the routine details to you, Jonathan," he added and left the other staring after him.

For the rest of the day Paul Russell was conscious that his visitor was never very far from his side. Wherever he went the benevolent-looking figure with the mild eyes peering from behind the pince-nez somehow happened to be there—as unobtrusive as a shadow but just as inescapable.

When the evening's surgery was completed the doctor came into the lounge where his wife and Tremaine were already seated.

"Anything on tonight, dear?" he asked.

"No—we're just Darby and Joan tonight," Jean told him, and he made a little grimace.

"Darby and Joan—and the shadow."

"The shadow?" she said, puzzled, and then she caught his significant glance and was silently embarrassed.

Mordecai Tremaine said nothing.

It was beginning to grow dark when a ring came at the door, and Jean opened it to find Sandra Borne on the threshold.

"You don't mind, Jean?" she said. "I'm an awful nuisance at such a time, but I've been in the house all the evening, and I was beginning to get the shivers."

"You're welcome anytime, Sandy," called the doctor. "Come along in."

Sandra Borne nodded to Mordecai Tremaine as she entered. "Hullo," she said. "You haven't caught our murderer yet?"

"Or murderers," he returned, accenting the plural. "No, not yet, Miss Borne."

He saw, as she sat down and he was able to observe her closely, that she was not as lighthearted as her tone had implied. He had thought as she had spoken that her remark had had a forced, unnatural sound; there had been a faint ring of hysteria in it. Her face still possessed its peaked look of strain.

Paul Russell watched her hands. They were twisting nervously, and she was unaware of the fact.

"Why don't you get away from that cottage, Sandy?" he said quietly.

He was faintly surprised by her answer.

"I think I will, Paul. I thought I would be able to go on living there in spite of what's happened. But I—I can't. It's nerves, I suppose—the reaction from it all. But tonight I found myself listening to every little sound. I've got to admit it. I'm—I'm afraid…" Her voice trailed away, and then her head went up and she smiled. "Now I'm being stupid. It's funny, isn't it? I know that it's only my nerves and that it's absurd to be frightened. I know exactly what's happening to me. And yet I can't do anything to stop it."

The doctor leaned forward.

"Look here, Sandy, you know our invitation's always open. Why don't you come over here with us? There's plenty of room for you."

She was frankly relieved at the offer. She gave Tremaine the impression that although she had not intended to ask for it, she had been hoping that the invitation would be given to her. Something of the tension passed from her face.

Gradually it faded completely. Long experience had given Jean and Paul Russell a sure grip upon such situations, and under their tactful handling, the conversation became free and lighthearted. Temporarily, even some of their apprehension regarding Tremaine was removed. Time went by imperceptibly but rapidly, stimulated by the atmosphere of friendly talk. It was with a feeling of surprise that Mordecai Tremaine saw that it was ten minutes past eleven. The others, too, suddenly became aware of the hour.

"It's time I made some coffee," said Jean, rising to her feet.

She was on her way to the kitchenette when the doorbell startled them with its clamor. It rang with a shrill, insistent note. Paul Russell's lips shaped a noiseless "Damn!"

"All right," said Tremaine, calling to Jean, "I'll see who it is."

He went into the hallway, switching on the light as he did so, and opened the door. The visitor's finger was already on the bell again, ringing demandingly, imperiously.

It was Jonathan Boyce. As he stood framed in the lighted

doorway Tremaine saw that the inspector's stocky figure was taut with a barely controlled emotion and that his face was stonily rigid.

"What's the matter, Jonathan?" he said, alarmed.

Boyce stepped over the threshold.

"When you spoke about a third murder, Mordecai," he said, his words clipped and almost devoid of expression, "what did you know?"

Tremaine could only gape at him, taken aback by the intensity of his manner.

"Why, what do you mean?" he managed to get out at last.

"I mean," said Boyce, "that we've just found Edith Lorrington. Dead. Murdered."

If Mordecai Tremaine had seemed bewildered before, now he was like a man who had received a devastating blow. He stared at the inspector. His eyes were incredulous, horrified.

"Edith Lorrington?" he said in a whisper. "*Edith Lorrington*! No, it isn't possible! It's wrong—*wrong*!"

15

Inspector Boyce stood motionless in the doorway, the grimness of his features emphasized by the light cast by the shaded electric globe in the hall.

"It may be wrong, but it's a fact," he said. "Edith Lorrington is dead. Someone beat her to death with a heavy brass poker and left her body lying on the floor of her dining room. We probably wouldn't have known anything about it until tomorrow, but one of the villagers who'd promised to do some baking for her called at the house, couldn't get a reply, looked in because the back door was open, and found her body."

Tremaine was still staring, as though even yet he could not believe what he had heard.

"You're sure—you're quite sure there's no mistake?" he said, and his voice was hesitant and unreal.

Jonathan Boyce spoke sharply.

"I've seen her," he said. "You don't make mistakes like that." A hint of accusation came into his tones. "What's the matter with you, Mordecai? You've been giving me the impression that you were expecting something to happen. That's why I'm here—to find out just what you were expecting."

"Not this," said Tremaine. "Not this."

He put a hand to his forehead. He was striving to think, striving to see where he had been wrong, striving to see reason in the chaos and the terror.

By now the sound of their voices had attracted the attention of the others. Paul Russell had come out into the hallway.

"What's wrong, Inspector?" he asked.

Boyce looked at him. Beyond the doctor he saw the drawn but inquiring face of Sandra Borne. And from the open door of the kitchenette he saw Jean peering curiously at him.

"I'm afraid I've some bad news," he said quietly. "Miss Lorrington is dead."

Russell gave a start.

"Edith? But you can't mean it, Inspector! I gave her a thorough overhaul only last week, and I'd have guaranteed her another twenty years!"

"Your guarantee wouldn't have covered a violent assault with a heavy weapon, Doctor," said Boyce levelly. "Miss Lorrington didn't die naturally. She was murdered."

"Murdered!" The word hissed involuntarily through Russell's lips. "Not—not *another*!"

"Another," said Boyce.

Tremaine saw horror dilate Sandra Borne's eyes. She

staggered, and he was only just in time to save her from a fall. She leaned against him, her hand searching for his arm to support her.

"No," she whispered. "Don't say that Edith—"

"I'm sorry, Miss Borne," said Boyce. "I'm afraid it's true."

Deep in the mists of confusion that were encompassing Mordecai Tremaine's brain, half-knowledge glimmered like a feeble flame a great way off. He struggled gropingly toward it through enveloping clouds. The glimmer strengthened. And then the half-knowledge became certainty and burst blindingly through the mists, shredding them into nothing and leaving him amazed that he had taken so long to realize the truth…and bitterly angered with himself that he had not seen it in time to save Edith Lorrington.

"What a fool!" he burst out, groaningly. "What a stupid, blind fool!"

Boyce gave him a sharp glance.

"Over what?" he asked.

Tremaine did not reply. He seemed, in fact, not to have heard the question.

"I should have saved her," he said. "I should have known."

The inspector looked as though he was going to say something further. And then, instead, he turned to Paul Russell.

"You've been here all the evening, Doctor?"

"Yes," nodded the other.

The news the detective had brought seemed to have stunned him. He uttered the word mechanically.

Boyce was apparently satisfied with his answer.

"I thought you might have had something to tell me, Mordecai," he said, addressing Tremaine once more. "Perhaps you will in the morning." There was a significant note in his voice. "I'll see you then," he added. "Good night all."

After the door had closed behind the inspector, Tremaine still stood in the hallway. It was clear from his face that his thoughts were still occupying him to the exclusion of his surroundings.

The others watched him. The horror behind Jonathan Boyce's visit was beginning to impress itself upon them. They were beginning to realize what it meant. Their eyes were haunted and fearful, fixed upon Mordecai Tremaine as if they were waiting for a lead from him before they dared to move or speak.

"Poor Edith," said Jean. "Poor Edith…"

Her trembling, too highly pitched voice ended the paralysis. Sandra Borne's white face turned jerkily toward her as she spoke.

"I can't believe it," she said. "First Lydia—then Philip—now Edith. What does it mean? What is happening to us all?"

Mordecai Tremaine drew a deep breath. He turned toward the doctor.

"I've got to go out, Paul."

The doctor was startled.

"At this time of night?"

"You're not serious, Mordecai?" broke in Jean. "After all, there's nothing—there's nothing you can do—"

"But there is," he told her. "There is." He added quickly: "Don't wait up for me, Jean. I don't know how long I'll be."

Almost before they had realized his intention and certainly before they could make any move to dissuade him, he had gone. They were staring at a door that had banged shut behind him.

There was determination in Mordecai Tremaine's manner as he walked quickly down the darkened road toward the village. He hesitated as he drew near the entrance to the copse, but it was only for an instant or two, and then he strode on as vigorously as before. He would reach Martin Vaughan's house a few minutes sooner if he used the pathway over the common, but he could find no enthusiasm to carry him through the darkness of that fatal copse. The black shadow of murder still brooded over it.

His mind was still trying to assimilate the shock of Edith Lorrington's death. This third murder must inevitably bring with it a desperate urgency. Tomorrow the village of Dalmering would be the most-talked-of spot in the country. Everything that took place in it would take place in the blinding glare of a frightening publicity. For the police there would be scorn, accusation, bitter criticism.

No one was more aware of that than Jonathan Boyce. It was that knowledge that had lain behind his manner at "Roseland." Tremaine knew as he walked breathlessly on that if he was to help his friend he must help him soon.

To his first ring at the door of "Home Lodge" there was no reply. Tremaine rang again. There was still no response. He placed his finger firmly on the bell and held it there. He heard the summons go shrilling through the house unceasingly.

This time he did produce a reaction. A sound above him revealed the opening of a window. He looked up to see a man's head and shoulders framed in the opening.

"Who the devil's there?" demanded an exasperated voice.

It was Vaughan himself. There was no mistaking the big man's harshly threatening tones. Tremaine stepped back from the doorway.

"It's Tremaine," he called.

There was a muttered exclamation.

"What the blazes do *you* want?"

"To talk to you," said Tremaine. "It's important."

Vaughan's bulk remained blocking the window for a second or two longer. It seemed that he was on the point of shutting it again without replying. And then: "Wait there," he said shortly. "I'll come down."

In a few moments his dressing-gowned figure was leading the way into the house. He pushed open the door of a room adjoining the hall and switched on the light. As the other drew together the heavy curtains, Tremaine glanced curiously around him. It was clear from the well-filled bookshelves and the desk, with its reading lamp held in the hand of a carved wooden figure with an Egyptian flavor, that this must be Vaughan's study. The figure, several bronze statuettes, and what appeared to be reproductions of examples of ancient pottery work revealed the big man's interest in archaeology. On the walls were many photographs showing work in progress at several excavation sites—some of them were signed, as though they possessed a personal significance.

"I'm sorry I dragged you out of bed," said Tremaine, feeling that some sort of apology was needed. "I thought your man Blenkinson might still have been up."

"Blenkinson's away," retorted Vaughan, unmollified. "He's gone to Mereham. His sister's ill. I sent him off this afternoon. Was it him you wanted to see?"

"Oh no," said his visitor quickly. "I came to see you."

Vaughan pulled forward a big leather-covered armchair and motioned him to be seated.

"Now," he said, the note of challenge still in his voice, "suppose you tell me the reason for this late call. I hope you haven't dragged me out of bed for nothing."

"I haven't," said Tremaine, dropping his air of apology

and returning the challenge with an equal sharpness. "Edith Lorrington was murdered tonight."

Vaughan's features suddenly froze, and his powerful fingers stiffened upon the back of the chair against which he was standing.

"Where did it happen?" he said, and there was nothing in his voice to suggest that he was talking of murder.

"At her home."

"How was it done?"

"She was beaten to death. The murderer attacked her with a heavy brass poker."

"Do the police know who did it?"

"No."

Vaughan gave a long sigh. His fingers slipped from the chair, as though the nervous pressure which had been holding them there had been suddenly relaxed. And then: "Why have you come to me?" he demanded.

Mordecai Tremaine looked him full in the face.

"I want to know whether you've been out this evening," he said deliberately.

A dull red began to spread from the big man's thick neck. A vein at his left temple became suddenly prominent.

"That's a damned impertinent question!"

"Will you say the same thing when the police ask you? They *will* ask." Tremaine did not wait to see the effect of his statement. He said: "Why were you so anxious that *Murder Has a Motive* should be chosen as the play for your production here?"

His abrupt change of subject acted as a curb to Vaughan's rising anger. He hesitated.

"What do you mean?"

"I mean why did you press for that particular play more than any other?"

The big man had recovered himself now and he was back on his guard.

"That's my business," he said.

"It may be the jury's," said Tremaine. His tone became sharper. "You're in a very dangerous position, Mr. Vaughan—perhaps you don't realize just how dangerous. Why did you want that play to be produced?"

"If that's all you've come for you're wasting your time. I've no intention of discussing it with you."

"Was it because someone else asked you? Was it because Miss Dare wanted it?"

There were danger lights in Martin Vaughan's eyes.

"Leave Miss Dare's name out of it," he said tensely.

"What reason did she have?" went on Tremaine, as though he was unaware of the warning that was being given him. "Why did she want that play above all others?"

Vaughan took a step toward him. His great shoulders were

hunched. His big hands, slowly clenching and unclenching at his side, were full of a dreadful menace.

"I've listened to enough!" he said thickly. "Get out of here, Mr. Paul Pry! I'm warning you—don't drive me too far!"

Mordecai Tremaine's heart had begun to beat uncomfortably. But he managed to stare back with an air of calmness into the threatening features that were thrust toward his own.

"Yesterday, Inspector Boyce couldn't make up his mind whether or not to arrest you," he said. "Tomorrow his mind will probably be made up for him. You haven't much time."

"Are you trying to threaten me?" said Vaughan, and there was a vibrant note of danger in his voice. "I've watched you on your prying ways about the village. I've heard you asking questions, trying to find out other people's business. Turn your attentions to someone else, d'you hear me? Try watching some of the others. That little scoundrel Hornsby, for instance. Why don't you try and find out what *he* wants? And Shannon—try your detective methods on *him*. Ask him what he was doing in Colminster when he was supposed to be in London!"

"It's *you* I'm dealing with at the moment," said Tremaine, trying to keep his voice steady. "You were in love with Lydia Dare. You had a motive for killing her, and you had the opportunity, too. Philip Hammond believed that you *had* killed her. You could quite easily have killed *him* to stop him from talking and to save your neck. There again you had the motive *and* the opportunity."

"I suppose I killed Edith Lorrington as well?" sneered Vaughan, and Tremaine nodded.

"Perhaps a motive could be found," he said.

He was not prepared for what happened. Vaughan's great bulk towered above him. The big man's hands swept out. He found himself held in a terrible grip that swung him back across the room and against the wall. The other's distorted face glared into his own with the frightening air of madness.

"You interfering little rat!" he snarled. "You won't carry any more tales to your precious detective friends!"

It was then that Mordecai Tremaine began to realize the extent of his danger and fear was plain in his eyes.

"Stop playing the fool, man!" he said gaspingly. "You're choking me!"

"Am I?" said Vaughan, mockingly, and the pressure of his hands increased.

Tremaine reached up his own hands, trying to free himself from the remorseless grip that was slowly strangling him, but he was helpless against Vaughan's massive strength. He could only grapple with a furious despair with the steel bands that were about his throat.

He opened his mouth and tried to shout, but only a hoarse,

croaking sound came out. Vaughan grinned and relaxed his grip a little.

"Why don't you call for help?" he taunted him. "Why don't you shout for your policemen?"

Falling waters were beginning to roar in Mordecai Tremaine's ears. The room was no longer stable and motionless. The electric light had begun to move mistily, and the bookcases that he could see dimly beyond it were advancing and receding in uneasy waves.

Now that it was too late he realized what a fool he had been to come to "Home Lodge" alone and without telling anyone of his intentions. He should have known the type of man with whom he was dealing. He should have been aware of the danger in which he would be placing himself.

What he had not bargained for was the absence of Blenkinson. He had expected that the manservant would be in the house and that Vaughan's attitude would be conditioned by that fact. He was paying now for that miscalculation. He was alone with fear and a madman.

Vaguely, as though it came from a great distance and was muffled by cascading waters, he heard the big man's voice.

"You're right—I *was* in love with Lydia. You've got it all worked out, haven't you? How I followed her out of the house that night, went around by the roadway, and waited for her in the copse and killed her! You know just what I did and why and how. You know just how I got rid of Blenkinson this afternoon so that I could go out and kill Edith Lorrington and get back without being seen! Or maybe that was something you didn't know. Maybe it didn't occur to you when you came here tonight that there would only be the two of us in the house. Maybe that was where your plans went wrong."

Vaughan was grinning mirthlessly. Tremaine was conscious only of the big man's wild eyes and of his form towering over him, grown monstrous in size so that everything else seemed to have been blotted out. The voice went on, telling his doom.

"It's almost foolproof. If I were to kill you no one need ever know. You'd just disappear. With all my experience it wouldn't be difficult to find a way of disposing of the body. It would be just another unsolved mystery. You've been too clever, Tremaine. You've walked right into my hands, and you're too dangerous for me to risk letting you go. You might talk. You might start asking all those questions of yours…"

All the horror of Dalmering was in the room. It was as though all the terror that had overlain the loveliness was concentrated in this tiny space, black and dreadful. Within this curtained enclosure in this lonely house they were cut off from the world as surely as though they were isolated on another planet, and with them there was only a great and terrible evil.

Mordecai Tremaine's mind was working in a hysterical incoherence. The lawless nature of Vaughan's early life, his obsession with ancient peoples with their savage blood cults, his deep-seated passions and his love for Lydia Dare, his dreadful madman's strength—his knowledge of all these coalesced suddenly to give him the final warning that unless he could force Vaughan to hear him, unless he could reach beyond the bitter rage that had mastered him, he was lost indeed.

"Wait, you madman!" he croaked. "They'll hang you!"

Vaughan laughed—a short, horrible sound.

"Only once," he said. "Only once. For Lydia, for Hammond, and for Edith. Only once for all of them!"

Tremaine made one last desperate effort and succeeded in forcing the big man's hands apart for one brief instant.

"For God's sake, stop!" he gasped. "I know you didn't kill them!"

A change came over Vaughan's features. Slowly the glare went from his eyes. He released his grip. Tremaine's knees seemed to dissolve beneath him as the hands that had been holding him against the wall fell away and Vaughan caught him under the armpits and lowered him into the big leather chair.

He opened a small cabinet and took out whiskey and a tumbler. He poured a stiff drink of the neat spirit. Tremaine was huddled in the chair. He was shuddering, and his hands were not under his control. Vaughan guided the tumbler to his lips and forced the whiskey between his chattering teeth.

It burned a fiery path down his bruised throat. He gasped with the sting of it. Vaughan allowed him a moment or two longer in which to recover. And then: "What was it you said?" he demanded.

Tremaine put up a hand to his neck and winced.

"I said I know you didn't kill them," he repeated shakily.

16

Pauline Conroy was not acting. She was displaying a stormy fury that owed nothing to her dramatic talent. Mordecai Tremaine found himself inclined to quail under the angry flash of her dark eyes. He thought of Kipling's line about the female of the species and ruefully acknowledged its apt quality. Pauline in this mood was undeniably dangerous.

It was the morning after Edith Lorrington's murder. The actress had stopped him in the village square, and it had been obvious from her first words that her friendly attitude toward him had undergone a drastic revision.

She had made no effort to conceal the reason for her antagonism.

"I want to see you!" she had said, as she had caught sight of him, and had stepped full in his path so that he had had no chance of avoiding the meeting. "Just what are you up to?"

Tremaine had blinked at her in a bewildered fashion, adopting the pose of ineffectiveness that served as his main line of defense.

"I don't understand," he had told her.

But she had brushed aside his protests.

"You understand all right! What's the idea of setting your detective friends to spy on me?"

It had not been a question but a statement. She had gone on to make other statements, all of them pointed and some of them vituperative. She was still making them.

"I trusted you! I thought that you were my friend, not a cheap spy! I'm not going to stand for it, d'you hear! I'm not going to be watched and followed everywhere I go!"

"My dear Miss Conroy," said Tremaine, trying to stem the flood, "surely you should be speaking to Inspector Boyce, not to me? After all, I can't order policemen to go around watching people or to stop watching them. I'm just an ordinary member of the community like yourself."

"Don't try and fence with me. Everybody knows that you and that Scotland Yard detective are as thick as thieves. *You* told him to spy on me. *You* told him to set those men following me around."

The hostility in her voice stung Tremaine into replying in kind. There was an edge to his own voice.

"Innocent people don't object to the police carrying out their duty," he said coldly. "From your attitude one might think that you and Mr. Galeski had something to hide."

Whether it was his suddenly uncompromising attitude or

his unexpected mention of Galeski's name that was the cause of her discomfiture he was not certain. But some of the fire died out of her eyes and was replaced by a flicker of fear.

"Why are you bringing in Mr. Galeski?" she said breathlessly.

"His name just occurred to me," said Mordecai Tremaine, "that's all."

But he was looking straight into her face as he spoke, and she read more into the words than their bare meaning. Her expression was momentarily overshadowed by anxiety, and then, without a further word, she turned and left him.

Evidently, thought Tremaine, as he saw her go hurrying through the village, Jonathan Boyce had taken (with a painstaking literalness) the advice he had given him to watch Pauline Conroy. So much so that she had very quickly become aware of it. In such a restricted area as that of Dalmering, of course, it was impossible to shadow a person for long without being detected. He saw the current shadow as the thought came to him. The man did not have the air of a policeman, and in a city he would in all probability have carried out his task unnoticed, but here in Dalmering he was an obvious stranger, and as a stranger he inevitably attracted attention, despite the influx of strange faces during the past few days.

However, the important point was not that Pauline Conroy had discovered that she was under observation but that she had revealed herself to be considerably disturbed over the fact. The extent of her angry outburst a few moments earlier had demonstrated just how disturbed she was.

Tremaine put up a carefully exploring hand to his throat and caressed it tenderly. It was painful and swollen, and he had difficulty in swallowing. Martin Vaughan's iron hands had left their mark. His investigations seemed to be leading him into deep waters. It still caused him a shudder to reflect just how near he had come to death on the previous night. The madness in the big man's eyes had held the promise of his destruction; he knew that he had been only just in time to save himself.

Exactly what had he told Martin Vaughan? He recalled that scene when he had sat huddled in the leather armchair in the big man's study, fearful that the other might repeat his attack. When one's life was at stake it was no time to indulge in scruples. One could not always employ strict accuracy in one's statements, and Tremaine was aware that he had said several things that were not altogether true. But in doing so he had gained his ends. He had been an immeasurably relieved man when he had been walking away from "Home Lodge," alive and free to breathe the night air that had seemed to possess the headiness of wine after the terror of the house.

While the thoughts were running almost idly through his

mind, his eyes had been scanning his surroundings for he had come out upon a definite errand. Outside the Admiral he spied Barry Anston's tall form, and he hurried toward him.

The journalist greeted him soberly.

"It looks as though things are getting out of hand," he observed. "I'll be believing soon that this place really has some particular hoodoo attached to it. Poor old girl—I was speaking to her yesterday morning. She wouldn't have harmed a fly. Who could have wanted to kill her?"

"Someone with a good reason," said Tremaine.

Anston looked at him inquiringly, and as he did so he saw the ugly discoloration on his companion's neck.

"Hullo, what have you been up to? Been having a nightmare or something?"

Tremaine clutched at the operative word with all the fervor with which the drowning man is alleged to clutch at the legendary straw.

"That's it," he said eagerly. "A nightmare. Must have been something I ate for supper, I imagine. I woke up trying to throttle myself."

Anston regarded him disbelievingly.

"You seem to have made a pretty good job of it," he remarked drily.

Tremaine was not anxious to undergo a cross-examination. He knew that questions were on the journalist's lips, and he did not wish to reveal his adventure of the previous night. He said quickly: "I wanted to talk to you about Shannon. You know something about him. I thought you were going to tell me what it was the other night when you produced Mrs. Hammond instead."

"I *think* I know something," returned the other. "I'm expecting confirmation today. It should be through by this evening, but until then I'm keeping quiet. After all, I may be wrong."

"I don't think you are," said Tremaine. "By the way," he went on, without offering any explanation for his statement, "I haven't seen Hornsby around lately—the private inquiry agent. Has Mrs. Hammond called him off? There's no further need for him now, of course. There won't be any divorce court evidence required."

"I wonder whether it would have been used, anyway?" said Anston slowly. "It was an odd business. Both those women were undoubtedly in love with Hammond. I didn't see much of Hammond, I know, but from what I did see he didn't strike me as being the sort of fellow many women would fall for. Yet he must have had some fascination for them. The woman he was living with here—Karen is she called?—is a lovely creature. You'd think she'd have had dozens of men after her, and yet she chose Hammond and was what we smugly call living in sin with him. And despite the way in which he was deceiving her and the fact that she was employing Hornsby to watch him, his legal wife didn't really want to divorce him, you know. That's pretty obvious from the way in which she talked to me."

"It's a queer, tortured business," said Tremaine heavily. "And God knows just how tragic it's likely to turn out to be." His eyes stared into the distance without seeing anything for a moment or two, and then he glanced up at his companion again. "Do you know where Hornsby is now?"

"Probably in Colminster," returned Anston. "He's been staying there. It's the next station up the line. I dare say he thought he'd be less conspicuous, although, as you know, plenty of people spotted him in the village here as it was."

Mordecai Tremaine remained talking to the journalist for a little while longer, partly in the hope that Jonathan Boyce might appear, but there was no sign of the inspector, and eventually he said goodbye to Anston and began to make his way back to "Roseland."

Had Boyce been able to report progress in his investigations to his superiors, or had the murder of Edith Lorrington left him groping in the same fog of uncertainty that had surrounded the two previous murders? He had no doubt that the inspector was a very harassed man. Dalmering was in the limelight now. Boyce had to get results and get them quickly. Three unsolved murders in rapid succession was the stuff of which Scotland Yard nightmares were made. Tremaine suspected that the commissioner himself would have been on the wire, demanding hourly reports, insisting on immediate results and leaving the hapless inspector with the uninspiring knowledge that his career hung dangling on a tenuous thread over the edge of the abyss.

For the newspapers, of course, it had been a sensation worthy of their fullest attention. The murder of Philip Hammond had given them every incentive to compete to produce the most arresting headlines; this latest tragedy could not have failed to move them to even greater heights. The evening newspapers would contain articles that would descend in a verbal deluge upon Scotland Yard and call forth even more fiery comments from the commissioner to blister Inspector Boyce's already suffering soul.

The next development was obvious. The inhabitants of Dalmering would be demanding protection. If there had been three murders, there might be a fourth, and a fifth. So far Scotland Yard appeared to have accomplished nothing. There was no knowing when the terror would cease.

Immersed in his thoughts Tremaine did not notice where he was walking and almost collided with someone coming in the opposite direction. He looked up hastily, an apology on his lips, and saw that it was Geoffrey Manning.

"There's no harm done," said Manning cheerily. "As a

matter of fact, we saw that you were preoccupied and were keeping a good lookout." His tone was noticeably carefree. Phyllis Galway was with him, and Tremaine saw that both their faces were flushed and that they shared an air of elation.

"You both look very pleased with life," he observed, a little surprised in view of the prevailing circumstances.

"We are," said Manning. He glanced at the girl and she appeared to give him consent, for he said: "You're the first person we've seen and I've just got to tell you. Phyllis and I are engaged."

Normally, Mordecai Tremaine would have warmed to the note of excitement Geoffrey Manning could not keep out of his voice. His sentimental soul would have been filled with delight, for to see the blossoming of romance was one of his keenest delights. But today he was too conscious of oppression, too much aware of the evil that was loose to respond with his wonted enthusiasm.

"Congratulations," he told them. "I hope you'll both be very happy."

His voice gave him away.

"I know." It was the girl who spoke. "You think that we shouldn't have done it—not now, not with all the tragedy there is around us. You think it doesn't—doesn't fit."

"Well—perhaps," said Tremaine. "Perhaps it is just a little premature, shall we say."

"I understand what you mean," she said. "After all, there've been so many terrible things. Poor Edith—"

"I don't wish to imply," said Tremaine hastily, "that you shouldn't become engaged. The world has to go on. Young people still have to live their lives even if tragedies happen around them. It isn't fair to cramp them. It was just that—just that I think it might be wise not to announce it just yet."

"I didn't really want to tell anyone yet," she admitted. "But you know how it is—you begin to feel that you simply can't keep it a secret. It's stupid, of course. People aren't all that interested in you. And I know that Geoffrey wanted to tell you—"

"Why shouldn't I?" Manning broke in quickly. "Why should we try to hide it?"

"I confess," said Tremaine, "that I'm a little surprised. When I came here a few days ago I didn't realize that you were on such close terms."

Manning seemed to be searching for an answer.

"Phyllis's parents don't altogether approve of me," he said at last. "They think I'm not settled enough in my career—I've ambitions to become an artist although I've a job with a firm in Kingshampton at the moment. We didn't let people suspect how we felt toward each other. There's always so much talk in a village."

"It isn't exactly that Daddy and Mummy don't approve of Geoff," said the girl. "It's just the money question. I suppose they think they're doing it for my own good. But they'll come around—I know they will."

"We're engaged now," said Manning. "I want them all to know. We're going to get married as soon as possible."

"You must forgive Geoff," said the girl, with a smile. "He's a little light-headed, I think. You'd imagine he had only a few days to live to hear him talk!"

"Maybe we have," said Manning. "You've got to enjoy things while you can. How can you tell what's going to happen next? Look at this place—last week it was just a quiet little village. Now, everybody's scared, even if they won't admit it. Who's going to be the next to go? That's what they're all asking. I'm scared for Phyllis. I want to get her away!"

"Geoff—you mustn't talk like that! You sound as though you think these dreadful murders are going to go on!"

Tremaine looked fixedly at Manning. There was an unnaturally tense expression in the other's face. He hesitated for an instant or two. And then: "I'd like to ask you something," he said quietly. "You say that I'm the first person you've told of your engagement. Would you keep it a secret just a little while longer?"

Phyllis Galway looked at him in a puzzled fashion, but the undoubted seriousness of his tone stayed her questions.

"All right," she said slowly. "Perhaps it would be better if we did, after all."

Manning looked as though he had been going to raise objections but had changed his mind. He nodded. "If Phyllis agrees I will," he said reluctantly. "We won't say anything just yet."

He appeared to be unwilling to agree to the proposal and yet equally unwilling to oppose it. Tremaine did not allow him any opportunity to retract.

"Thank you," he said, and he was speaking chiefly to Phyllis Galway. "I can assure you that I've a very good reason for making the request."

With that he nodded and left them. He walked at a brisk pace, for he knew that even yet Manning was uncertain whether or not to let him go unchallenged.

He had taken his stand now. He was committed to the course of action he had been turning tentatively over in his mind before he had met Manning and the girl. And for that it was essential that he should find Jonathan Boyce.

It took him an hour to locate the inspector, but at length he found him—coming from the house where Edith Lorrington had lived, where he had evidently been superintending the painstaking search for clues his men were undertaking.

Tremaine did not allow himself to be swerved from his purpose by the Yard man's air of almost desperate preoccupation.

"Found anything?" he asked.

The inspector swung around upon him. Beneath the bushy eyebrows his eyes held a challenge.

"I've been wanting to see you, Mordecai," he said, a trifle shortly.

Tremaine affected surprise.

"Have you?"

Boyce glanced significantly at the plainclothes men who were in their neighborhood, almost within earshot.

"We'll talk going along the road," he said. And when they were some yards away and there was no further danger of their being overheard, he added: "Things are bad, Mordecai—damned bad. Three murders and nothing to show isn't the sort of program that makes you popular at the Yard."

"I suppose not," said Tremaine commiseratingly. "What's the situation now? Are you up against another blank wall?"

"There isn't even anything resembling a clue," said Boyce. "Whoever killed Edith Lorrington seems to have walked into the house, picked up the poker, killed the old lady, and walked out again without leaving a trace. We've no fingerprints—nothing."

"Anything in her past to give you a lead?"

"Not that we've been able to discover, but it's too early yet to say much about that. She seems to have led a pretty quiet sort of life here. She had a few friends but no very intimate ones." Boyce spread his hands wide, as though he was giving voice to a thought that had been weighing on his mind. "Who could have *wanted* to kill her? With Lydia Dare and with Philip Hammond there was at least some sort of reason behind each killing, even if we can't prove anything definite as yet. But with Edith Lorrington there's nothing at all— nothing except brutal, savage devilry."

"I told you once, Jonathan," observed Tremaine quietly, "that every murder has a motive behind it. This murder isn't the exception."

Boyce took him suddenly by the arm.

"You know something, Mordecai. You've something in your mind—some theory about all this. You were expecting another murder."

"Perhaps I was," returned Tremaine slowly. He said: "If I'd known—if I'd dreamed what was going to happen to Edith Lorrington I would have told you. I don't think there is anything I know that was concealed from you." And then he added, apparently incongruously: "Did I ever tell you I lost several hundred pounds in the Roydale Trust Company?"

Boyce looked at him in a puzzled fashion.

"No," he said, "you didn't. Although you did tell me once that you'd lost some money in a bucket shop that was supposed to be producing a new kind of shock absorber. But the Roydale smash is ancient history. Why are you bringing that up? Roydale got fifteen years, didn't he?"

"That's right," said Tremaine conversationally. "He got fifteen years."

"What the devil is all this leading up to?" demanded Boyce irritably. "We're not discussing your history as a stock market operator. Let's forget the red herrings and get back to where we were."

Mordecai Tremaine was immediately contrite.

"Sorry, Jonathan," he said. "I suppose you are facing a pretty serious crisis."

"Crisis," said Boyce, "seems to me to be a mild understatement. I'm heading for an explosion that is going to blow my pension to the never-never land. I'd hate to repeat what the commissioner told me over the phone this morning."

"You've let him know what results you've obtained so far?"

"The trouble is that there are too many results," said Boyce. "When I put someone in the dock I like to be sure that it's the right someone. Here there are too many people who might have done it. They can't all be guilty."

"Three of them could be."

"*If* all three crimes are unconnected. Which I'm inclined to doubt." The inspector waited a moment or two, and then he said: "There's a shortcut from Edith Lorrington's house to 'Roseland.' You can go from one house to the other in four or five minutes…if you're familiar with a path that isn't very easy to find." He added, casually: "You were with Dr. Russell all the evening, weren't you, Mordecai?"

"Yes," said Tremaine, waiting for the next inevitable question.

"I don't suppose you actually sat with him all the time. Didn't he work in his surgery for a while, for instance?"

"I believe he did."

Mordecai Tremaine did not know what to say next. It was plain enough what Boyce was hinting at. He decided that the only thing he could do would be to recognize the obvious, and he said, after a pause: "What makes you think that Paul might have killed her?"

Boyce gave a sigh of relief.

"I'm glad you're taking it this way. I know that Dr. Russell is a friend of yours. But we've got to face the facts. There's that legacy…that could have been a reason for killing Lydia Dare. The others might have been unpremeditated. Perhaps Hammond and Miss Lorrington looked like becoming dangerous. He had to kill them to cover himself."

"If Paul killed Lydia Dare," said Tremaine, "why did he ask me to do my utmost to find the murderer?"

"An added precaution. He thought he was safe and that it would help to divert suspicion still further. Of course, at that time he didn't bargain for any more killings."

"Last night," said Tremaine, "when you called at the house you were going to say something to me and then you stopped. Was it because Paul was there?"

"Yes, it was." Boyce added, as though a surprising thought had just occurred to him, "Do *you* think he did it?"

"I might," said Tremaine evasively. "And I might not. You may be interested to know," he went on, changing the subject in a blatant fashion, "that our friend Shannon was actually at Colminster on the occasion when he was supposed to be in London discussing business with his acquaintance Millward."

"I've seen Anston," said Boyce. "I know all about it. Don't," he added, "make such obvious attempts to head me off."

"It's all right," said Tremaine. "Tonight you'll have your murderer."

He spoke so casually that at first Boyce did not realize what he had said. And then he stopped short in the roadway, and his voice was sharp.

"*What* did you say?"

"I said," repeated Mordecai Tremaine, "that tonight you will have the murderer. *If,*" he added, "you'll do what I ask."

He told the inspector what it was he required and it was significant that Jonathan Boyce heard him through and raised no objections.

17

There was no rehearsal of *Murder Has a Motive* in progress, but there was a drama being enacted on the stage of the village hall. Perhaps it was imbued with an atmosphere even more compelling than that of the play by virtue of the very fact that it was a drama in which there were no consciously effective lines being delivered by hardworking actors under the stress of an artificial emotion. Words, when they came, were hushed, their banality betraying the nervous tension by which the speakers were actuated. They crept into the silence as if they knew that they were intruders and faded hesitantly into nothingness again, leaving an uncomfortable air of apology behind.

Mordecai Tremaine looked fleetingly around at his companions. His action was barely perceptible, but he could have closed his eyes and painted a vivid verbal picture of the scene.

He could have described the heavy figure of Martin Vaughan, overflowing the inadequate chair upon which the big man was seated and lowering over the rest of the company like some brooding colossus, out of place among pygmies and at the same time suspicious and afraid of them. He could have described Howard Shannon, plump hands nervously clasping and unclasping in front of him, darting sudden, furtive glances all around.

Next to Shannon he could have given an accurate portrait of Pauline Conroy, sulkily dark, with rebellious, conscious beauty in every exaggeration of her seductive form, still posing for the audience despite the sharp quality of the fear that was racing unpleasantly inside her. It was a measure of her apprehension that she had allowed her right hand to drop secretively below the edge of the table and search out Serge Galeski's left. She was holding it tightly, her palm moist against his.

Tremaine was aware that she was clinging both literally and figuratively to Galeski for support, although the producer was betraying no sign of it. He seemed unaffected by his companion's agitation. The expression on his face was that of self-recognized superiority; his too-frequent glances around the table were a supercilious if unspoken challenge. It was as if he was saying that they could prove nothing against him and that he sat despising them, aloofly secure.

Would he still be so blatantly contemptuous when the evening's drama had run its course? Mordecai Tremaine reflected grimly that before he left the stage Mr. Serge Galeski's air of assurance was likely to be dissipated.

He peered beyond the stage lights into the gloomy body of the hall. He could not see clearly, but he fancied that in the deeper shadows at the back there was an occasional whiteness that was a face, and by keeping his eyes focused in that direction he thought that he could recognize Barry Anston and Gerald Farrant.

He had expected the journalist to be there. Anston knew that another chapter in the story that he had been sent to Dalmering to cover was about to be released for publication. Whether he expected it to be a sensational one Tremaine did not know, but even if he had been completely skeptical over the likelihood of any developments the other would still have been present as a matter of routine. However, it was possible that it was not only routine but a significant word from Inspector Boyce that had been responsible for his appearance. The Yard man would undoubtedly have told him that it might be worth his while to pay a visit to the village hall.

It was by his eyes that Tremaine knew Gerald Farrant. They burned out of the gloom, so that it was only after you had been gripped by their fierce intensity that you became aware of the taut white face in which they were set. Farrant had come for vengeance.

There were others in the hall besides the journalist and Farrant. There was no one on guard at the doors to keep them out, and somehow the whisper of what was to take place must have traveled through the village. No doubt they were mainly reporters. It was too late to worry about them now, but Mordecai Tremaine hoped that they would remain quiet and not bring attention upon themselves.

There was a tingling in his veins. This was his hour. The elaborate theory he had built up was about to undergo its test. If it failed, if it crumpled uselessly beneath the impact of his experiment, then he had laid himself open to being labeled as an object of contempt and scorn, and he would have no words with which to face Jonathan Boyce. There would be no alternative but to leave Dalmering immediately and take his shame and his confusion with him.

But he knew that it would not fail. Confidence was flowing strongly within him, like the steady, irresistible surging tide of a triumphant sea.

His glance traveled again around the table at which he and his companions were seated. It rested briefly upon Karen Hammond. No one in the village knew that she had not been Philip Hammond's wife. The dead man's real wife had made no statement to the newspapers, nor had she uttered any word to lead to a public scandal or a muttering of tongues in the village. She had, in fact, behaved with a surprising amount of discretion and forbearance. Tremaine suspected that the answer lay in the fact that she had been in love with her husband. She had kept silence in order to preserve Philip Hammond's name as long as she could.

Karen Hammond's blond hair, freed from the closely fitting hat she had worn to the hall, was in vivid contrast to the severely cut dark costume that served to indicate what was believed to be her widowhood. Its tumbled, gleaming tresses framed a face that was stonily impassive in its marbled grief. There was no sign now of the nervous fear that had previously marked her; it was as though Philip Hammond's death had frozen both her terror and her heart. She was sitting motionless at the table, and the blue eyes that were fixed steadily in front of her could see none of the things at which she appeared to be staring.

Tremaine looked beyond her to the head of the table, where Sandra Borne occupied the position of chairman. Her eyes were bent sympathetically upon Karen Hammond. She sensed his glance, and her head turned to meet his gaze. An appeal came into her face, and he nodded understandingly and made a gesture toward the two vacant chairs at her right hand.

Jean and Paul Russell had not yet made their appearance. Until they had arrived he did not wish the business of the evening to begin. It was essential for his purpose that all the actors in his cast should be in their places.

Martin Vaughan noticed their exchange of glances. His chair creaked as his big frame moved.

"What are we all waiting for?" he demanded. "If it was so important to call this meeting why don't we get on with it instead of sitting here like a lot of dummies?"

Sandra Borne looked full at him.

"We're waiting," she said, "for Doctor Russell and Jean. We can't start until they're here, but I don't think they will be long now."

Her level, patient tones seemed to placate the big man. Oddly for him he even looked a little shamefaced.

"Sorry, Sandra—I didn't mean to be short with you. It's just this waiting about with nothing happening…"

The unusual meekness of Vaughan's attitude sent a tremor of movement around the table, as if an electric current had been suddenly passed through a wire linking up all the people who were seated there. Shannon moved his head quickly; the flabbiness in his cheeks quivered jerkily as he turned. He eyed Vaughan suspiciously, almost as if he had been made abruptly aware of danger from an entirely unsuspected source.

Tremaine surveyed his companions critically from behind the inevitably insecure pince-nez that lent him such a harmless appearance. He was watching for all signs of reaction among the little group about him.

Phyllis Galway was looking across the table at Vaughan. Her lips were slightly parted. She had the air of a child who had been invited to a grown-up party and who was tremendously excited but a little scared. Tremaine thought that her youthful loveliness had never been more marked.

He glanced at Geoffrey Manning with a slight pang of what might have been the envy of an old man who was regretting the opportunities of a youth that he could never see again. The pang momentarily gained in force as he saw that Manning was paying no attention to the girl he was to marry. He should, said Mordecai Tremaine's sentimental soul wrathfully, have no eyes for any other person but her. If he could ignore that fresh appealing beauty he did not deserve his good fortune.

Even as the thought was born, Manning ceased to look at Serge Galeski and his gaze rested upon the girl. The grimness in his face softened, so that his always somewhat rugged features lost something of the carved ugliness that had been marring them and he looked more like the agreeable youngster of a few days previously. It was, however, only a brief metamorphosis. The hardness and the strained expectancy came back. His eyes left the girl's eager figure and took on once again their look of shadowed brooding.

Under Manning's gaze an angry flush had spread to Serge Galeski's face. The deliberately untidy, long-haired producer had already lost a little of his satisfied composure. He was searching Manning's face in his turn, as if trying to find an assuring reason for the prolonged stare the other had given him. His eyes flickered uneasily to Pauline Conroy. He cleared his throat.

"Miss Conroy and I can't afford to wait much longer," he announced, assuming an air of importance. "Our time is valuable."

"I'm sorry, Mr. Galeski," said Sandra Borne's tactfully persuasive tones. "I hope we don't have to keep you much longer."

Despite his protest Galeski had made no attempt to move. His utterance had been purely a face-saving one. Tremaine knew that the man would not leave until the grand climax had been reached.

He was aware of a stir of admiration within him as he watched Sandra Borne. Her nervous tension was certainly no less than that of any of the others, but she betrayed the least sign of it. She was still occupying the position she had been occupying for so long in the village—she was the hardworking, willing horse, who accepted all the least enjoyable tasks and received none of the limelight. It was taken for granted that if there was anything to be set right, anything to be organized, it was Sandy who would shoulder the burden. It was Sandy who would see that everything was all right on the night.

During his brief stay in the village Tremaine had discovered the truth of it in a dozen little ways. To do the other members of the community justice it was partly her own cheerfulness and readiness to accept new responsibilities that was the cause of the variety of the tasks she performed in the common good. Sandy was a village institution. She could always be relied upon.

But although she was outwardly still the same, still ready to carry on with her self-imposed work, Tremaine was certain that she was very near the breaking point now. The lines of fatigue and exhaustion in her face were more deeply etched than they had been even a day or so before; the shadows under her eyes had become larger and more pronounced. Her self-possession was a pose that she was finding it increasingly difficult to maintain; the cost to her nerves of preserving it was reaching the danger point.

Howard Shannon shifted uneasily. He had not the same degree of control over himself; the strain of waiting was becoming more than he could endure without making some effort to reduce the tension. He licked his lips furtively. He seemed to be on the point of saying something when there was a sound at the back of the stage, and in a moment or two Jean and Paul Russell came into view, having evidently entered the hall by the back way.

Paul Russell gave a quick, uncertain glance around him.

"Sorry we're late, everybody," he said, a little jerkily. "A last-minute call held us up."

"That's all right, Paul," said Sandra Borne. She indicated the two vacant chairs. "Will you and Jean sit here?"

The gathering was complete now. Mordecai Tremaine wondered what the watchers sitting silently and almost invisibly at the back of the hall were thinking of it. There must be a strange air of fantasy about the scene, so many of them crowded around a table in the center of the lighted stage and the hall stretching gloomily empty behind them except for those few unofficial observers.

Paul Russell fumbled with his chair as he sat down. It was not usual for him to be so uncertain in his movements. He avoided looking at Mordecai Tremaine.

"You're still driving yourself to death for us all, I see, Sandy," he remarked, but although the words were normal enough his tone was a betrayal.

Tremaine glanced in his direction—and caught Jean's eyes upon him, apprehensive and unhappy. Dr. Russell and his wife were in an undoubted state of agitation. Jean flushed and turned hurriedly toward Sandra.

"I hear a rumor that you're leaving us, Sandy. Is it true?"

"Yes, it's true, Jean," she returned. "I've tried hard, but I can't stay here any longer. There are too many—too many memories."

Martin Vaughan coughed. She looked down the table at him.

"Of course," she said. "Sorry, Martin. You don't want to hear about me. Now that Jean and Paul are here we can go ahead." Her glance swept around the table, including them all in its scope. "We all know each other, so that there isn't any need for me to attempt to be formal." She hesitated, choosing her words. "I hope no one minds my taking the chair. I don't want any of you to feel that I'm attempting to—to run things. But I've—well, I've had a good deal to do with the various arrangements we've made, and it seemed to be the best thing to do."

Vaughan leaned forward. Momentarily the bitterness was back in his voice.

"It's all right, Sandy. One of us had to do it, and you're more qualified than most of us. We all know that it's the winding-up meeting."

"Well, yes, I suppose that is the best way to describe it. After Lydia's death we all decided that we'd carry on with the play, but I don't think there's anyone who is in favor of it now. There's been too much real tragedy around us for any of us to want to go on play-acting." Sandra Borne looked questioningly at them. "*Is* there anyone who thinks we ought to go on? I've been in touch with the people at Kingshampton," she added. "There's no question of our being under any obligation to go on with the production. They understand our position."

There was a silence. She looked at them all in turn. She said: "Paul? Geoffrey? Pauline?"

She lingered over the last name. Pauline Conroy shivered.

"No," she said, in a strangled voice bereft of her usual dramatic tones. "No, I couldn't play in it now."

Martin Vaughan's clenched fist came down hard upon the table with a force that startled them.

"The damned play's a hoodoo! We've seen the last of it. We all know that." He glared truculently around at them. "And we all know that we didn't need a meeting to decide that there wasn't going to be any production. We didn't come here to discuss whether we're going to continue with *Murder Has a Motive*. We came because we *had* to come. All of us were told that we'd be here or else!"

"Martin—"

Sandra Borne's hurried protest was doomed to be unheeded before it was made. The big man had exploded the dynamite. And because they had all known it was there they sat breathlessly expectant, waiting for the next development.

Vaughan's head was thrust forward challengingly.

"It's true, isn't it? It was all very polite, but that was what it meant. We're here because the police wanted us to come."

Mordecai Tremaine's voice cut into the strained silence that followed Vaughan's outburst.

"Almost correct," he said quietly, "but not quite. You are all here because *I* wanted you to come."

His calm shouldering of the responsibility disconcerted the big man, and before he could return to the attack Tremaine had forestalled him and was on his feet.

"I owe you an apology, ladies and gentlemen," he told

them. "That is, all except one of you—the person who killed Lydia Dare and who also killed Philip Hammond and Edith Lorrington."

There would be no interruption now. He had known what the effect would be before he had spoken. Even Martin Vaughan's aggressive attitude had vanished; the big man had ceased to loom across the table and had retreated to his chair, his truculence no longer there. Tremaine squared his shoulders. He had his audience. Before him was a lake of silence into which his words would drop effectively and unopposed.

"I wanted you all to come here tonight," he said, "because I wanted to talk to you. I wanted to talk to you about *Murder Has a Motive*. I have a copy of it here." He indicated the square, brown-paper parcel that lay on the table in front of him. "You know, of course, that I attended two of your rehearsals, and during the past few days I've also studied the script very carefully. And I would like you all to consider it very carefully yourselves—perhaps from a different angle to that to which you have been accustomed."

He paused to allow them to appreciate the significance of what he had said. And then: "Some of the remarks I am going to make," he said, "may seem to you to be unwarrantably personal. I am a stranger here among you, and I have no official status. But I would ask you to remember that three people have been murdered in this village and that the murderer is still walking freely in our midst—*perhaps preparing to add a fourth murder to the list*."

"Do you think," said Vaughan sharply, "that there will be a fourth?"

"I said that *perhaps* the killer is planning a fourth," said Tremaine. "Let that serve as justification for anything I may say."

"I don't understand what all this is about," broke in Serge Galeski suddenly, "but if you know something, go ahead and say what it is."

"I'm aware that it hasn't been an easy time for any of you, Mr. Galeski," said Tremaine, asperity in his voice. "I know that suspense isn't pleasant. But I'm dealing with this in my own way."

He went on: "In the play a woman is murdered by a man who loves her, because she is going to marry someone else. In your production, Miss Galway played the woman and Mr. Vaughan played the murderer. There was a real-life parallel, as I believe you all realized at a rehearsal that followed shortly after the death of Miss Dare and at which I was present. Mr. Vaughan was in love with Lydia Dare. She was to have married another man—Mr. Farrant, to state his name. And she died. She died in circumstances that placed Mr. Vaughan in a very dangerous position and brought him to the notice of the police."

As though he had expected that it was here that he might begin to face interruptions, he continued quickly: "Later in the course of the play, a man—played by Mr. Shannon—is murdered by his wife because he has been unfaithful to her. In real life Mr. Philip Hammond was murdered. It was suspected by at least one of you—and probably more—that he had—to express it without mincing words—a mistress whom he had been seeing in London. Again, you will observe, there was a remarkable parallel between the murder in the play and the murder that actually happened. And just as Mr. Vaughan had been compromised by the first murder, so Mrs. Karen Hammond was seriously compromised by the second. To point out their guilt beyond all doubt their motives had already been clearly revealed on the stage in the crimes in which you were acting."

Tremaine stole a quick glance at Karen Hammond. Her blond head was lowered and he could not see her face, but he knew from her stillness that she was listening to him in fear.

He drew a deep breath. He had skated over the thin ice of her relationship with Philip Hammond, and so far there had been no challenging note. For the moment at least the murders were holding the full interest of all his listeners.

"One coincidence," he went on, "could have been overlooked. Two were impossible to accept. There was, in my opinion, only one answer, and that was that the murders in the play and the real murders were connected. In other words *that the person who wrote the play wrote it with Lydia Dare and Philip Hammond in mind, knowing that they were going to die.*"

Serge Galeski had completely lost his air of superior detachment. There was no trace of careless unconcern in his manner now.

"You mean," he said hoarsely, "that the play was *written by* the murderer?"

"Yes," said Mordecai Tremaine, "that's what I mean."

Martin Vaughan said: "In that case, where does the murder of Edith Lorrington come in? Where is your parallel in the play for *that*?"

"There isn't one," said Tremaine. "Because it wasn't intended that Edith Lorrington should die."

"Then why *was* she killed?"

"To save the murderer's neck. She knew too much."

"If she knew enough to make the killer run the risk of getting rid of her why didn't she go to someone with her knowledge? It wasn't like Edith to keep silence. Why didn't she tell your friend Inspector Boyce?"

"I think," said Tremaine, "that the answer is that she didn't know she knew."

There had been tension before; now fear and suspicion had broken loose and were running wild among them. The people seated around the table were no longer friendly members of the same community. They were hostile strangers, eyeing each other with furtive glances, afraid of their neighbors who had suddenly acquired the dark, terrifying quality of the unknown.

Howard Shannon's plump fingers plucked at his tie in a nervous gesture. He swallowed hard, as if to compel his vocal cords to do his bidding.

"How do we know," he said, with an attempt at bluster, "that you're not inventing all this?"

Mordecai Tremaine looked at him and through him.

"I'm not inventing it, Mr. Shannon," he said. "Any more than I'm inventing the fact that on the night that Lydia Dare was killed you weren't in London as you stated but in Colminster. You might, indeed, quite easily have spent part of the time in Dalmering. You could have walked back to Colminster in less than an hour and a half, and no one would have seen you."

Shannon's face was ashen. His hands shook. He placed them beneath the table in an attempt to hide his agitation, but he could not bring the color back to his flabbily gray cheeks.

"You're trying to trap me," he said. "You can't prove anything—"

"I have no doubt," said Tremaine, "that by now Inspector Boyce is able to prove it beyond question." His eyes held Shannon's. "I want you to understand," he said, "that I am not speaking in the dark. I *know* how all the murders were committed and by whom."

Someone gave a little gasp, stifled frantically as it came. All their eyes were fixed upon Mordecai Tremaine, and no one but the person responsible knew from whence it emanated.

"For God's sake," burst out Geoffrey Manning, "if you really know, don't keep this up!"

"The more I studied the play," went on Tremaine, as if he had not heard, "the more convinced I became that it could only have been written by someone who knew Dalmering intimately and that 'Alexis Kent' was a pen name hiding the identity of one of you. I'm a little surprised that the same thought didn't occur to anyone else. I wonder if it *did* occur to Philip Hammond? I'm told that he was offered a part but that he refused it. The reason must be obvious to you now—he didn't wish to play the unfaithful husband because that is precisely what he knew himself to be. It may have been because he realized that someone knew his secret that he came back here after the rehearsal that night without telling even his—wife—where he was going."

His hesitation over the word "wife" was unintentional. The term had come to him instinctively before he was aware of it. Karen Hammond was looking full at him now, and he saw her wince.

"Probably a note was given to him," he went on. "A note

that he felt he dare not ignore. That, admittedly, is guesswork, but I think the deduction is justified. We know that Philip Hammond came to the hall, and the murderer must have been waiting for him. He was struck down without warning by a blow from the hammer the murderer knew was kept there. His body was dragged into the gas stove, and the killer watched him die.

"Can you imagine how gruesome that scene must have been? A man's life slowly ebbing away with the moments, and the murderer standing by with a fearful, thumping heart, listening to every sound, in mortal dread that someone might come in but knowing no repentance. It must have needed cold-blooded devilry to do that, a callous, vicious purpose.

"But the murderer was—*is*—cold-blooded. The death of Edith Lorrington also tells us that. No doubt she smiled a welcome as she turned to greet her visitor, in whom she saw a friend, but in the next moment she had been beaten down, brutally and with premeditated force.

"From the very first moment of discovery the implacable intent of the murderer has been made evident. There was no mercy in the hand that struck Lydia Dare to her death, no pity in the heart and mind behind the knife buried so murderously in her breast on that dark and lonely path. Poor Lydia! She'd been so happy. She'd been looking forward to marriage and life with the man she loved. Whoever was responsible for the destruction of all those dear dreams of hers must pay the penalty for that black crime. It was a dreadful, villainous thing that was done in the darkness there."

He stopped. His glance went to Sandra Borne, sitting stonily at the head of the table. He said: "Not one life was wantonly broken but two. Which one of us but would have done our utmost to stay that tragedy could we have been at hand? Most of you, I know, would be prepared to swear that Sandra, for instance, would have risked anything to prevent that brutal crime."

She lowered her eyes.

"Of course," she said shakily. "Lydia was my friend. I—I loved her."

"Oh no," said Mordecai Tremaine quietly, "you hated her."

And then, suddenly, his figure was stiff and terrible, and his voice held an icy anger that lashed her soul.

"You hated her! Didn't you!"

18

Sandra Borne was crouching back in her chair, one hand to her mouth and her eyes dilated with terror. It was as though fear had paralyzed her.

Mordecai Tremaine said: "You hated her. You hated her because you were jealous of her. And you were jealous of her because she had all the things you yourself wanted. She was able to make friends easily; she occupied the limelight; people sought her out; she was admired by men. While you told yourself that you were always in the position of having to do all the drudgery and that you were perpetually left out of things where men were concerned.

"Everyone regarded you as the loyal, willing, uncomplaining Sandy who was always ready to take on the jobs other people were too lazy to bother about; always prepared to do all the unpleasant tasks for the good of everyone else; always treating difficulties with a smile. You were regarded as a standby for everything in the village; you were always being required to organize or to help. People thought that you enjoyed doing it; that you liked being always busy, always engaged in running some local charity or arranging flower shows, doing the routine duties attached to any village function and not coming forward for any bequests or publicity.

"But, although no one suspected it, all the time envy was gnawing inside you and was slowly poisoning your heart. You smiled at people with your eyes and uttered words of friendship with your lips, but all the while you were jealously hating them, wishing you could destroy them for leading lives that seemed to be so much fuller and richer than your own. You envied the fact that they apparently had all they wished for without having to exert themselves to obtain it. I say 'apparently' because only the owner of a warped and twisted mind could have argued like that, could have believed that no one else knew strain and sorrow and anxiety.

"Gradually you came to hate everyone belonging to the circle of your acquaintances whom you believed to be more fortunate, more favored by life than yourself. You hated Karen Hammond. You hated her because she was happy and had a husband who seemed to idolize her. You hated Lydia. You hated—others.

"And you nursed your hate. You nursed it and allowed it to grow until it became a festering, evil thing, obsessing your soul, and until it finally drove you to kill. To kill—not suddenly, in the passion of a moment, but cunningly, secretly, your purpose working itself remorselessly out through the weeks and months.

"I think that it was when you learned that Lydia was going to marry Gerald Farrant that your jealousy reached its climax. You knew that Martin Vaughan was in love with her. And when you heard that two men wanted her enough to want to marry her, and yet not even one had ever suggested marriage to you, it was the last indignity to your unhappy, perverted mind. You began to plan your revenge.

"You wrote *Murder Has a Motive*. You wrote it with the deliberate intention of seeing the murders in the play paralleled in real life. You wrote it so that it would be a pointer to the police as to the identity of the guilty persons when the crimes were being investigated.

"It was in your cleverness that your mistakes began. You took the manuscript of the play to Kingshampton to have it typed. You told the typing agency that it was a play that was out of print and of which you wanted a copy. That move was careless—especially as Edith Lorrington was on friendly terms with the people who run the typing agency in question—but it happens to be the only one of its kind in this area, and I don't doubt that you relied upon the fact that even if inquiries did happen to be made and the question of the original manuscript was raised, you could always say that your friend Lydia had asked you to take it over for her. And Lydia, being dead, would not be able to deny your story.

"But you overlooked one little point. A lot of people in the village could have written parts of *Murder Has a Motive*. More than one of them probably suspected or guessed that Martin Vaughan was in love with Lydia Dare. But at the time when the play must have been written there was only one person who could have known so much about the lives of Dalmering's inhabitants and who could also have known that Lydia was in love with someone else—and that person was her closest friend, Sandra Borne, in whom it was natural that she should have confided. *Because at that time no one else in the village knew that Lydia Dare had even met Gerald Farrant, still less that she was in love with him!*"

Tremaine paused. There was no sound in the hall—only the harsh, spasmodic, overemphasized noise of the labored, unnatural breathing of the woman he was indicting. The others were sitting perfectly still, not looking at Sandra Borne, waiting for him to unfold the remainder of the grim tragedy under whose shadow they had been living.

"A little while ago," he said, "I took the manuscript of the play up to Anita Lane, the London stage and film writer. She happens to be a friend of mine, and I asked her to read it and let me have her opinion. She told me that she thought that the author was a woman and that in places her own thoughts and desires had crept into the dialogue she had written for her characters. It confirmed my belief that, if I wanted to find 'Alexis Kent,' I need look no farther than Sandra Borne.

"When I was at Dr. Russell's house on one occasion," he went on, still speaking directly to a white-faced woman whose staring eyes were not looking at him, "you tried to give the impression that you hadn't known of Farrant's existence for a long while; that Lydia hadn't confided in you. It was too close to my arrival here for me to have developed any real suspicions, but it didn't seem to me to tally with what I'd been told about the closeness of your relations with Lydia Dare. And when, one by one, the other points began to arise, I was certain that you'd lied.

"You remember why you called that evening, don't you? Ostensibly it was to relieve your mind because you'd not been frank with Inspector Boyce. You said that you hadn't told him the truth because you hadn't wished to injure your friend's reputation or to throw suspicion on Martin Vaughan. Your real reason was to reveal to the inspector that Martin Vaughan had been in love with Lydia and to make quite certain that suspicion *was* thrown on him. You knew that if you came to Dr. Russell he would be forced to do his duty and advise you to tell the police the whole story.

"You see, your plan didn't stop at killing Lydia. You wanted to kill Martin Vaughan as well. You wanted him to be hanged for the murder. You knew where Lydia was going that night and what time she would be returning. You stole the knife from Vaughan's house—you would have had ample opportunity during one of your visits to him with Lydia. And you stole a pair of gardening clogs from the shed in Dr. Russell's garden. You wore those on the night of the murder. They were big enough to slip over your shoes—you have a very small foot—and they left a footprint that was sufficiently misleading for your purpose. It was clever of you to stand on the only patch of soft ground so that the police would have what looked like a valuable clue, but perhaps it was just a little overdone. It seemed too good to be true that the murderer should have stood so thoughtfully on just that spot, especially as it was too far from the bushes to make it likely that he was waiting in hiding there for any length of time. I was dubious about those two prints from the beginning. And there was that cigarette butt—it was another piece of local color that didn't seem to ring quite true. It hadn't been stamped into the ground, as it might have been if a person who smoked so much that a cigarette had been a necessity even during those tense moments of waiting had thrown down the stump in a moment of forgetfulness and put a foot upon it automatically. It had been only half smoked, and it had clearly been pinched out between finger and thumb—almost as though it had been deliberately left there.

"When Lydia Dare came along the path you leaped out

upon her and killed her. She was your friend, but you struck her murderously down; hate strengthened your arm, drove the weapon deep into her yielding body. The knife, of course, you left; it was part of your plan that it should be discovered and traced to Martin Vaughan. The gardening clogs, which you had stolen several days previously, you returned at the first available moment. It had to be at a time when both Dr. Russell and his wife were out, and your opportunity came when they drove together to meet me at the station. When I was introduced to you for the first time you'd just appeared from behind the garage at Roseland—you'd obviously come from the garden. I didn't realize it at the time, of course, but you'd just returned the clogs. The shed had been locked, but you had been able to pitch them in through the window. Dr. Russell found them later lying on the floor."

Paul Russell had given a start when Tremaine had mentioned the gardening clogs. As he heard the explanation of their theft and return, a look of surprise and understanding came into his eyes. It mingled with the horror that had been there since that first accusation had been leveled at Sandra Borne.

"Your plan seemed to be going well," went on Tremaine's level, implacable tones. "Lydia was dead, and you were already doing all you could to embroil Martin Vaughan. If the question of *Murder Has a Motive* came up, you knew that suspicion would fall upon him again because his name had been connected with it from the very beginning. Everyone in the village believed that that particular play had been chosen because Vaughan had wanted it. The truth was that Lydia had asked him to use his influence to ensure its being performed and had asked him not to mention her name in connection with it. I've had a—a talk—with Mr. Vaughan"—Tremaine caressed his neck significantly—"and he's told me all that happened. He sponsored the play for Lydia's sake. She asked him to do so for *your* sake. I don't know what arguments you used in order to persuade her, but as the person she believed to be her dearest friend, she obviously would have been only too willing to help you and to keep your interest in the play secret.

"The next step was the murder of Philip Hammond. You knew that he was on intimate terms with another woman. You pretended to blackmail him and instructed him to come to the village hall alone after one of the rehearsals. You were waiting for him in the darkness, and before he could defend himself you struck him with the hammer you had ready in your hand. You aren't a big woman, but you had hate and desperation to nerve you, and the hammer was a vicious enough weapon to enable you to strike a blow that stunned him. You dragged him into the room at the back of the stage, and when you were certain that he was dead, you lifted him into the trunk that was used in the play.

"There was a rehearsal on the day of Lydia Dare's funeral.

People thought that it hadn't been canceled because in the emotional upheaval everyone had overlooked it. But *you* hadn't overlooked it. You didn't cancel that rehearsal because you knew that Philip Hammond's body was in the trunk and you wanted it to be discovered dramatically. You wanted to exact the last ounce of good measure from your revenge. You wanted to terrify and shock; to see fear and horror in people's faces.

"You knew that sooner or later the fact that Philip Hammond was having an affair would become known. I dare say that you would have taken good care that it did leak out. That would have set the stage for Karen Hammond's torture and the next scene in your devil's plan. You wanted her to die for the murder of her husband.

"By that time I was beginning to make progress. I thought I knew what you had done and what you would do next. I thought I knew whom it was you had intended to be the next to die. I made arrangements to prevent your succeeding again, to prevent your destruction of another human life. But something went wrong. You didn't strike where I had expected. It was Edith Lorrington who was your victim.

"At first I thought that my theory was false, that all the time I had been following the wrong track. And then I recalled what I should have recollected before, and I knew why you had been forced to kill Edith Lorrington instead of your intended victim. She was a menace to you. She herself was unaware of it, but you had no guarantee that she wouldn't one day awake to the significance of what she knew. And when she did that, her knowledge might hang you.

"Edith Lorrington suffered from insomnia. On the night that Lydia Dare died, she was walking about the neighborhood and she happened to pass your cottage. She confirmed that you were in—as you had told the police—because she had seen the light and heard your wireless. But without realizing what it meant, she told Dr. Russell and myself that there had been a swing program on. And it's a well-known fact that you can't stand swing and that whenever a program of that type comes on, *you invariably switch off your radio*!"

There was triumph in Mordecai Tremaine's voice. The triumph of a man who sees the steady, patient labors upon which he has been engaged coming to sure fruition. He said: "Edith Lorrington also told us that she wished to see you and lend you a new novel that she thought you would like. She said that she had tried to give it to you before but that she hadn't been able to catch you. She didn't *say* that she'd done so, but, knowing her, I'm certain that, seeing the light in your cottage and being anxious to give you that novel, she not only passed by but made an attempt to attract your attention. She didn't succeed because, although the wireless was playing loudly and the light was burning, those things were merely to build up your alibi. You yourself weren't there. *You were*

*waiting outside in the darkness for Lydia Dare, with murder in
your heart!*

"Unfortunately it wasn't until it was too late to save Edith
Lorrington that I awoke to the truth. But after Inspector
Boyce had brought the news of her murder I suddenly connected the fact that everyone knew that you didn't listen to
swing programs with what Edith Lorrington had said, and I
knew why you had killed her.

"It's the simple things that cause murderers to hang," he
added grimly. "You should have studied the radio programs
covering the period for which you intended to be away from
the cottage and made certain that there would be no changes
that might make things awkward for you."

There was a cold, chilling note in the quiet words; a note
that seemed to breathe an icy, accusing wind and that carried
Sandra Borne's doom. Mordecai Tremaine stood looking
down upon her with the dispassionate face of a judge. He
said: "Lydia Dare used to say that she had the feeling that
horror was lurking in Dalmering; that some evil presence
seemed to be hovering over the village. Other people have
talked in the same way. The newspapers have printed articles
on the same theme, and at first, I, too, thought I could sense
what others had apparently experienced.

"But I discovered that all the fears, all the whispers, all the
hinted terror had a common origin—Sandra Borne! It was

you who built up the atmosphere of suspicion and horror. It was you who slowly spread fear through the village. You preyed first of all upon Lydia's mind. You pretended to be uncertain and afraid yourself, and gradually you wore down her nerves. After her death, of course, things became easier for you. With the aid of your carefully planted suggestions there were plenty of susceptible people who were willing to fall in unknowingly with your plans and spread the report that the village lay under some malign influence. You had only to wait and watch the campaign you had started to steadily develop.

"There *was* a malign influence, but it was a human one." Tremaine's voice became harder, icier, more laden with accusation. "There *was* evil in Dalmering," he said. "But it was the evil in your heart!"

Sandra Borne raised her head.

"Damn you," she said. "Damn you, damn you, *damn you*! *You knew it all the time!*"

She moved with a tigerish fury. Tremaine's voice rapped out sharply in warning: "*Look out, Paul!*"

Paul Russell reacted swiftly. He flung himself backward, and as he did so his left arm went up to ward aside the woman's right, the hand of which was holding the viciously stabbing knife. Before she could strike again the quick scuffle of feet sounded urgently on the stage behind her.

Biting, spitting, snarling, like a cornered hellcat, Sandra Borne was overpowered by the efficient combined strength of Jonathan Boyce and two of his men.

"I have a warrant for your arrest on a charge of willful murder," said the inspector. "I have to warn you that anything you say may be taken down and used as evidence."

Mordecai Tremaine drew a long breath of relief.

"I think that was what you wanted, wasn't it, Jonathan?"

Inspector Boyce nodded.

"Yes," he said, "that was what I wanted."

Disheveled, her hair streaming down over a passion-contorted face, Sandra Borne's wild eyes glared at them.

"All right," she said. "I did it! I killed them! I planned it all, just as you said! I hated them. I wanted to see them squirm and suffer. I wanted to smash their smug, complacent lives!" She struggled in the arms of the detectives who were holding her, thrust her face forward. There was no trace of the eager little woman they had known. She had disintegrated into an evil fury. "I hate all of you!" she screamed. "All of you—you hear me? You—!"

She uttered a filthy word. Mordecai Tremaine felt a little sick. He turned his head away. Jonathan Boyce made a gesture to his subordinates.

"Take her away," he said quietly.

It seemed a long time before anyone spoke. And then Paul

Russell said, shakily: "Thanks, Mordecai. She meant to kill. It was only your warning that saved me. I don't know how you realized so quickly that I was the person she intended to attack."

"I remarked just now," said Tremaine, "that Sandra Borne was forced to change her plans when she killed Edith Lorrington. The third victim had originally been designed to be someone else."

"You mean," said Russell incredulously, "that *I* was booked to be the next on the list?"

"Not directly. Your part in *Murder Has a Motive*, Paul, was one in which you were supposed to kill an actress because she was deserting you for another man after you had had for a long while what amounted to control over her life." Tremaine glanced significantly at Pauline Conroy and Serge Galeski. "Perhaps you can see what was to have happened? Miss Conroy would have died. *You* would have been suspected. I don't know just how you were to have been embroiled, but you can guess that Sandra Borne would have found some way of linking you with Miss Conroy so that it would have looked as though you had killed her because she had deserted you for Mr. Galeski. The third parallel would have been complete, and there would have been a triple revenge for the author of it. Pauline Conroy would have been dead, you would have been standing in the dock accused of her murder—and Jean's happiness would also have been destroyed."

The doctor was struggling to arrange his thoughts. He said, slowly: "It sounds incredible, and yet—and yet I'm not so sure. Now I look back she did have a habit of trying to link me with Pauline and of trying to throw us together at rehearsals. I didn't think much about it at the time, but it looks now as though that *was* the reason." He added: "So that was what lay behind what I thought was your suspicion of me! That was why you seemed to be watching me. You were expecting Pauline to be killed, and you thought that, if you could account for every moment of my time, you would be able to give me an alibi!"

Tremaine smiled.

"You're getting warm, Paul," he said, and his friend presented an appearance that was a mixture of bewilderment and contrition.

"Sorry, Mordecai," he said awkwardly. "I thought—"

"You thought I was trying to get you hanged," said Tremaine. "And I don't blame you. You had every reason to!"

Pauline Conroy had been listening to their conversation, understanding dawning in her face. She was a very subdued Pauline Conroy. She said: "I owe you an apology, too. I thought you suspected me and that that was why you were having me watched. But you really had those detectives to shadow me because you thought my life was in danger and were trying to protect me."

"You were certainly in grave danger, Miss Conroy. In fact, I suspected that, if I could break Sandra Borne's nerve tonight and drive her to confession, she would make a last attempt to attain her end and would attack either yourself or Dr. Russell. You were seated too far away from her, as it happened, for her to have any hope of injuring you before she was seized, which meant that it would almost certainly be Dr. Russell upon whom she would turn. That was why I was able to warn him so quickly."

Mordecai Tremaine looked around the table. His glance rested understandingly upon Phyllis Galway.

"I don't think you need delay over that announcement any longer," he said, with a twinkle. "I think you know now why I asked you to keep it secret for a little while. There was always a danger that if Sandra Borne learned of it, her twisted, jealous reaction might have taken the form of trying to do you some violence. But that danger is past now."

"Thanks to you," said Geoffrey Manning fervently. "I'm afraid you must have found me a little difficult at times. I knew that someone here must be the killer, and I was half off my head with anxiety for Phyllis."

"You were in love," said Tremaine. "That excuses a lot of things." He said: "We know the answer to the question we've all been asking ourselves. It's been an unhappy, difficult time, but the murders have been solved. There are no more questions we need ask." His gaze sought out Howard Shannon. "None," he said firmly, and he saw the relief that came into the plump man's eyes.

When Mordecai Tremaine left the hall, Karen Hammond was waiting for him. He had known that she would be. She stepped toward him out of the shadows surrounding the doorway. Diffidently, she put a hand on his arm. She said: "You know—about us?"

"Yes," said Tremaine gently, "I know. I saw his wife."

Her face was averted.

"You don't—you don't think I'm a terrible person?" she said, in a low voice.

"I haven't any right to think anything of the sort," he told her.

"It was because I—I loved Philip."

"I'm quite sure you loved him. That was why you said that he was at home with you on the night that Lydia Dare was killed. You knew that if you admitted that he was in London he would be asked to state where he had been, and that would have revealed the fact that he had been with his wife—his legal wife. You might have lost him." She nodded. He could see that her beautiful face was lined with grief, and he knew that she was crying. He could think of no words to say that would be adequate in the face of her tragedy. All he could say was: "You will be leaving Dalmering, of course?"

"Yes—tomorrow. I thought it would be best to go as quickly as possible. Officially, I'm going up to—up to Philip's funeral. It's to be at Harford Row. I'm not coming back. I—I just wanted to say 'thank you' for being so—so understanding just now and not saying anything."

"There is no need to thank me," he said and took her hand. "There was no reason why I should have said anything."

She returned the pressure of his fingers and turned quickly away. Tremaine waited for a few moments longer before he himself set off up the road.

It was five minutes later when he saw Jonathan Boyce. The Yard man came toward him with a springy step. He was smoking a pipe, and he looked like a man from whose soul a crushing weight had been removed. Which was, indeed, the fact.

"Well, Mordecai," he said, "it worked. It was theatrical, but it worked."

"It worked because it *was* theatrical," returned Tremaine. "All the things I said on that stage were true, but I couldn't prove they were true. A lot of it was theorizing. The only thing to do was to pretend that I knew everything and try and crack her nerve. It was a big chance, of course, but I've been watching her, and I knew that she was breaking up. She was bound to go under sooner or later."

The inspector puffed out contented smoke clouds.

"I'll admit that I felt dubious about it right up to the last.

That woman, doing all those cold-blooded things, planning them for months beforehand. You wouldn't dream she could be capable of it. Until tonight," he added soberly. "The mask dropped tonight all right."

"A jealous woman," said Tremaine, "will do a great many surprising things. I told you when you started on this case that murder always has a motive. Mix jealousy and hate and a woman, and you have a motive that's dynamite."

"The whole picture seems complete now," observed the inspector. "Howard Shannon's real name, as you surmised, is Herbert Roydale. He came down here under an assumed name after he'd finished his sentence. He's been going straight, but he's been living in fear all the time that someone would find out who he really was, and when Hornsby came down to watch Philip Hammond, the thing he'd been afraid of actually happened—and in the worst way. Hornsby—as Anston said—doesn't mind doing a little blackmail when he gets the chance, and when he discovered that Herbert Roydale, the man who'd got fifteen years for the Roydale Trust Company fraud, was living in Dalmering under the name of Shannon, he didn't waste any time in putting the squeeze on him as a sideline to his detective activities. Roydale, or Shannon, didn't want his identity known—he'd got himself pretty well established, and he wanted to stay in Dalmering—and agreed to pay. He used to board the

London train as if he was going right through, but he'd get off at Colminster, meet Hornsby, pay him his hush money, and then continue his journey the next day. That was what he did on the night of Lydia Dare's murder. He couldn't tell the truth without giving himself away, so he invented that story about having a business appointment. That's why he's been such a mass of nerves.

"It didn't make matters any better for him when Martin Vaughan found out that he'd been in Colminster on the night of the murder and tried to do some investigating on his own account. Vaughan, of course, has been laboring all the time under the shock of Lydia Dare's death. That's why his attitude was so strange. He didn't show any confidence until he stumbled on the fact that Shannon was hiding something and felt he had another suspect whom he could work upon."

"When I decided to take a chance after Edith Lorrington's death and go to his house and ask him for the full story about how he came to insist on *Murder Has a Motive* being performed," said Tremaine, "he tried to turn my attention to Shannon. I think that part of his unhelpful attitude was due to a feeling of genuine hurt that, loving Lydia Dare as he had done, people could even suspect him of having killed her."

Jonathan Boyce gave his companion a sideways glance.

"Talking about suspects," he remarked, "I think you gave your friend the doctor a few bad moments."

"I'm afraid I did," said Tremaine. "Poor Paul. He really believed I was after him. But I daren't tell him the truth in case it accidentally got back to Sandra Borne and put her on her guard. That legacy, of course, made matters worse for him, although it had nothing to do with the murder. Martin Vaughan was intended to hang for Lydia Dare. Paul was being reserved for Pauline."

They had reached the gate of "Roseland." The inspector stopped. He said: "I'm giving the commissioner a full report. I haven't said 'thank you' yet, Mordecai, but you know how I feel. The fact that I took the risk of using my authority to persuade those people to go to the village hall tonight is a proof that I was at my wit's end. I won't forget what you've done."

"It was nothing," said Tremaine, somewhat awkwardly, for Jonathan Boyce was not an emotional man, and he knew the depth of his feelings. "It was just a bluff that happened to come off."

He said good night to the inspector and pushed open the gate. But he did not go into the house. He walked into the garden and stood looking up at the stars studding a clear sky. He was troubled within himself and vaguely dissatisfied.

Lying darkly under a new moon, Dalmering was still and peaceful. The air about him was tranquil, and the faint swish of the sea was just audible. It called to mind the loveliness he had seen in his surroundings on that long-ago day when he had crested the hill in Paul Russell's little car and seen the village lying below him.

But he knew now that its loveliness was an illusion; that under the beauty there was evil and decay. Greed and hate and jealousy and fear and murder lay beneath its placid, false surface.

He thought of the hysterically screaming woman who had been taken from the hall. He thought of Howard Shannon, nursing the fear of being exposed to the neighbors who respected him as the man who had caused the ruin of thousands and prepared to pay heavily in blackmail to keep his secret safe and remain in hiding under the name he had assumed. He thought of Pauline Conroy and her guilty intrigue with Galeski. He thought of Philip Hammond and the woman Karen, the beautiful, unhappy woman for whom there could be no peace.

Everything he had touched had turned to pitch under his hand. His investigations had revealed only rottenness lying beneath the veneer of a happy, peaceful community. There had only been terror and intrigue, jealousy and dreadful murder. Was the heart of man just corruption, mocking his outward splendor?

And then a fresh, caressing coolness was gently fanning his cheeks. He squared his shoulders, as though he was brushing the depression from him. It was only a night breeze from the sea, of course. It possessed no magical powers. But suddenly his mind was clear again.

You couldn't see only beauty in the world. You had to see the disfiguring stains, the sordid and sprawling things, too. Because that was life. Life *was* ugly and untidy besides being beautiful and marvelous and full of wonder. You had to see the dirt as well as the stars. To see the dirt and not become a cynic, to hold fast to one's ideals, to preserve one's belief in the underlying decencies of humanity—that was the real purpose of living.

He went slowly back toward the house, and as he walked his feet made a little crunching noise upon the gravel path.

ABOUT THE AUTHOR

Francis Duncan knows how to write a good murder mystery, and from the 1930s through the 1950s, his whodunits captivated readers. His character, Mordecai Tremaine, was the best at unraveling a narrative. However, there was one mystery that went unsolved: Who exactly *was* Francis Duncan?

When Vintage Books, an imprint of Random House UK, decided to bring back Duncan's *Murder for Christmas* in December 2015, questions still loomed around the author's unknown identity. In fact, there wasn't a trace of biographical information about the author to be found, and Vintage republished the book without solving the puzzle. Francis Duncan remained a man of mystery.

That is until January 2016 when, after seeing *Murder for Christmas* on shelf at a Waterstones bookstore, Duncan's daughter came forward to the publishers, revealing that Francis Duncan is actually a pseudonym for her own father, William Underhill, who was born in 1918. He lived virtually all his life in Bristol and was a "scholarship boy" boarder at

Queen Elizabeth's Hospital school. Due to family circumstances he was unable to go to university and started work in the Housing Department of Bristol City Council. Writing was always important to him, and very early on he published articles in newspapers and magazines. His first detective story was published in 1936.

In 1938 he married Sylvia Henly. Although a conscientious objector, he served in the Royal Army Medical Corps in World War II, landing in France shortly after D-Day. After the war, he trained as a teacher and spent the rest of his life in education, first as a primary school teacher and then as a lecturer in a college of further education. In the 1950s he studied for an external economics degree from London University. No mean feat with a family to support; his daughter, Kathryn, was born in 1943, and his son, Derek, in 1949.

Throughout much of this time he continued to write detective fiction from "sheer inner necessity," but also to supplement a modest income. He enjoyed foreign travel, particularly to France, and took up golf on retirement. He died of a heart attack shortly after celebrating his fiftieth wedding anniversary in 1988.

Look for the next book in Francis Duncan's classic Mordecai Tremaine mystery series

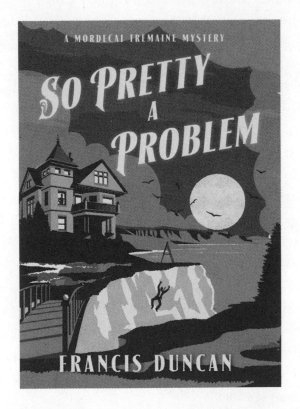

A MORDECAI TREMAINE MYSTERY

SO PRETTY A PROBLEM

FRANCIS DUNCAN

"It all looked innocent enough, but who could tell? It wasn't until attention was focused on one particular spot that one realized just how many odd things could go on under the eyes of unsuspecting neighbors."